Here
Comes
the Corpse

Here
Comes
the Corpse

MARK RICHARD ZUBRO

ST. MARTIN'S MINOTAUR ⚹ NEW YORK

www.minotaurbooks.com

ISBN 0-312-28098-X

First Edition: August 2002

10 9 8 7 6 5 4 3 2 1

Thanks to Barb, Jeanne, Rick, and Kathy

Here
Comes
the Corpse

1

The man looks good in anything: white cotton briefs, black silk boxers, a leather thong, baggy Bermudas, tight faded blue jeans, his baseball uniform, a hand-tailored business suit, leather pants, a muscle T-shirt, or torn old sweatpants, but he is especially gorgeous in a tux. That afternoon I watched him dress. I do that on occasion, and this occasion was more special than most. Size thirty-two, white Jockey shorts, black socks, a Hugo Boss tux, white shirt tucked into black pants, his bow tie tied, his jacket shrugged into. I enjoy the fact that I'm the only one who is intimate with the body that is encased in clothes he'll show to the world.

"Ready," he said.

I stood in front of him. Scott always ties my bow tie. I know I could learn to do it and he knows that, too. It's just a moment we enjoy before attending a big, dress-up, formal event. Facing a full-length mirror, I stand with my back to him. His arms reach around me, and he leans in close. I snuggle my backside into him. His hands twirl the ends of the bow tie into the requisite knot. I inhale deeply the smell of him, almost masked in his aftershave and deodorant. The feel of him enfolding me in his warmth before venturing out in public is sublime ecstasy. I shut my eyes. I try to stop all conscious thought and melt into his presence around me.

This day he took his time with the bow, then placed his hands on my shoulders and murmured in my ear, "You are a very sexy man, Tom Mason."

I turned around. Our arms entwined and we held each other. I said, "I love you, Scott Carpenter."

"I love you, too," he said, and we kissed.

Further passion was pointless at this moment. We were off to be married, and we weren't about to be late. Besides, both sets of our parents were waiting in the living room. No, they wouldn't hear us if we became amorous. The penthouse was huge and the walls were well constructed, but there wasn't time, and something about the proximity of parents can cool the fervor of the most ardent lovers.

"Nervous?" he asked.

"Yeah, you?"

"Yep." He smiled. "Luckily there ain't nothin' we can do about anything now."

Everything was set and planned for to the last detail: the caterers, the flowers, the banquet hall, the band, the emcee, the deejay, all the requisite marital accouterments ready to go. With all that could go wrong on such a day, you either laughed hysterically or had a nervous breakdown. With any luck we'd get laughter.

Unfortunately, I'm a worrier. This is not good when facing a party of the scope and diversity of this one. Keeping a lid on my ability to worry had been one of the things Scott had insisted on as we discussed having an elaborate wedding. No matter how perfectly anything is planned, doesn't everyone still worry? I wanted everything to go right, for people to have

2

a good time. And with the amount of money we were spending a whole lot of people should have one hell of a fantastic time.

Our wedding day was certainly special. Unique. Amusing. A hit. A marvel. We got nothing but raves until the corpse turned up.

With a stunning amount of good fortune, we had got through the planning without a major fight. We'd both realized early on that we'd created a monster. In the abstract, getting married is a great idea; reaffirming our commitment, a fine concept. Having a big party is not inherently an evil undertaking.

Here's a wedding tip. No matter how tempting, don't invite a dead body to the reception. Even at the exchange of vows at the church, the presence of the deceased is an iffy proposition. Trust me, in either venue the reactions of your nearest and dearest will most likely range from distinctly miffed to decidedly overwrought. Even the more distantly related, or those invited more out of obligation than desire, tend to become disconcerted. Those more sensitive might have a physically negative response. Leaving aside normal human reactions, things don't go better with corpses. The flowers are not prettier, the food doesn't taste better, and the band doesn't play more popular songs. Nothing good comes of a corpse at the wedding.

Although with the addition of a corpse, you can be sure everyone will talk about your wedding for years. If you're going for a sensation, for a day that will be gossiped about by everyone's grandchildren, if you're after a "we want CNN at our wedding" effect, then by all means invite a corpse. It will be just the thing you're looking for. Miss Manners might be hard-pressed to approve of our having a dead body, but the Pope was already pissed off at us, so what did we have to lose? And we didn't actually invite the dead guy. Ethan Gahain would never have been invited to the wedding or the reception.

The Pope was pissed because we were having a gay wedding. Yes, Scott and I had lived together for years, but we wanted to make it official, and we wanted to make a statement. It was not going to be just your run-of-the-mill, let's-quietly-pledge-our-love-and-not-bother-anybody affair. We were going to do it right, and we were going to do it big.

And none of this "commitment ceremony" crap. We were having a wedding, and by God, we were going to call it a wedding. Besides, to me, a commitment ceremony sounds as if the community is ritualizing the placing of an unfortunate and sometimes criminal person in a psychiatric facility. Not the image I was going for here. We knew we were more than a couple of "out" gay people declaring our true love. This was a loud, garish affirmation for ourselves and maybe as well a statement for all those gay and lesbian couples who'd like to make a public pronouncement but couldn't.

We weren't getting married because we wanted to be just like straight people. There's a legitimate division in the gay community about the importance or validity of being just like "them." Trust me, no matter what position you take on an issue, someone in the community isn't going to like it, will make a stink about it, and/or picket and protest, all for generally insane and illogical reasons. What these people mostly desire is their fifteen minutes of fame while tearing down something they perceive is better than they are, or something that someone else has that they want. My general response to this more-than-sharklike political feeding frenzy in the gay community is "fuck 'em." Which very much summed up how I felt about anybody's disagreement with what we were doing. We loved each other. We were getting married. End of story as far as I was concerned.

Our wedding would be major news. We were public figures. Scott, as an openly gay baseball player, and I as his lover had both been on numerous talk shows. Notice would be taken even if we didn't want it to be.

We knew the right-wing screamers would make a big deal out of what we were doing. We'd never be able to keep even a small ceremony out of the tabloids. Because of the hatred felt toward us by many, when gay people do something publicly, that public thing often becomes a political statement whether we like it or not.

So, if it was going to be big, we figured why not make it really big? The actual rite of committing our lives to each other would be reasonably quiet, but also make a political statement. Our immediate families and six select friends, three for Scott and three for me, would witness this ritual. Three hundred sixteen clergymen and clergywomen would officiate. That little oddity happened for several reasons.

We got the idea for a clergy-infested ceremony from two incidents. In Chicago, one United Methodist minister had performed a gay commitment ceremony and gotten the sack. In northern California, fifty-seven United Methodist ministers had performed the same ritual and had not gotten in trouble. If there was to be safety in numbers, we would have a ministerial mob officiate at the ceremony. I'd gotten in contact with gay-friendly clergy in numerous denominations. As word spread of our plan, all kinds of brave priests and ministers came out of the woodwork. The notion of doing it en masse appealed to the willing but timid. We wound up with United Methodists, Presbyterians, Episcopalians, Unitarians, Lutherans, United Church of Christ, Congregationalists, Reform rabbis, and Catholic priests. Even six daring Southern Baptists came forward.

Admittedly, Scott and I were doing a bit of rubbing it in

the right-wing's faces. The right-wing might have its moments, for example, when a gay Republican congressman addressed the Republican convention and delegates protested before, prayed during, and claimed after that it wasn't precedent-setting. This was ours. We decided we would make our marriage a bigger deal than any right-wing fools could.

It was the thirty-nine Catholic priests' participation that got the Pope pissed. Or maybe he was angry because he was one of the few people we didn't invite. Then again, maybe not. When the Vatican got wind of that many priests taking part in such a ritual, the powers that are decided to send out orders and decrees. Not a one of the priests backed out. What with the brouhaha about gays in Rome during the Catholic "holy year," and censoring a priest and a nun who had been working with gay Catholics, and us officially being "intrinsically disordered," it was impossible to ignore us.

Before getting a final commitment from each of the clergy, we sent them a copy of the vows and an outline of the ceremony and asked for feedback. We wanted to be sure they were absolutely clear about what they were getting into. We'd decided beforehand that anyone who insisted on major changes would be told no thank you.

One danger with so many clergy in attendance was the possibility that they might burst into spontaneous prayer. We'd checked the credentials of all of them, so no loony religious-right fanatics were likely to slip in, but you never knew. We didn't want our ceremony beginning as a number of high school football games in the South recently had with well-orchestrated, spontaneous prayers. What was never made clear to me about this passionate, public praying was why they didn't do this spontaneous ritual at opera performances, the movies, professional football games, or a vast array of other venues? School-sponsored or non-school-sponsored, praying at football games always struck me as a very medieval/Crusades thing to do. I've always frowned on and never fully understood how Christianity and the perpetuation of violence became synonymous so often throughout history. Since our wedding did not involve any proposed violence, I wasn't too worried about untoward prayers marring the proceedings.

We'd divided up the responsibilities for planning the day-long festivities. I was to take care of the vow-exchanging ceremony and the politics. He was to take care of the reception. This actually worked out far more harmoniously than I'd imagined. The political stuff, especially organizing the clergy, was kind of fun.

We did collaborate reasonably well on the guest list for the reception. Our families were easy. No matter how remotely connected, they were invited. We'd offered to pay for hotel rooms and transportation for relations traveling great distances; mostly his from the South. When you're as rich as Scott's income made us, it's not hard to add an extra few hundred people here or there.

The attendance of so many politicians and the media at the reception was a bit of a hassle. Early on, movie and television stars began lining up for invitations or having their representatives call for them.

Then there were the anti-us demonstrators. How many people do you know who have to plan for protesters showing up at their wedding? Sure, most folks have the danger of an odd or angry in-law or two, but these were bona fide crazies. They threatened to come. We expected them. Other than coordinating response with the police, we chose to do little about them. The protesters would have their own little space a block and a half from the hotel. Afterward I was told that no more than twenty were ever present at any one moment.

I was slightly glad they were there. Nothing like nutty pro-testers to spice up an event. The hate-filled signs and the il-logic of that ilk are sometimes the best arguments in favor of pro-gay legislation.

At the entrance to the reception we did wind up having to have—along with nasty-looking metal detectors—burly, grim-faced security guards carefully checking the guest list. This was more to keep out the dementedly curious and any overzealous interlopers than from any real belief that some kind of concerted effort to disrupt the proceedings would occur.

Scott, with my mother's eager assistance, concocted and orchestrated the elaborate reception. They'd stick their heads together with the wedding planner, and the three of them would giggle and laugh for hours on end. The wedding planner cost more than the annual budget of some third-world countries.

My father early on gave me excellent advice: "Whatever they tell you, smile and nod, ask one or two questions, smile and nod again, then agree enthusiastically. Keep that formula in mind. You'll thank me."

I did exactly as he said, and it worked magnificently. The smiles and nods I realized were for amiability. The questions to show that I cared and was interested. The agreement be-cause I knew I didn't have much choice. They were doing the work.

Along with my political and ceremonial duties, I was in charge of domestic arrangements. We decided we were not going to cram overnight guests into our homes. Simultane-ously entertaining domestically and running a massive party were more than we were prepared to endure. Nevertheless, both his penthouse and my place in the country had to be scoured within inches of their lives. People would be in and out of both of them all week. The rehearsal dinner two nights before was in his penthouse. The bachelor party the night before had been in my home. I cleaned enough in the two weeks prior to the wedding to last until the next accumulation of dust bunnies turned into dust elephants.

We chose to recite our vows at Rockefeller Chapel at the University of Chicago. It was a perfect setting on a gorgeous fall Saturday afternoon.

At the church all the clergy were in the pews with a detailed outline of what was to happen and a specific script for who was to say what when. We opted for reasonably conventional vows. The whole ceremony mixed the traditional with the hopelessly romantic and the pointlessly melodramatic. This was topped off with a generous sprinkling of liberal politics. A neat trick if you can pull it off. It was a gay wedding. If you can't do excess and melodrama at a gay wedding, when can you? I ask you, where would it be more appropriate? Okay, grand opera, but short of that?

Our parents walked each of us down the aisle. What I hesitate to admit to many people is that I've always wanted to walk in some kind of glorious procession to the strains of the last half of the fourth movement of Tchaikovsky's Fifth Symphony. I figured this was my one chance, and I wasn't going to blow it. Besides, the whole Wagner "Here Comes the Bride" shtick didn't make a lot of sense with the two of us looking more butch and masculine than several professional football teams combined. (Turned out the orchestra should have tuned up with "Here Comes the Corpse.") For his processional Scott proposed using the "Grand March" from *Aida* but without the elephants. I think the only reason he didn't insist on the elephants was the size of the pooper-scoopers that would have been required. Hard to tell when logic is going to set in when you're making excess into a lifestyle. When he found

9

out what music I wanted to have as I walked in, he insisted on the *Aida*. He didn't have the benefit of my father's advice, but the opening music was the only thing he insisted on. I have no idea why. He hates most opera, except *Carmen* and the "Grand March." Go figure. Maybe I'm not the only one who has secret dreams about music and processions. Besides a little cliché opera at a gay wedding is no bad thing. I mean, I *had* held back on playing the "Alleluia Chorus" at the ceremony. I didn't want to get too religious. Besides the chorus is about God. Didn't have much to do with marriage that I could see. Even this small impulse toward a modicum of restraint was totally absent from the reception.

At the exchange of vows, both of us, our families, and our guests stood at the altar in front of the assembled ministers, priests, and rabbis.

A gay men's choir began the ceremony with Judy Collins's song "Since You Asked."

During the ceremony, we faced each other and held hands. The early-afternoon light flooded the richly wood-paneled interior. The golden-hued light struck wisps of his blond hair. It was supposed to be a magical moment, and it was. I remember thinking about how beautiful he was and how much I loved him.

Of course, there was the stunningly annoying and possibly lethal party to follow, but for the moment, all else was forgotten.

A retired Illinois Supreme Court justice led the clergy in performing the ceremony.

Scott spoke his vows first, then me. This was because of a mad whim of mine. Since I'm an English teacher, I figured go with alphabetical.

Our words echoed in the hushed chapel. When I finished, I said, "I do. I love you," closed my eyes, and kissed him.

It was odd hearing a churchful of ministers intoning, "We now pronounce you a married couple."

After the vows and the kiss, we turned to the crowd.

The weight of the new gold band on my left hand felt perfect. Both of our rings were gold. His had a great blue sapphire, mine an immense red ruby, symbols of two of the great rings of making and healing from our favorite book, *The Lord of the Rings.*

Our parents beamed and smiled, both mothers crying. The clergy rose to their feet. Along with our parents and friends, they cheered and clapped. Scott smiled and murmured, "This was perfect."

For the recessional we had a full choir, a host of trumpeters along with a small orchestra, and the church's organ performing the "Ode to Joy." When a lone trumpeter began the opening chords solo, it could not have been a more magical moment.

Now, if you thought there was bit of excess (or even a lot) at the exchange of vows, you should have seen the reception. As Paul Rudnick put it in *The Most Fabulous Story Ever Told,* the entire operation looked as if it had been done by someone for whom "too much is just a starting point." We rented the Grand Ballroom of the Hotel Chicago, one of the newest hotels and by far the largest space available for such an event in the city, short of renting out McCormick Place. (A possibility, but not very practical. The lead time for getting space at the larger lakefront venue for the date we wanted was years.)

This was the biggest party we ever expected to throw. We'd invited well over a thousand people, not counting as many of those clergy as wanted to attend, and a horde of reporters, too. Here's another tip. Keep the reporters well fed and their drinks full up. You'd be amazed how much more positive your press coverage becomes.

11

No need to winnow the guest list when you can afford to invite everyone you know.

The mayor of Chicago, the governor of Illinois, and their wives stayed far longer than I thought they would. The guests were numerous and varied: movie stars and media hounds, half of Scott's teammates, many of my fellow teachers, old friends, three teammates of mine from our championship high school football team and our old coach, all of my brothers, sisters, nephews, nieces, aunts, uncles, and cousins. Over half of Scott's relatives showed up from the wilds of backwoods Georgia, the most important being his mom and dad. We invited every sports reporter from around the country who'd ever said a kind word about Scott in print or electronically. Anybody who worked for the gay newspapers in town was given credentials to cover the affair. Special spots were reserved for entertainment columnists from the *Trib* and *Sun-Times,* E! network television, and all the national gay magazines that wanted to cover the event.

In the Hotel Chicago the twenty-story atrium ballroom had two vast walls of solid glass and a dome of intricate stained glass. Rainbow-flag bunting around the ceiling's four edges. Vast displays of flowers—sheets of roses, rainbow colors again. Then orchids and more orchids, all living, white orchids in vast redwood tubs filled with sphagnum moss. Gargantuan balloons and twenty-foot-long, rainbow-hued feather boas swirled around gold, Godiva-chocolate centerpieces. Huge banners held photos of Scott and me from our childhoods, teenage years, and adulthoods with the pictures blown up to twelve feet tall. Yes, they had the ones of each of us as infants with our bare bottoms prominently exposed. Those embarrassing treats were festooned behind the head table. I especially liked his high school photo with him in his baseball uniform. He claimed he liked best the one of me bare chested and clad in marine fatigue pants taken at boot camp. There was also a two-story-high collage featuring pictures of relatives and friends. There was one collage of his coach and team from when they won the Georgia state baseball championship, and one of me, my teammates, and coach from when we won the Illinois state football championship.

Mirrored balls above the dance floor, mars lights dimmed for the moment, a string orchestra to play quietly during dinner, a wait staff inspired by pool-boys-r-us, each wearing tight, tight black pants and a muscle T-shirt. A bell choir, all of whom were in red toreador pants. An ice sculpture of the skyline of downtown Chicago that extended fifty feet. Five different restaurants catered the dinner, one for each course of the meal. More trumpets were in there somewhere. And a laser light show that ran continuously. Enough candles to lower the local supply for months. Along with an open bar, we had an immense buffet awash in hors d'oeuvres catered from a sixth restaurant to keep the crowd fed and lubricated as the reception line went on and on.

While I was aware ahead of time of most of what Scott and company had prepared, I was still a bit awed. My lover, the calm, reasonable, never-do-anything-to-excess country boy, had put to shame all the drag queens on the planet. We had more glitz and glitter than a stadium full of drag queens' wet dreams.

The receiving line was immense. It took hours, but we shook hands with or hugged all of them.

Until we found the dead body in the bathroom, it was a reasonably fun event.

2

The first hint of something being amiss came in the reception line. Everything was all I expected and more until Ethan Gahain appeared in front of me. Rachel and Perry Gahain, my parents' best friends since before I was born, had been invited to the wedding. Ethan was their younger son. When I saw him, the smile that had been plastered to my face remained intact, barely. Standing next to him was my sister, Caroline, and her husband, Ethan's older brother, Ernie.

There was history here. Big history. A lot of it was kind of sad, sentimental, and nostalgic. Some of it was true love, betrayal, and heartache. My first memory of Ethan was of us playing together in my backyard when we were both five years old. He'd taken a red truck from me. It was my favorite toy at the time. My mother had come out to find out what the squalling was about. I'd gotten a lesson in sharing and the unfairness of the world. Our getting in trouble was his fault. He'd swiped the truck. The tears then were a harbinger of things to come. For thirteen years we went to the same kindergarten, grammar school, and high school. We played on all the same sports teams. When we were kids, our families went on picnics, took camping vacations together, and shared numerous holiday events. My mom and dad still frequently socialized with his.

During my sophomore year in high school, I developed a mad crush on him. Ethan was the first guy I made love to, my first boyfriend. I was his first as well. We were passionate with each other in that supersecret teenage way. This feeling of and need for secretiveness was made even more acute because of our being frightened little gay boys.

Even in that reception line at such an incredibly happy, busy moment, the flash of remembrance of that first sexual encounter was as clear as if it had happened less than ten minutes ago. I would never forget the fear and ecstasy of intimately touching and being touched for the first time. Does anyone ever forget their first time? I doubt it. On that late-Saturday night so long ago, we admitted we were both scared, but willing to go beyond experimenting.

I thought Ethan was gorgeous then. As he stood before me, he was, if possible, even more handsome. The skinny kid had become a well-muscled adult, into his thirties and looking fine. He obviously kept himself in shape. His suit, shirt, and tie matched perfectly and fit beautifully. He was a Harrison Ford type, kind of rugged, kind of daring, but with warm and fuzzy not far underneath. Ethan's brush-cut red hair might have receded a trifle since I'd last seen him.

We had had a sexual relationship for over a year and never did get caught. His house was the best place. Both his parents always worked until after six.

While we were in love, we'd made all kinds of unrealistic teenage dream-plans together. As adults we would own a farm in Nebraska and grow old together unbothered by society. We'd make love endlessly under the starlight. We'd ride motorcycles through the Sahara desert and camp through Europe. We'd never lose touch. We'd always be in love.

We broke up during junior year.

I remember precisely what caused the split with almost as much clarity as our first sexual encounter. The day before Christmas vacation, I caught him after school in a classroom with the lights off. He was having sex with a female substitute teacher just out of college. She had fled instantly. He and I had stayed and talked. His cruelty during that hour had left nasty welts on my teenage psyche. I remember distinctly that he said, "Our sex wasn't any more meaningful to me than the sock I use to cover my dick when I beat off." I thought we'd been engaging in heavenly bliss. It sure felt like that to me.

I'd planned to go on a trip to Disney World with his parents and family over that vacation. I couldn't think of a way to get out of it. I still went, but I was totally depressed and miserable the whole time. Going on the trip probably turned out for the best. At least I wasn't at home and didn't have to face all kinds of questions from my mother about what was wrong. Even more, I saw clearly how cold and unfeeling Ethan really was. Worst of all, the whole trip he acted as if nothing had happened. If the breakup had bothered him, I might have felt better, but he seemed happy and content every single instant. Not a bit worried about me or what might have happened to the substitute teacher. No teenager is that good at acting. It was real and hurtful. That vacation, he always managed to make sure we were in a crowd so even if I knew how to talk to him about what had happened, I wouldn't be able to. By the time the trip was over, I thought I would hate him for the rest of my life.

Certainly, I was taught one of the tough lessons of life, that we do not always get what we want, no matter how sincere or eloquent or desperate we are. The harsh lesson that loving someone truly and deeply does not guarantee that he will love you back.

I have no idea what happened to the teacher. She never subbed in our school again. I know my sixteen-year-old heart was broken. I remember not having anyone to confide in or cry with. By necessity I was very closeted when I was in high school. Now or then little sixteen-year-old closeted gay guys don't have a lot of options. Although I think that is slowly changing for teens.

To this day I don't think either his or my parents had a clue to the sexual nature of our friendship. Combined family events were a strain for me for years after that. I hid our breakup as secretly as our intimacy. When we were in college, my sister helped bring about a reconciliation of sorts.

We were never close again, but my hurt and anger slowly dissipated. Our parents were still friends. We had the same close-knit circle of friends. We had to work together and be in one another's presence. We were still both starters on the same football team. After one collision at practice looked more like a war than a tackling drill, our coach had to pull us apart. He'd asked us if there was a problem. We'd both said no in that hide-the-problem-from-adults teenage way.

We'd gone to different colleges. After his first marriage, he seldom attended any family events, so I saw even less of him. We had talked only sporadically over the ensuing years. He'd coached for a number of years at Carl Sandburg University in Wheaton and then moved to Lafayette University just outside St. Louis. Several of the athletes he'd coached at both schools had gone on to win medals in the Olympics.

Usually my parents were my main source of information about the events in Ethan's life. At last count he had a total of nine kids from four different marriages. His offspring included those that were biological, adopted, and blended. I'd

17

heard he'd just divorced his fourth wife. We hadn't talked in nearly two years. I remember exactly what he said that last time. I'd been traveling with a stopover in St. Louis and had a half a day with nothing to do. My mother was always urging me to call him. In a fit of nostalgia, I'd phoned and suggested we get together for a cup of coffee. He said, "Taking the time to get together with you is not worth the bother."

Before I could shut myself up, I had blurted out, "Why not?"

I remembered his next words exactly: "I want you to keep your faggot ass out of my life."

I was hurt and mystified. What do you say to a statement like that? I don't know how I had the presence of mind to simply say, "I hope you have a happy life." Even if I had thought of a brilliantly cutting and witty comment, it would have made no difference. He'd hung up before I began speaking.

What kept our lives intertwined and made things even more complicated was that just after I got out of college, my sister married Ethan's older brother, Ernie, a stunningly attractive man in his own right. I'd had an unrequited crush on Ernie when I was little. That attraction had been one of my first clues that I was different. As an adult, Ernie had developed numerous health problems. He had been hospitalized for one illness after another, culminating a couple of years ago when he'd been diagnosed with multiple sclerosis. He was generally okay, but was often forced to take it easy and occasionally needed to use a wheelchair.

And now, here was Ethan at my wedding, smiling happily.

Mrs. Gahain said, "Ethan called this morning and asked if he could be at the reception. I hope it's all right."

Well, of course, it wasn't all right. It was all wrong, but you don't say that to a grandmotherly woman who's your mom's best friend. You don't make a scene, especially not at such a moment. I'd read my Miss Manners.

Ethan held out his hand and said, "Congratulations."

I shook his hand, nudged Scott, and said, "Look who's here." I introduced them.

Scott looked at Ethan, then back to me. He knew the history and the hurt although they'd never actually met. But Scott's got as much social sense as I. He held out his hand, smiled, and said, "I'm glad to meet you at last."

Ethan smiled broadly, leaned close to me, and whispered, "I need to talk to you."

I remember thinking this was a monumentally dopey time to say such a thing. We're in the middle of this vast, once-in-a-lifetime party, and he wants to talk? This wasn't some silly soap opera. At any rate, in less than thirty seconds the moment was over. The line eddied around us with the fabulously prominent mingling with the dearest of old friends. The mayor's wife gave me a hug. Ian McKellen smiled cheerfully. A Hollywood producer in the mob had been trying to convince us to let him use our life stories for a movie of the week on some obscure cable channel. We sicced our agent on him. An hour later the line finally ended and the festivities commenced in full.

Three hired videotapers. Three still-picture photographers. The buffet, the free drinks, and then the meal itself. An entrée of Hawaiian fillet of beef; vegetarians got vegetables; noncaffeine people got noncaffeine drinks. Gifts, as if we needed them, on an immense gift table. We'd registered to the hilt. Our biggest disagreement had been pro and con about accepting presents, Scott for and me against. Our compromise was to agree to donate all gifts to charity.

Cutting the wedding cake was fun. No, we didn't do that stupid shove-the-cake-in-the-other's-mouth bullshit, which I consider to be possibly the most singularly idiotic and moronic part of any ritual on the planet.

The toasting was kept to a minimum. My dad's awful jokes were strictly limited by my mother. What threats she used to cut him off, I can't begin to imagine. Scott's toast was sweet. He simply lifted his glass and said, "To the man I love." Mine was equally as simple: "I will always love you."

I think the best part was when the lights went down, a spotlight shone on us, and we shared the first dance together. Scott dancing used to be a sight to behold—this wonderful stud athlete turning total klutz and forcing himself to be propelled around the dance floor. No question, he's game, especially for a slow dance. We'd taken some lessons. He was no longer horrible. Over the years I had graduated from wild flailing about to rock and roll, to above average at some pretty complicated steps. We weren't ready to enter a tango contest, but we could hold our own and not embarrass ourselves.

As the crowd watched and applauded, we began to sway together. I remember shutting my eyes and melting into his arms. It was a perfect moment. He is so gorgeous and so strong, and I love him so much. Dancing together with him in public is wonderful. I felt his arms, and shoulders, and torso, and legs, and it was fabulous. And then we danced with our moms. We were prevented from making a decision about dancing with our dads by the expedient of Scott's dad flatly refusing to be coerced out onto the floor with anyone. He claimed he didn't dance, and Scott averred that this was true. I think my dad might have done it, but I'm not sure. My brothers and sister danced with both of us. It was a little weird, but they're so great and so supportive. I thought about trying to ask some of Scott's teammates, but I thought that would be pushing my luck.

The dancing thing turned into this gender-bending extravaganza. People were laughing and carrying on with same-sex and opposite-sex couple switching. I remember doing a bit of the Charleston with a guy I had played football with in college and the polka with my old high school coach. I used to baby-sit for his kids. I danced with a punter from the NFL and his date, a college basketball player. They hadn't arrived to-gether, and as more and more people danced in same-sex couples, their two daring whirls together weren't noticed. There are all kinds of closets. I even managed a sweep around the floor with Ethan's brother Ernie, who was in a wheelchair.

The crowd did a lot of good old-fashioned whooping and hollering as everybody whirled and twirled, twisted and shook, throughout the ballroom.

Through the chaos and the fun, I saw Ethan only twice, at a distance. No opportunity presented itself for a tête-à-tête with the negatively remembered. I didn't seek him out.

3

An hour later the band had swung into its second set of wild rock and roll from the late fifties and early sixties, and I needed a break. I eased out to stop in the washroom. The closest one was jammed. We'd made sure there was another, more private one for the use of the bridal party. It was behind the dais, up several sets of stairs, and down a hallway. This bathroom had only one urinal and one stall. The place was crammed with multisized, ornate, bronze sculptures. It had blue-green tile walls and was topped off with the odd flourish of a lavender porcelain urinal. Standing there pissing, I was just barely able to hear the sound of the band. As I zipped up, I heard a soft moan. I looked around. Nothing. Another soft moan. I looked under the stall partition. I saw a foot resting at an odd angle. For the foot to be in that position the person sitting on the commode would have to be a contortionist. This wasn't good. The trickle of blood I noticed next was alarming.

The stall door wouldn't open. I called out. No answer. Blood was rapidly spreading. I knelt down to get a better view under the partition. I saw the back of whoever it was, leaning against the door. I couldn't fit under the stall walls. I took the fortuitously rectangular trash can, toppled it on its side, stood on it, and looked into the stall from above.

I recognized Ethan. He reached up a hand and whispered, "Help me."

I whipped out my cell phone, dialed 911, and then hotel security.

I gripped the top of the partition with both hands and pulled myself up. The bottom of my dress shoes, bought for the occasion, were slippery, so I had to scramble for a foothold. As I looked down from above, I could see even more blood, but no specific damage or wound. Ethan's eyes followed my every movement. With one leg over the top, I sort of hopped/fell over. I heard my pants rip. I ignored them. As quickly and carefully as I could, I eased myself down the other side of the partition. I slipped the last few feet. I teetered for a moment and almost fell on Ethan. My left leg rested for a few seconds on the rim of the toilet and then began to slide off. I slipped and landed with one hand on Ethan's knee and the other on the floor. My face was near his.

I repositioned myself on my knees next to the top half of his body. Even though the stall was wheelchair accessible, the space was still cramped. He was bent nearly double. "Help me," he gasped again. This time his voice was weaker. He raised his hand. I held it.

I said, "Help is on the way. Who did this?"

Ethan tried to lift his head. This movement showed me the results of what must have been one massive impact or numerous vicious blows. The entire right, rear side of Ethan's skull had been shattered. Bits of bone mixed with hair and blood as I cradled him in my arms.

I didn't even think about the blood soaking into my tux as I held him. All the hurt and pain he had brought into my life were out of my waking memory. I was holding the boy I'd loved those many years ago. Ethan breathed deeply several times, then said, "I love you, Mike." His eyes lost their focus. Seconds later he closed them. He stopped breathing.

He never answered my question.

I moved the body so I could open the stall door and laid him flat. Hotel security arrived just as I began CPR. The paramedics appeared before I had time to wonder where they were, but nothing anyone could do helped. Ethan was dead.

I had no notion who Mike might be. Whatever Ethan had wanted to talk to me about earlier would remain unsaid forever.

As the paramedics tried desperate measures, I stood in the background. I could still see the inside of the stall. I saw blood on the tank, the bolt on the door, the toilet-paper holder, and the side of the bowl. The porcelain commode was cracked. The metal paper-holder was bent. I couldn't imagine any way he could have fallen and hurt himself this severely. Obviously, someone must have taken his head and repeatedly bashed it against the various protrusions in the stall. Most of the blood was on the floor.

Sometime in there the thought flashed through my head that Scott and I were going to miss our plane. We had first-class reservations on an overnight flight to Paris. I also remember thinking this wasn't the usual kind of thing that goes wrong at a wedding. I'd imagined the food running out or maybe my fly being open during the ceremony or possible fights among various factions of relatives—mostly his, if truth be told. Who knew how his fairly prejudiced crowd of relatives would respond to this Northern liberality? Of course, there was always the random chance that any reveler, liberal or conservative, straight or gay, might cause a scene. I'd even pictured the protesters gathered outside the hotel making a mad rush to crash the party, with valiant faggots holding off the invading hordes. Okay, that was kind of silly, but I certainly hadn't imagined what I was witnessing.

Early on, I asked one of the assembled security people to get Scott. He and I stood in the hall outside the washroom and talked.

"We'll have to cancel the rest of the party," I said.

He nodded. "You found him. You'll be a suspect."

"I know."

"And you knew him."

"Intimately." I rubbed my hands over my face. "The first guy I ever loved is dead. I wonder how many people keep in contact with their first love or know where they are after so many years."

"The breakup was a long time ago."

"It's still a painful memory."

He put his arm around my shoulder. "I know. I'm sorry."

After watching cops busily working to and fro for a few minutes, Scott said, "I don't remember his name on the invitation list."

"It wasn't. He came with his mom and dad. In the reception line, he told me he needed to talk to me. I wonder if it was guilt from years before that he wanted to expiate, or if he was in some kind of trouble."

"I love it when you say *expiate,*" Scott said. "I get all goosebumpy."

"I'll swallow a thesaurus just for you."

"If he was in trouble, wouldn't he have talked first to someone in his immediate family or even to one of his ex-wives?"

"Why would he confide in an ex-wife?" I asked.

"If they were close? If he was in trouble, why you and not them?"

Scott had a point. Why me? I said, "I wonder if he just

happened to be in town or if he deliberately planned to come to the wedding all along." I shrugged. "I guess it's not important. I'm going to have to tell his parents."

"Do you want the police to do that?"

"No. I think it would be better for me or maybe my parents to be the ones to break the news."

Uniformed Chicago police officers had entered the corridor and cordoned off the area. I noted that a few small storage closets were between the reception and the washroom, but no possible exits. My mother showed up. She's got that built-in "mom" radar for when things go wrong. I explained the situation to her. They sent my older brother to his hotel room to get me a pair of pants. The rip in the tux from crawling over the partition extended from the top of my left butt cheek to behind the knee. The tux pants and coat were blood-soaked. The shirt had miraculously escaped with nary a fleck. In light of the death, I wasn't all that concerned with my appearance. My mother pointed out the extent of the blood on my clothes and said changing was the sensible thing to do. When I thought about Ethan's blood drying on me, I got a chill. As I thought of being caked in blood while talking to people at the soon-to-be-halted reception, I realized that while changing wasn't essential, it was sensible. Plus, I really didn't want my underwear in full view of any passerby for the rest of the night. My brother and his family were staying for the weekend in the hotel. He brought me a pair of his jeans, which were a trifle too big. I wound up wearing the tux shirt, bow tie, and faded jeans, a little odd, but serviceable. Before I changed, I washed Ethan's blood off my hands.

I was questioned. The cops told me not to leave. I told them I'd be with the guests from the reception. I wasn't going anywhere.

I returned to the head table. You don't keep partying

when there's been a death. I wouldn't miss seeing the all-drag-queen rock band. I could do without the finale of the evening, a balloon and confetti drop. I would never get to see how they pulled off the indoor fireworks without burning down the place. Scott assured me it could be done. I'll never know. Probably for the best.

First, we took Ethan's parents aside. The hotel provided a quiet suite for the family. Scott and I left my mother and father with Ethan's parents. My mom and dad had volunteered to break the news to them, and it made sense for someone from their own peer group to tell them the awful news. I'm not sure anyone is good at making such a tragic and unexpected announcement, but my mom has great comforting abilities. In the face of the hugest of calamities, she's the one in the family you can count on to remain calm.

While Ethan's parents were being told, we stopped the music and dancing. I made the announcement to the crowd. The cops informed them that they would all have to be interviewed.

If the killer was an invited guest, he or she was probably still present. Leaving at the height of the festivities might have looked suspicious. Of course, a random stranger could have come in the back way to that washroom, then left the same way. It was open and easily accessible from the rest of the hotel. Looking at the milling mob, I thought, counting the hired help, we had nearly two thousand suspects.

My lawyer was at the reception. Todd Bristol stuck reasonably close to my side. Uniformed cops and detectives began taking statements. We'd promised them the guest lists and names and addresses of everyone who was invited. Even for the Chicago police department, this many people to interview takes a lot of time. Our security guards would have a checklist of everyone who'd actually showed up for them to cross-reference. Despite the bevy of cops present, the interviews took quite some time. In the end many of the guests simply gave their names and addresses and would be talked to later. We left when they stopped the interviews.

4

Outside in the cold, crisp October night, we found a small crowd of reporters gathered near the entrance to the hotel. With as much good grace as we could summon, we put them off until later. The protesters had long since disappeared.

It was a little after eleven. Next to our limousine in the parking garage, the chauffeur was talking to a man I didn't recognize. I figured it was some clever reporter who had gotten to our driver. We didn't use anywhere near as much security as we once did. The chauffeur was supposed to keep unwanted intruders away. The stranger looked to be in his middle twenties. He wore a black leather jacket open over a white T-shirt, faded blue jeans, running shoes, and white socks. His brush-cut, blond hair was cut off a quarter inch from the scalp. He had gray, very aware eyes.

As we approached, the blond took a card out of his jacket pocket and handed it to me and said, "I'm Jack Miller, a private investigator. I need to discuss Ethan Gahain with you." My mask of politeness in the face of strangers remained rigidly in place. Such reserve is necessary even for those on the fringe of celebrity such as myself. The vast majority of people who gawk at the barely-to-truly famous were at least aware enough not to be intrusive. However, there were always those determined to go too far; the kind of people blind to their arrogance, immune to self-awareness and their impact on others. Guarding against the truly demented was vitally necessary. In addition we needed to feel as if we still had some control of our lives. Coolness to all is necessary because it is impossible to predict which ones might be the out-and-out crazies who might wish us harm.

"Andrew," I said to the driver, "what's he doing here?"

"Don't blame him," Miller said.

I said, "Who else is there to blame?" Although Andrew had originally simply been scheduled to drive us to the airport, the limousine service trained them to know better.

Scott said, "Make an appointment."

Miller said, "I might know why Mr. Gahain was murdered."

That stopped us.

"Why haven't you talked to the police?" I asked.

"Unlike Lestrade and countless other bumbling, clueless, and inept police officers, the Chicago cops don't seem to have learned the wisdom of consulting their wise and kindly local private investigator."

I was tempted to smile at this truism. I was too tired.

Miller said, "I don't work for the police. They saw my private investigator ID and told me to go away. They didn't seem interested in what I knew. I'm not sure if what I know is connected to the murder. I'm not sure if what my client wanted to know might or should become public knowledge because of the murder. My client's goal did not include publicity."

I asked, "Who was your client?"

"Ethan Gahain hired me to find Cormac Macintire, son of Cecil Macintire."

Cecil Macintire, a right-wing radio screamer, was more hated and vilified among gay people than Dr. Laura. He freely used the phrase *fag-pedophile* when referring to gay people on the air. He claimed a rise in child molestations in recent years had led to an increase in gay people. Besides the error in the basic statistics, the theory itself was full of shit. His most bizarre statement was his implication that a male adult reading any of the Harry Potter books was at least effeminate, probably acting gender-inappropriately, and was most likely a pedophile and gay. Macintire was single-handedly attempting to turn ignorance into bliss, following directly in the footsteps of the Pope.

"Why did Ethan hire you to find Cormac?" I asked.

"Because he was missing?"

I said, "I am truly not in the mood for smart-ass answers. I figured he was missing. Why was Ethan concerned about him being missing?"

"They were business partners. He was supposed to deliver some work to Mr. Gahain. He didn't. He missed several other appointments this week. Even if he spontaneously decided to leave on a vacation, he didn't take his toothbrush or his shaving gear. Two empty suitcases were in the back of his closet."

"What kind of business were Ethan and Cormac in?"

"At first Mr. Gahain told me it was an Internet computer operation doing Web site designs. He didn't give me a lot of details. At the time it didn't seem necessary. There were no other coworkers to talk to. At least that's what Mr. Gahain told me when he hired me."

Scott said, "I thought Ethan was a college PE coach."

Miller said, "It's not illegal to try to supplement your income. I visited their company's Web site. It seemed pretty innocuous, advertising their services for Web site design.

31

Nothing on it suggested a reason for his disappearance."

"Was Cormac married?" I asked.

"Yep, with two little kids," Miller answered. "His wife was at least as concerned as Mr. Gahain, but she had no more answers than he did."

Scott asked, "Why didn't she hire somebody?"

"She was going to, but Mr. Gahain beat her to it. She did call the police. They filed a report."

"Maybe his fascist father had something to do with Cormac going missing," I suggested.

"I haven't been able to establish much of a connection between father and son."

Scott said, "Cecil Macintire holds himself up as a paragon of familial virtue."

Miller said, "I don't care if he does, unless it has something to do with helping find Cormac. Neither Cecil Macintire nor his people were very forthcoming. I got the impression there was some kind of estrangement."

"You no longer have a client," I said. "What's the point in talking to us? Do you have any reason to believe Cormac was involved in Ethan's death?"

"The whole case doesn't add up. I don't like one dead client with one missing business partner. My client may be deceased, but I feel an obligation to myself to find out what the hell is going on. Early this morning I uncovered some data in St. Louis that I needed to talk to Mr. Gahain about."

"At the wedding?" Scott asked.

"Mr. Gahain sounded desperate to find Macintire. He was spending a lot of money and demanding very quick answers. The new data I found might have led to the missing man. I hurried up from St. Louis. I was going to push hard to get some clear answers. I found out Mr. Gahain was here to attend a wedding. I almost decided to wait until tomorrow, but I thought I'd give it a shot. By the time I got here, he was already dead. My police contact confirmed what his fourth wife told me, that you grew up together and that he came to town specifically to talk to you. You may have information I need."

"We haven't been close for many years," I said. "He may have come to talk to me, but he died before he could tell me anything."

Miller said, "Close or not, there had to be a reason he chose you."

Miller motioned us away from the limo. "I'm trying to be discreet. The man is dead. I don't want to ruin a reputation. I was hired to find Cormac. What I found out was that Mr. Gahain lied to me. They had an Internet business all right. Two of them. The one he told me about and another, a pornographic Internet operation. I don't like being lied to or misled by a client."

"How did you find this out?" I asked.

"A guy named Josh Durst, who was connected to both Ethan and Cormac. He thought I was coming to audition for some pictures. I didn't disabuse him of the notion. He seemed eager to talk and I let him."

Scott said, "There's always rumors that the mob controls a lot of pornography."

"I don't know whether or not his murder or the pornography was mob-connected. I certainly didn't find any of the usual signs of illegality: drugs, fraud, money laundering, embezzlement, and until tonight, no violence of any kind."

"Exactly how long had Cormac been missing?" Scott asked.

"Ethan Gahain last saw him four days ago. He hired me two days ago."

"Did Cormac have a reputation for unexplained disappearances?" I asked.

"No. He had a reputation as dull, boring, and ordinary."

"You said pornography," Scott said. "That's a wide range of possible stuff. What exactly are we talking about here?"

"Photographs. Videos. DVDs. CDs. Lots of pictures of athletes in locker rooms, male athletes in various states of undress, some naked, showering, pissing. Videos and photos that looked like they were taken with hidden cameras, most likely without the consent of those involved."

"Naked guys?" Scott said. "With all those marriages you'd think he'd be straight."

"You don't have to be gay to make gay porn," Miller observed.

"Yeah, but I bet it helps," I said. "He had at least one fling with a guy, me."

Miller didn't comment on this bit of information. He said, "I was supposed to find Cormac. What I found was evidence of a sophisticated pornography ring. Mr. Gahain may not have overtly lied to me, but he concealed the nature of their business."

"What difference would it make if you knew what business they were in?" Scott asked. "What if they were carpet salesmen?"

"Whether or not producing or acting in porn is illegal, there's an aura of inherent danger. You've got possible illegalities connected with it. Either of those could be significant. Everything connected to a missing person has to be checked thoroughly because you don't know which bit will lead you to them. That's a huge chunk of a mutual relationship to leave out. I was pretty pissed as I drove up here. I do not like clients who lie."

I knew it was very true that Ethan was a concealer from way back.

Miller was saying, "I haven't found evidence that they produced and financed full-length pornographic movies. They seemed to be more distributors of productions they made themselves. My understanding is the pictures were taken at a large number of venues around the country over quite a number of years. Before I left, I confirmed that at the time some of the videos were made, Mr. Gahain was in those cities at those venues."

I asked, "How many venues and how many years?"

"I've only seen a few pictures, but some of those look like they go back to when Ethan was in college."

"How big an operation was it?" I asked.

"I wasn't able to pin it down exactly."

I asked, "Five bucks or five million bucks?"

"Certainly thousands, maybe hundreds of thousands. I'm not sure. They had the Web site and a few ads in porn magazines. I only had time to check a few of the ads connected to Mr. Gahain and Cormac Macintire. As far as I have been able to determine, they placed only a very limited number of very specific ads. I haven't found any of the people in the porn. There's lots of those ads for specific fetishes and odd quirks in the back of some magazines. I tried tracking down athletes in the few pictures I saw. I had no luck."

Scott asked, "What's the big deal now? If there were porn-picture problems, are you saying someone in them may have killed Ethan?"

"It's possible."

I said, "I still think you should tell all this to the police."

Miller said, "I'm sure you wouldn't want your friend's reputation sullied. I'm hoping we could be of help to each other."

Scott asked, "How do we know you didn't have a reason to kill Ethan, or that you are who you say you are? Business cards are easy to make."

Miller held out his PI license and said, "You're a little late asking for proofs. Just so I'm very clear here, I don't do dead. The state frowns on it. They take away your private eye license for that kind of thing. I am not a hired killer. With rare exceptions, gunmen such as you're probably imagining don't exist much outside the grimmer Hollywood movies."

"I wasn't imagining much of anything," Scott said.

"Look," I said. "We're both tired. I'm not willing to stand out here all night and discuss this." I looked at Scott. He nodded. "We'll check out your credentials and get back to you."

Miller could do little but acquiesce and leave.

5

On the way home we discussed our now postponed plans for a honeymoon. I'd taken two weeks off from school without pay; one the week before the wedding, the other for the honeymoon the week after. We didn't want to get married around any of the holidays, and during the baseball season would have been awkward. It had simply been easier for me to be off work for two weeks in October. We were a famous enough couple that all the kids and parents at school knew I was gay. I'd even invited a few parents and former students to the wedding.

Because of Ethan's death I wouldn't feel right leaving so quickly. There were too many connections past and present. We could put the honeymoon off indefinitely. We had been scheduled to be in Paris for the first three days and in New England for the fall colors for the last three.

The limousine pulled up to the penthouse. As I exited, I noticed a teenager sitting on the three-foot-high brick wall that lines the north side of the semicircular drive up to Scott's building. The kid wore baggy black pants, a lengthy and over-large T-shirt, and an open jacket. He was smoking a cigarette. I didn't recognize him as one of the building regulars. I peered closer. It was one of Scott's nephews. He spotted us, eased himself off the wall, and slouched over. He sported a pronounced scowl. Halfway to us he flipped the still-lit cigarette onto the pavement and didn't bother to crush it out. He jammed his hands into his pockets. He was Scott's oldest brother's fifteen-year-old, middle son. His parents had not come to the wedding.

I remembered him from our only visit to Georgia, when Scott's father had been seriously ill. The boy had shown up at his grandfather's farm in a beat-up, old, red pickup truck one afternoon with a couple other cousins to see their famous uncle Scott. The kid had brought the same scowl with him that afternoon. I didn't remember his name. He had buzz-cut black hair and an unblemished, pale skin. The kid was six feet tall and maybe 170 pounds. From that summer visit, I remembered him giving a couple of fleeting smiles. They would have been pleasant but for the constant scowl lurking at the edges of his mouth. When the scowl wasn't lurking but blazing forth, it made him look as if an overfertilized piece of produce had been jammed up his ass.

I tapped Scott on the shoulder. He looked in the direction I pointed. He smiled widely when he saw his nephew. "Donny," Scott said. He held out his hand, and they shook briefly. The scowl disappeared for several seconds. I noticed his hands tremble before he stuffed them back into his pockets.

Scott asked, "Did your parents change their mind about coming to the wedding?"

"Uh, no."

"They aren't here?"

Donny shook his head no.

"Do they know you're here?"

Another head shake.

"We better get upstairs," Scott said.

Donny's only luggage was a smallish, black backpack. As the elevator doors closed, he announced, "I'm not going back."

"Donny, you hungry?" Scott asked.

This time we got a nod yes.

"First, we're going to get you fed. We're going to call your parents to assure them you haven't run off to join the circus, been kidnapped by aliens, captured by fire-breathing dragons, or trampled in a rhinoceros stampede. Unless one of the above is true, and this is just a stop on the way?"

For his attempted humor Scott got a you-must-be-nuts look. Then Donny restated, "I'm not going back."

"How did you get here?" I asked.

"I got plane tickets over the Internet with my parents' credit card number." Bragging now. His voice included the occasional squeak of a teenage male whose voice hasn't finished changing. "A friend's older sister drove me to the airport in Atlanta. I took the train from O'Hare to downtown Chicago. I knew the wedding was today. I got here too late. Even though I showed my ID, they wouldn't let me in. They said IDs were easy to fake. So I walked here. The guard tried to make me go away. So I had to wait out near the street. This was the first time I traveled by myself. I've never even been on a plane before."

It was late and it had been a spectacularly exhausting day. I wasn't really up to dealing with him, but I wasn't about to go to bed before I found out what the hell was going on. I gazed carefully at Scott. He was still beaming at the kid. Was he missing the snarls Donny made little attempt to conceal?

In the kitchen Donny sat at the black marble counter. He dumped his backpack at his feet. From the refrigerator Scott pulled out cold chicken, dill pickles, mayonnaise, mustard, olives, celery, carrots, milk, and soda. He got rye bread from the cupboard and a glass from the cabinet over the sink. The kid began shoveling in great gobs of food even before Scott had everything out.

"They didn't feed you on the plane?" I asked.

Donny shook his head, then gulped half a glass of milk.

"What happened at home?" Scott asked.

"Lots of stuff. Teenage stuff. I thought about killing myself."

When I hear about teens and suicides, especially the unexplained deaths, I always suspect a gay connection. Statistically gay teens are 30 percent more likely to try suicide than straight kids. I was willing to condemn Scott's older brother and sister-in-law on general principles, although, for the moment, I was prepared to keep this to myself. This wasn't a good time to start criticizing the in-laws. Yet. Scott said he'd gotten over the fact that some of them had chosen not to show up at the wedding, but I suspected it still bothered him. How could it not?

"Why did you think about committing suicide?" I asked.

I got half a snarl and, "Shit happens."

The kid continued eating most of what was put before him, including what was left of the half gallon of M&M's candy ice cream in the freezer. Obviously, he wasn't going to starve himself to death. After he'd wolfed down half the contents of the refrigerator and cupboards, he was no longer pale and trembling.

"Have you talked to your mom and dad since you left?" Scott asked.

Repeating the lament of countless legions of teens before him, Donny said, "I can't talk to them. They won't listen. I couldn't think of what else to do, so I came here."

"Whatever's wrong," Scott said, "I know your mom and dad would not want you to be dead. They'd want to try and help."

"You don't get along with them. They don't like you. You can't talk to them. Why should I have to?" The soothing burr of Donny's Southern drawl did nothing to make his responses less of a whine, less combative, or more charming or easier to listen to.

"But I'm not going to kill myself over it," Scott said.

"I can't talk to them," Donny reiterated.

Scott said, "We need to call them and tell them you're safe."

"I won't."

"You know if you don't, I'll have to."

"I don't care. I'm not going back. Can't I stay here with you?" These bits of defiance and bravado and pleas were delivered in ascending tones of hostility, mixed with whining and indifference.

I thought most of his attitude was driven by fear of rejection. We knew little about his home life, but I'd seen the same thing at the school I teach at. A kid's home is awful, but the mix of rejection, indifference, and poor parenting rarely leads him or her to embrace a hand held out in concern. Hollywood movies and television might be able to get warm, fuzzy endings from caring teachers intervening with troubled teens. Unfortunately, the reality I'd seen seldom worked out so easily, neatly, or warmly. The rejection and indifference from a parent is seldom monolithic. The hand of love has been held out to the kids and then betrayed them. What rules many of these kids' lives is the betrayal they feel. Even stronger is the uncertainty about if they will ever have or deserve the unconditional love of a parent. I said all this to Donny. When I finished, he said, "Huh?"

Scott said, "We will help you. We care what happens to you, but we will not put up with teenage hostility or whining. You ran all the way to us for a reason. Because you are here does not mean you are in control."

"I could leave. I could run away again." But he didn't move.

"Yes, you could," Scott said, "and that's a type of control. You stated you wanted to stay. We'd like to have you. There would be rules here for however long you would stay. There are always rules. I am not going to hold you down and make you call your parents." The kid nodded. "Sometime tonight they need to be communicated with. If necessary, I'll call them. They undoubtedly have the police looking for you. To not call would be criminal and cruel."

Donny focused his eyes on Scott.

Scott said, "Why don't you tell us what caused you to run away?"

Abruptly the kid began to cry. As the tears fell, he said, "I'm not going to cry. They can't make me cry." I handed him a box of tissues. After several minutes, he drew a deep breath, gave an enormous snuffle, and told the story. "Sometimes my dad hits me. This year most of our fights were about my being on the basketball team. My dad always wanted me to play sports. I was the MVP on every basketball team I played on in junior high and so far in high school. He was always more interested in how I played than I was. I had some injuries this year."

I sometimes wondered about teenage athletes with major health problems. Did some of them incur the injuries simply to get rid of the pressure?

"What does your mom do when he hits you?" Scott asked.

"She's scared of him. I'm not going to hide behind my ma.

I'll be as big as him soon. I've tried to run away before. I've left for good now."

"Was there something specific that happened in the last day or so?" Scott asked.

"We had a big fight. Practice was supposed to start last week. I refused to go. He never called me a wimp to my face, but I heard him say it to Ma one night. Then they found pot in my room. He really hit the roof. I had only a tiny amount. I never use it. I was holding it for a friend."

I almost laughed. Scott said, "Don't give me that holding-it-for-a-friend bull crap."

Donny looked startled and frowned. After a moment he resumed, "Okay. I smoke a little. My friends are kind of wild. Then one time my parents caught me with a girl. They were supposed to be out till late. They came home early. Nothing happened with the girl."

Scott raised an eyebrow.

"I swear." Donny held out his hands palm up. "Honest. I really wanted to date her brother. He's a year ahead of me in school. That's why I came to you guys. I hoped you'd be sympathetic."

So, the kid was gay. A reasonably big deal, but not as big of a deal as it might have been a few years ago, although he was from rural Georgia. From what I knew of Scott's older brother, Donny's father, he would be hostile to the news.

Throughout Donny's narrative, in the back of my head I kept getting a niggling little feeling that something wasn't right here. I sensed there was more of "Are they buying this?" in his recitation than a need for affirmation or a desire to be comforted and helped. I could have been wrong. I'd taught teenagers a long time and listened to a lot of truth and lies. His tale of woe didn't sound quite right to me, but I didn't know what it was about what he was saying that I didn't trust.

I said, "Some of your other relatives are in town. Some are staying in that hotel. Why didn't you go to them? You could have waited outside the reception and caught people as they were leaving."

"Why are you questioning me? I didn't do anything wrong." He was rapidly moving beyond thinly veiled hostility and whining to blatant defiance.

Scott held up a hand to me. He asked Donny, "Why didn't you ask the guards at the doors to the reception to get one of us or one of your uncles, aunts, or your grandparents?"

"I didn't, okay? I just didn't. You'd think you'd want to help me."

I was moving beyond willing to help a kid in trouble to being fed up to the gills with the little snot.

"Why should we?" Scott asked. At least Scott's questions were beginning to indicate less than an infatuation with this possibly toxic teenager.

"I think I heard what happened in the washroom to that guy," Donny announced.

I was thunderstruck. I thought I caught a hint of a smirk on the kid's face. That pissed me off. I didn't think Scott caught it, and I couldn't be absolutely sure that's what I saw, but I was now even more suspicious. Was this a big slip in the heat of anger or a planned revelation, or evidence of overwhelming emotion in the face of unexpected death?

Scott said, "Are you okay? Did anyone try to attack you?"

"No. I'm okay."

"You know he's dead?" I asked.

"Yeah, I had to sneak around the guards to get out of the hotel. I heard them telling people why they couldn't leave."

"How'd you get out?" If the kid had been able to sneak out, certainly the killer would have been able to do so as well.

"I pretended I was with another family. I hung close to

some teenagers who had nothing to do with the wedding."

I said, "Very slowly and carefully, tell us the exact sequence of events from when you entered the hotel until you left."

"I tried to sneak into the wedding. I got stopped at the main entrance to the ballroom. I tried going around to different hallways. Finally, I needed to use the bathroom. I heard these guys hollering at each other. I didn't actually go into the john or see them."

"Are you sure there were only two?"

"I only heard two voices. I wanted to use the john, but I thought I'd better wait. They sounded pretty violent. I hid down the corridor so no one would see me. Then I heard a big yell and a couple thunks. A door opened and closed. Then it was quiet. I heard footsteps moving away from me. The hall was carpeted, but I could still hear the footsteps. They walked away from where I was, toward the party, not toward the exit. I wasn't going to hang around. After I was sure he was gone, I ran."

"What time was this?"

"I don't have a watch."

I asked, "You're sure whoever was in the washroom didn't walk past where you were?"

"I would have seen them."

"Then wouldn't he have been able to see you? Hanging around at that moment was pretty risky. If someone had just committed murder, they weren't going to want to leave witnesses."

"Well, I was kind of hidden. At the time I didn't know anybody'd been killed. I heard him walk the other way. I didn't hear anybody walk past me."

So according to Donny the killer had almost certainly walked back to the reception. I remembered I had passed no exits and only storage closets on the way to the washroom. I presumed the cops had checked them. The killer couldn't have simply waited until everyone left and walked calmly out. Certainly no one had mentioned a blood-covered killer waltzing around the reception. Either he or she managed to avoid most of the blood, had a quick change of clothes, or washed it all off. Then again, I'd held and tried to help Ethan. The killer might have had little blood to conceal.

I asked, "Why didn't you call the cops or at least tell someone?"

"A runaway reporting a crime? I figured I was safe hanging out in the crowd. Then I heard all kinds of people talking about a dead body in a washroom. I was scared. I didn't know who killed him. They might think I did it, or maybe the killer would come back. When I left the hotel, I didn't know what to do. I decided to come here."

"How'd you know where we lived?" Scott asked.

"I got the address from Aunt Mary's computer when we were there for Grandpa and Grandma's wedding anniversary party. No one saw me copy it down. I knew she'd have it because she likes you guys."

The kid had heard the murder take place. He needed to talk to the cops. He could certainly eliminate the possibility of escape out the back way.

"You're going to have to talk to the police at some point," I said. I was tempted to tell him that when I'd found Ethan, he was still alive, and that if they'd found him sooner, they might have been able to save him. I'd have to ask the authorities if that was true. Even though I didn't like Donny, my suspicions would have to turn to certainty before I'd try to put that amount of guilt on the kid.

Donny said, "I know I should have called. I guess you're right. I don't want to talk to the police." At the moment I felt

46

extremely uneasy about what the kid had told us. Many of his earlier answers seemed too facile or even rehearsed. The stuff about the murder seemed genuine. I wasn't going to confront him just yet.

We set him up in the guest room with a view to the west.

After the kid was in bed, we returned to the kitchen. Standing against the Corian countertop, we discussed what to do next.

6

Scott said, "We should call his parents. Do we tell them about Donny's connection to the murder?"

I said, "I'd hate to give that kind of information to a parent over the phone. The kid probably should be the one to do that."

"If he doesn't, we'd have to consider it. Do we tell the cops he probably heard the murderer?"

"I don't think we have much choice there. He can almost certainly eliminate one avenue of escape. His story means it is very likely that the killer was at the reception. Donny's version might help keep me from being a suspect. After I found the body, emergency people showed up pretty fast. On the other hand, according to his story, he can't accuse anybody." Even though he was Scott's nephew, I wanted to get the next question out in the open. "Could Donny have killed him?"

Scott gazed at me for several moments, then said, "I sure as hell hope not." He shook his head, sighed, and said, "Let's get the parent call out of the way."

It was two in the morning. Scott found the number and

dialed. He put the call on the speakerphone. It rang twice. A very alert, nonsleepy female voice answered.

"Cynthia? It's Scott, Hiram's brother."

Silence.

"Donny is here in Chicago. He's safe."

"Thank God. We've been frantic." She didn't bother to cover the receiver as she gave the news to whoever else was in the room. The phone clunked several times, someone putting it down. Several moments later we heard weeping. The phone was picked up. A gruff male voice said, "You put him on the next plane home."

"Hiram," Scott said, "I think maybe you should come and get him."

"I want to talk to him."

Scott said, "He's asleep. He said he didn't want to talk to you."

"He's my kid. He'll do what I tell him."

"Yes, he's your kid, but for the moment, he's here."

Cynthia's voice came back on the line. "We'll come pick him up."

There was a deep-voiced squawk. Cynthia spoke firmly: "We'll be on the first plane in the morning." Seconds later we heard a dial tone.

As we undressed for bed, I said, "I wonder if Donny was telling us the whole truth."

"Why wouldn't he?"

That's the problem with people such as Scott who are inherently truth-tellers. They are more likely to believe those who lie. Scott may pride himself on how good he is with little kids, but he's not used to teenagers. He doesn't see them daily. He hasn't experienced up close their desperate need for secrecy combined with their wild desire for attention and affirmation. They passionately desire an identity and security.

They are often ill equipped to conceal their needs or to articulate them intelligently. Their needs are always out there at the raw edges of reality. All of that is pretty normal. How far beyond the ordinary adolescent angst Donny had gone, I wasn't sure yet. Something was amiss. Simple lies or depths of criminal complexity, I wasn't sure.

I said, "I just got a sense there was more to the story."

"He's a good kid. I don't think he'd lie. Which part sounded incomplete to you?"

"For one, that part about abuse by your brother. You know him better than I, but when we were in Georgia, he didn't strike me as abusive." I did think of him as a bigoted redneck, but not a violent one. I didn't think this was a tactful thing to say.

Scott said, "Hiram puts on a macho, tough image, but he isn't mean."

"I wonder if the kid is really gay."

"Why would a straight kid want to make that up?"

"Maybe he thought that's what we'd like to hear, and he figured saying that would make us be more sympathetic to him. I'm not saying I have definite answers here. I'm just saying I have doubts."

"I believe him." Scott stated this as absolute fact. "I asked him some tough questions and he gave reasonable answers."

"I thought they were more like snarls."

"He's a teenager. He's had a rough time. What do you expect?"

I backed off. I had no proof, and it was his nephew.

Scott amended what he said. "I believe him for now. We'll have to talk to his parents and get their side of things."

I agreed.

In bed we caressed each other and snuggled close. He

murmured, "This isn't quite where I planned to be on our wedding night."

"Funny, this is exactly where I planned to be." It was late and a horrible deed had impinged on an emotionally rough-edged day. I kissed him and we cuddled contentedly for a while. I wanted him close, but it didn't seem like the right moment for mad passion. In a short while I felt his muscles relax. He usually falls asleep faster and sleeps longer and deeper than I. I held him until my arm fell asleep. I pulled it gently from under him and turned over on my back. I laced my fingers together, placed my hands behind my head, and stared at the ceiling.

For the moment I eliminated the murder from waking memory. I thought of our wedding day and our commitment and our love. I thought of how lucky I was to have found a man who loved me as much as I loved him, that I had found someone to share all of life's little oddities. And I do love him. Deeply and completely and happily. No question, he was the one I wanted to spend my entire life with. I looked at the ring on my finger. This would be the first time I would be sleeping with it on. I could see his on his left hand.

My thoughts took a maudlin turn for a while into usually unexpressed fears. I wondered how long we would be to-gether. An accident on the freeway could end everything to-morrow, or we could live for fifty more years together. I wondered which of us would die first and how tough that would be for whichever of us was left. I couldn't imagine a life without him.

When we were kids, Ethan and I had vowed to each other that our relationship would never end. Silly promises of a cou-ple of kids they might have been, but at the time they felt permanent and enduring. As a teenager I'd never confided such dreams to anyone else. Our breakup had felt like the most horrible betrayal. Time had blurred my memories of those awful days. The hurt as a child combined with the more recent rebuff as an adult burned like the sting of an old memory that comes back unexpectedly. Vestiges of heartache remained. My relationship with Scott, the reason and calm of adulthood, and the forgetfulness of years kept me from the soap opera tears those moments might otherwise merit.

I had Scott to tell all my secret hopes and dreams to, and it felt very right. If they needed a picture of bliss for the dictionary, I was ready. I touched his brush-cut hair with the tips of my fingers, let them linger on the nape of his neck, on his left ear, the line of his jaw. I leaned over and whispered, "I love you." I was in love with a man who loved me, and we had just had a day that had been near perfect, until ten minutes to seven.

Finding a dead body at the wedding didn't fall into the category of amusing anecdotes to tell the grandkids. I know that into every relationship a little rain must fall. This was more like a deluge. I had a brief view of the two of us walking hand in hand down a street with dead bodies flopping in our wake. I shuddered at the thought that the story of our lives might become more like a demented amateur sleuth's than I preferred to imagine. Who would invite an amateur sleuth to town? They're a crime wave waiting to happen and certifiable menaces to society. Here's another tip: never invite Miss Marple or the rest of her cozy crowd to anything. When amateur sleuths show up, people die.

I awoke an hour or so later. When we have houseguests, especially the first night they stay, I sleep poorly. It's not that I expect them to cart off the crown jewels; after all, they are invited guests. It's not as if I can hear them. Maybe it's something primitive and instinctual. Someone's in my territory. Or despite Scott's assurances, maybe we had a killer sleeping down the hall. Or maybe I'm a neurotic moron and need to get a grip. Or maybe I was wakeful because of the excitement of the day and night we'd been through.

At any rate, I was restless. I put on some white athletic socks, Jockey shorts, and a tatty old T-shirt that reached to midthigh. I stopped in the kitchen for a sip of diet soda. I heard a noise in the electronics room.

Calling it an electronics room was not descriptive enough by half. If it was digital or made noise or produced the slightest electronic blip, even if it barely breathed technology, we owned it. Scott loved playing with all this junk. I enjoyed using it, but nowhere near as much as he.

I stopped in the darkened doorway. Donny Carpenter was backlit by the myriad digital displays on the resting machines, four of which were now in the middle of the floor, unplugged and disconnected. Donny was in his stocking feet and boxer shorts. He was busily working on a fifth machine and quietly humming to himself. One of the computer monitors glowed. I distinctly remembered shutting down everything in this room after we'd showed it to Scott's parents the day before. The monitor indicated the computer was turned to the search engine for the Internet.

I leaned against the doorjamb and waited for Donny's inevitable realization that he wasn't alone. He turned with the receiver he'd been manhandling and walked to his pile of loot in the center of the room. Just before he added it to the stack, he looked in my direction. The electronic component in his hands thudded onto the gold, plush carpet. I heard several bits of electronic innards rattle.

"Rearranging the furniture when you're a guest something they teach in Georgia?" I asked. "How kind and thoughtful."

"Uh" was the first noise he made, then he switched to muttering. I caught the word *Motherfucker.*

I pressed the button to turn the lights up. He didn't meet my eyes. He didn't gaze at my underwear-clad torso. Mostly he looked at the ground. Occasionally, he stood on the side of his feet. I said, "I suspect most of what you told us earlier wouldn't stand up to a lot of scrutiny."

"I did run away." Full teenage snarl.

I sat down in a comfy, high-back swivel chair, draped a leg over the side, stretched out, and said, "So all the rest was lies?"

He raised his voice. "I did hear the shouting in that bathroom at the hotel. I don't have to put up with this shit!" He strode toward the door.

I rose to my feet, glided to the portal, and stood in his way. I was several inches taller than he and at least twenty or thirty pounds heavier. I said, "I'm trying to decide if I care enough to take that snarl and shove it down your throat."

"My uncle won't let you threaten me. I'll tell him you did."

"We could race to tell him. If you don't tattle, I certainly will. His problem is that despite the slings and arrows he's endured, he still has a naive belief in the goodness of all mankind. I, however, have been a schoolteacher for far too many years. I can recognize a teenage lying sack of shit when I see one. I expressed my doubts to him earlier. He didn't believe me."

"I'll run away again. You can't make me do anything. I can do anything I want."

I hate it when people disconnect from reality. I said, "What a stupid thing to say. Only moronic twits without a brain in their heads would say such a monumentally boneheaded thing. Where on this planet does anyone do whatever they want? You may be trying to say you will make all the decisions controlling your life, but there you would be wrong again."

"I don't care what you say."

"Caring isn't the problem. Your fatuous stupidity is."

"Fuck you"—delivered in a full-throated roar. No snarl when he was truly pissed.

"I've got a question, several in fact." I pointed to the monitor. "What were you looking for on the Internet?"

"Nothing."

"I can download the history and find out where you've been."

"Not if I went there when I finished and erased it."

I hate how kids know so much about computers. Even more I hated the triumphant tone in his voice. I asked, "How were you planning to get this stuff out of here and where were you taking it to?"

Now I got a silence filled with oceans of defiance. His arms were folded across his chest. His jaw was set. The eyes were focused on the middle distance, a trick usually reserved for inhabitants of B-list British novels.

I thought I'd try logical progression of thought. This doesn't work often enough with your average recalcitrant teenager, but it's better than torturing them painfully in a dark, dank dungeon, no matter how tempting this last alternative might be. I said, "I don't understand how you think silence is going to help right now. You either did or did not think the whole thing through: coming here, lying, and ripping us off. I'm curious about your thought process."

No response.

"Why didn't you just run away somewhere closer to home, to a friend's, why here?"

Nothing.

"It's a little late to put everything back right now. Why don't you go to bed, and we can resume our lack of discussion in the morning." I paused at the doorway and looked back. "In case you're planning to leave tonight without telling us, be aware the doorman in the lobby is on duty twenty-four hours a day. The parking garage always has an attendant on the premises. As far as I'm concerned, you are free to leave. I'm just letting you know your departure without merchandise would be noted. With merchandise, you'd be stopped." I didn't wait for a reply. I wasn't about to trust the little creep. I watched him leave.

Almost everything about him made me uneasy. Not trusting him was one thing. There was something very not right about this kid. I returned to the computer that Donny had turned on and checked the Internet history. In fact, I couldn't even find evidence that he'd gone on-line. The kid was either very good at covering his tracks, or he hadn't had time to use the thing much. Then again, he could have just turned it on out of curiosity. Yeah, right. I believed that. He had to have a reason for turning it on. I doubted if he was ever going to tell me what it was.

We had thousands of dollars' worth of equipment in this room. We'd had security devices installed on all the exits to the penthouse and on rooms with valuable items such as this one. I set the electronic lock and watched the quarter-inch-thick glass door glide shut. I called security, then sent the elevator to the ground floor. He'd be unable to recall it without the key. He wasn't getting out downstairs without us knowing. I set the alarm on the emergency exits to the stairs. Up here he couldn't leave without breaking a window and jumping. With the kind of glass we had on this floor, he'd probably need a cannon to break it. He didn't strike me as a jumper. A user, a taker, a manipulator—sure. Suicidal? I figured he was making that up, too.

I crawled back into bed next to Scott. He stirred in his sleep. I lay close to him and shut my eyes.

. 7 .

The bright morning sun flooding through the floor-to-ceiling windows brought with it a ringing phone. It was the doorman announcing my parents, my sister and her husband, and Ethan's parents, Rachel and Perry Gahain. Scott was in the shower. I threw on jeans, white socks, tennis shoes, and a logoless sweatshirt. It was seven in the morning. We'd gone to bed at three. I'd confronted Donny around four. I called to Scott to tell him they were here. He said he'd hurry. There was no sign of Scott's nephew as I unblocked the elevator. As I passed Donny's room, I glanced in. He seemed to be sound asleep.

I let the six of them in. If we had slept little, they had obviously slept less. Mr. and Mrs. Gahain's eyes were red-rimmed with dark circles around them. They were still in the clothes they'd worn to the reception. We sat in the kitchen. I switched on the automatic coffeemaker and set it to brew. Several years ago we'd gotten the properly exotic brewer with the properly exotic packets filled with properly exotic and annoyingly perky coffee. I got out regular cream for my mom, the fake cream my dad likes, sugar, blue and pink diet-sugar packets (my mother likes to use one of each), and honey for Scott. I placed the tray in the middle of the breakfast nook. As we all filled our coffee cups, Scott entered the room.

My mother said, "We've been up with the Gahains all night. We've been trying to make sense out of Ethan's death. Of course, we can't. The police talked to Rachel and Perry, but either the police didn't know anything or wouldn't tell them anything."

Mrs. Gahain said, "We need to understand why."

"Ethan insisted he had to come to the wedding to talk to you," Mr. Gahain said. "What did he say?"

"In the receiving line, he said we needed to talk, but we never did."

My mother said, "Rachel called me yesterday morning. I told her it was okay to bring Ethan along even though he wasn't on the guest list. I told the security guards to admit him. I didn't think you'd mind."

Mrs. Gahain said, "Thank you, Dolores, I know you were always close to Ethan. He didn't say anything to anyone?"

Everyone shook their heads no. I said, "Not to me. I'm sorry."

Mr. Gahain said, "Ethan arrived late Friday night. We knew something was wrong, but he wouldn't talk to us. If there was anyone he could always talk to, it was you, Tom. He always trusted you."

At this moment I was not about to say their kid and I hadn't exchanged more than a few words in years and hadn't confided in each other in far longer. Quite obviously they assumed their son and I were still close. Whether this misperception was due to Ethan's lies or their lack of insight, I couldn't be sure.

Mrs. Gahain said, "We weren't as close as we should have

been. Many people don't confide in their own families, certainly not after they're grown and out of the house."

"That's very true," my mother said. "That happens in all families."

Mr. Gahain said, "We want to know who killed him. We want the son of a bitch who did this caught, tried, and executed."

Mrs. Gahain said, "What's important is that we want to know what was wrong. We want to know what was in his mind. We can't ask his ex-wives. We were never close to any of them. Some we met only a few times. We never got more than a week's notice of when the ceremonies would be. It was almost as if he wasn't really serious about them. We didn't usually find out about the divorces until after they were finalized. Tom, you'd be the one, of all the people we can think of, who would know or be able to find out what was going on. You were best friends."

I wasn't so sure their knowing what was wrong was a good thing. A lot of the time I think it's better for parents not to know what their kids are doing. Certainly I'd done things as a kid I'm not prepared to confess to my parents. What's the point? Total honesty is a myth.

"I don't think I can help you there," I said. "We haven't really talked in the last couple years." I was not about to say I'd been rejected twice in particularly odious ways. How could I say that kind of thing to a parent who had just lost a child?

She continued, "He told us he was planning to move up here, but first he had to talk to you. He said it was important."

My mother said, "If Tom knew, he'd tell you." This was accompanied by the look I remembered from childhood that always meant I want the truth and I want it now. I'd long since built up immunity to blabbing under that fearsome glare. My mother was good. Even though I had nothing to tell, I was not immune to the tendrils of accompanying guilt that followed when I was the recipient of that storied gaze.

I confirmed her statement. "If I knew, I would tell."

Big sigh from both Gahains.

"We can't go down to St. Louis to talk to people," Mrs. Gahain said. "We've got to arrange the wake, the funeral. They're going to be here, where he grew up." Trembling pause. "Get used to him being gone." She began to weep. We were all silent. My mother patted her hand. Mr. Gahain put his arm around his wife's shoulder. Tears coursed down his cheeks. I didn't have the comfort of tears.

Some minutes later when they were more composed, Mrs. Gahain said, "We're wondering if there isn't some clue, some reason. We knew almost nothing about his current life." She gulped. "I'm almost afraid what we'd find if we went down there."

Mr. Gahain said, "We want to know why this happened."

I asked, "Ethan was being secretive about what he wanted to say. Do you have any reason to believe his reluctance might have been because he was involved in something criminal?" I was certainly not going to ask his parents if they knew their son was into making and distributing pornography.

"No," Mr. Gahain said, "but he was always so distant. We rarely talked."

Mrs. Gahain began to cry again. "We tried to be good parents."

My mother said, "You were and are good parents."

"He loved you," I said. "That I do know for sure. He told me so." And he had. Years ago we were sitting in a bar with a crowd of friends the night after he had come back from college graduation. The same night he had also said his parents drove him nuts even faster than his wife did. At the time he was married to wife number one.

60

Mrs. Gahain turned her teary eyes on me. "We want to find out what happened. Would you go to St. Louis and look in his house? We're the executors of his estate. We'll pack it up at some point in the future, but maybe there'll be a clue there, a hint, a reason."

And sometimes there weren't reasons or rational explanations. Sometimes, many times, I found that which is irrational ruled the world. (Think the Taliban, Jerry Falwell, and Pat Robertson.) I wasn't about to mention that either. This was no time to be less than comforting.

My mother said, "You'll go, Tom, won't you?" Her best friends were in pain. I knew she was, too. She'd watched Ethan grow up and genuinely liked him. I wanted to know what happened. I wanted to know who this Michael was that Ethan used his last breath to mention.

I asked, "Had he given out even the smallest hint about what was bothering him?"

Mr. Gahain said, "No. We've gone over and over everything we can remember that he said to us since he came home. We can't think of one thing." He shrugged.

"He didn't reveal anything specific, but you suspected?"

"Something was wrong," Mrs. Gahain said. "We had no idea what or how serious it was. I think he was frightened of something. He should have known he could talk to us. He always could."

I was glad they believed that.

I asked, "Did he have any enemies that you know of?"

"No," Mrs. Gahain said, "although we didn't know a lot of his friends either."

Mr. Gahain added, "At least one of his ex-wives hated him."

"Why?" I asked.

"I think there were some alimony and custody issues," Mr.

Gahain said. "We never knew precisely what the problem was."

Ernie and my sister had sat silently through all this. I turned to them. "Do either of you have a notion about what was bothering him?"

Caroline said, "No," quickly and emphatically. My sister was always good at being definitive.

Ernie said, "We haven't been close in a long time. Our age difference was somewhat of a factor, but it was more him than me who put distance between us as we got older."

"Ernie, please!" Mrs. Gahain said.

I knew Ethan worshiped his older brother when they were kids. According to Caroline, as adults Ernie and Ethan had fought often and loudly, causing no amount of grief at family gatherings. Caroline had informed me that she thought it was both their fault. Ernie refused to give her details about the background to the fights. He never pointed to one specific incident in the past. When she had first told me, I had suggested that maybe it wasn't one specific thing that had caused the break. Maybe it was just the result of being brothers who rubbed each other the wrong way. Then again, maybe Ethan had done something recently that had made Ernie angry enough to commit fratricide.

Ernie said, "We can't hide things if we expect the truth to come out. I need to lead a quiet life. Ethan always had to be going and moving and doing, just being more intensely than anyone else. I'm afraid it finally caught up with him. I should be the one to go to St. Louis. I just can't handle it physically. I figured something was bothering him, but, no, I don't know what it was."

I asked, "Have any of you remembered any connection he had with someone named Michael?" I had told them about his last words.

All of them gave various forms of the same puzzled frown. Mrs. Gahain said, "Since you told us that earlier, we've tried to figure out who he may have been referring to. We haven't a clue. I assume he must have known people named Michael, but we aren't aware of anyone he knew well enough to say he loved him."

"He wasn't gay," Mr. Gahain said. "Why would he say he loved Michael?"

This was delicate. I was not about to discuss their son's sexuality with them. Not at this point. Not if Ethan hadn't. "None of his kids were named Mike, were they?" I asked. "Or maybe a nickname for one of his wives like the movie with Pat and Mike that Spencer Tracy and Katharine Hepburn made?"

Mrs. Gahain said, "No. That can't have been what his last words meant."

My dad corrected me, "Hepburn was Pat so that comparison doesn't work." Then he added, "It sure was an odd thing for him to say."

I said, "I'll keep asking about that name especially while we're down in St. Louis."

We agreed to go that day. My mother pulled me aside in the hallway. "I know the Gahains think you and Ethan were still close. I know you haven't been since you broke up when you were kids."

"You knew about that?"

"That silly grin you had on your face for over a year when you were in high school could only mean one thing. You weren't dating any girls. You would have told us. Then you went into that heavily morose period that one winter. It wasn't hard to figure out."

"Oh. All that agony I went through to come out to you guys . . ."

"Probably wasn't necessary. Perhaps you're a stronger person for it."

"I'd rather be a stronger person without it. Pain hurts."

"I understand, dear. It's over. The Gahains are good friends. I'm glad you agreed to go."

"They were like a second set of parents to me when I was a kid. Do the Gahains know Ethan and I were lovers as kids?"

"They've never mentioned it. I never brought it up. It's not my secret to tell." She hugged me and gave me a little kiss on the cheek.

As the rest of the crowd drifted toward the elevator, my sister fell in step beside me. She put a hand on my elbow to slow me down. She gazed carefully at me. "I know you, Thomas. You're suspicious by nature. Ernie did not kill his brother. We both know they didn't get along. Ernie is in a wheelchair, for Christ's sake. He can't even maneuver that freely." I knew there were logistical problems to Ernie having been the killer, but the stall in the washroom had been wheelchair accessible. When I didn't immediately respond, she said, "Ethan was not to be trusted. Look at all those divorces. Ever ask yourself why?"

"I'm not sure I cared enough to think about it much at all."

"Then think about it now. Every single marriage failed in less than two years. You and he didn't get along. Ethan and Ernie were estranged. It is not Ernie's fault that Ethan didn't get along with people."

I said, "I don't think Ernie did it."

"Good," she said. We rejoined the others.

After they had left, Scott went to begin preparations for breakfast, and I went to take a shower. He slid back the door as I

64

began to shampoo my hair. I smiled at him. "Did you want to join me?"

He asked, "Why is there a stack of video equipment in the middle of the electronics room?"

"Your nephew was making a pile. I don't think he came all the way from Georgia to help us rearrange the furniture." I told Scott what had happened when I'd awakened earlier.

"He was going to rip us off," Scott said.

"I believe that would be the medical diagnosis."

"The little shit. You were right about him."

When I finished my shower, I joined Scott in the kitchen. The recently referred to piece of excrement walked into the room. He glared at me, smiled at Scott. Donny was wearing faded jeans, white socks, and a wrinkled T-shirt emblazoned with a picture of the rock group Metallica. His hair was mussed. Bags under his eyes indicated insufficient amounts of sleep.

"You were ripping us off," Scott said.

"No, I wasn't."

It was the blatant lie that did him in. Scott's got a big heart, especially for kids, but he hates being lied to.

Scott said, "What the hell did you think you were going to be able to do with that stuff? You couldn't possibly walk out the door with it."

"I was just looking at them."

I loved the thought of Donny confessing the truth and pleading for forgiveness. The stubborn pout on the kid's face didn't lend itself to the possibility of that fantasy being fulfilled. The ensuing moments of extended silence added nothing to the situation. As he had earlier this morning, the kid simply shut down. Finally, Scott said, "Donny, you look like you could use a shower. Under the sink in the bathroom connected to your room, you'll find clean towels and wash-

65

cloths." The teenager looked from one to the other of us, shrugged, turned, and left.

I said, "Direct confrontations aren't working."

"We could try to borrow a tank and run him over repeatedly."

"Much too tempting."

"We could look through his backpack while he's taking a shower. Maybe we'll find some clue to what he's really up to. Although maybe that would violate his rights. I'm not sure I care about his rights. The little creep lied."

I said, "I like it when you do both sides of an argument."

"Come on."

We trooped down the hallway. Through the bedroom door we could hear the shower running. Scott tapped softly. There was no answer. We walked in. The jeans, socks, and T-shirt Donny had been wearing along with a red-and-gray-striped pair of boxer shorts lay on the floor. I checked the pants pockets while Scott rummaged in the backpack. I found two quarters and a penny in one front pocket. I extracted a wallet from the left rear. I found three five-dollar bills and two ones, a learner's permit from the state of Georgia, a picture of a pleasant-faced girl, a picture ID from General Gwinnet High School, and a condom.

Scott whispered, "I found something." The shower water continued to run. I hurried over. Scott had scattered the contents of Donny's backpack onto the bed. I saw a comb, a toothbrush but no toothpaste, deodorant, three more pairs of boxer shorts in muted reds and grays, two more T-shirts with rock-group logos, and two more pairs of white socks. Scott held out a pencil pouch, the kind they used to have when I was a kid, ten inches by three inches of vinyl that zipped on one side. In it Donny had stuffed a thick roll of bills including some hundreds and fifties, a credit card with his dad's name on it, and the remnants of a plane ticket, one-way from Atlanta to Chicago.

"Why did he come here?" Scott asked. "What wild and romantic dreams were in his head?"

"Lot of money."

The shower stopped. I scooped up everything except one pair of boxer shorts and stuffed it all into the backpack. We dropped his possessions in a hall closet. We sat in the kitchen to wait. The explosion wasn't long in coming. He marched into the room, hair still wet, boxer shorts on, a towel in his left hand. He had small tufts of hair around each nipple. He was skinny to the point of emaciation, belying the amount of food he'd devoured last night. He had a tattoo of a scorpion around his navel.

"What the hell is going on!" he demanded.

"Precisely." Scott's quite cryptic when he's pissed.

"Where's my stuff?"

"Safe," Scott said.

"You took my money."

"Yes."

"You guys are perverts. I'll accuse you of trying to molest me."

I remained impassive. Scott scowled. While the kid glared from one to the other of us, Scott let the silence build several more beats, then said, "Of all the places on the planet to choose from, you came here. Why?"

"Can I at least have my pants?"

"Why here?" Scott asked.

"I told you last night."

"Why?" Scott reiterated.

"I want my pants."

"Where'd you get all that money?"

"Savings. I want my pants."

I got up, left the room, made sure I wasn't followed, retrieved his pants, and brought them back. The kid was standing at the window looking out at the lake. I handed him his pants and sat back down next to Scott. The kid yanked his pants on and then glared at us.

"Silence is not going to work," Scott said.

"You can't keep me here," Donny said.

"That presumes we want you to stay," Scott said.

Donny looked a trifle disconcerted at that.

The intercom phone buzzed. I picked it up, listened, and hung up. I turned to Donny. "The police are here," I announced.

"You can't make me talk to them," Donny said.

"What's the big deal about giving them a statement?" Scott asked. "There was a murder at our wedding, and if they have a few questions, why would that cause you such anxiety? Unless you lied to us last night."

"I didn't lie." Donny had added a bit of a snap to his usual snarl.

"Then I don't see the problem," Scott said.

"You can't let them question me. You can't tell them I was there."

I left the room to let the cops in.

8

When I got back to them, I introduced Detectives Rohter and Hoge from the night before.

Hoge said, "We stopped by to check a few things." The detectives sat three feet apart on our white couch. Scott and I sat opposite them with our knees touching. Donny sat to our left, their right.

Rohter said, "We've got thirty-seven people at the wedding who knew Mr. Gahain."

I said, "That sounds right. There were a lot of folks there from the old neighborhood. My parents, old friends, people from high school."

"And you guys," Rohter said.

I said, "Scott had never met him until last night."

Rohter added, "Except for his relatives and you, none claimed to have talked to him in the past five years."

"I haven't talked to him much recently."

"Why is that?"

"We drifted apart as adults. He moved to St. Louis a couple years ago."

Rohter said, "We haven't been able to pin down his movements at the reception. No one admits to seeing him heading to that washroom. Mostly he's reported to have been sitting by himself in a corner or at a table with no one on either side of him."

"It was a big party," I said. "No one was expecting to have to remember details as possible murder witnesses."

Hoge said, "We were hoping we'd find someone."

Scott pointed to Donny. "He heard the murder take place."

The stoic gazes of the detectives rested on Donny. The teenager said, "Hey, what! I didn't see anything. I don't know anything."

The cops looked at Scott, me, and then the kid. Donny said, "You can't question me without my parents here."

Everybody's a lawyer these days. Although, anyone with half a brain, as opposed to most suspects on television shows, would ask for a lawyer and shut up.

Then it hit me about why the kid made me uneasy. Here he was facing being questioned by the cops, and he didn't look troubled or concerned. I saw petulance mixed with excitement. It was the same look as the night before when he'd first told us what he'd heard. For most of us there would have been some kind of strong reaction or worry or at least concern. He asked no questions about what had happened nor evinced the slightest bit of curiosity. Someone had been killed, and it didn't seem to bother him. I didn't detect any feeling from him that he should or could have done something to help. No residual realization that he had been in the presence of or in close proximity to a violent act that took a human life. He may not have completely understood what was happening at the time, but when he heard the news, it should have at least given him pause. Earlier this morning he'd been far too casual and composed for any fifteen-year-old.

Scott said, "He ran away from home. He came here. Maybe because much of his family is here for the wedding, or maybe he had nowhere to go nearer to home. His parents are on their way to pick him up." Scott gave them the details of Donny's arrival, then said, "Here's what he told us about the murder." Scott finished, "We didn't call you then because it was the middle of the night. He hadn't actually seen the killer."

Rohter kept an impassive gaze on Donny as he said, "You're not a suspect. You might be able to help us. Wouldn't you want to help catch a killer?"

Donny seemed to contemplate this for a minute. Then he folded his arms over his chest and set his jaw. I noted the familial resemblance to Scott at that moment. Scott has that same look on his face on the mound when he's facing a fearsome hitter or when he's particularly irritated with me.

Donny said, "I ain't saying nothin' till my parents get here."

I love teenage logic. First, he hates his parents, then he runs to them for protection. The dyad of bravado and ego chasing the triumvirate of angst and immaturity and fear.

I said, "I'm curious. How does this work? First you want to be free of your parents and be independent, but as soon as trouble rears its head, you run and try to hide behind them."

"I'm not hiding behind my parents."

"Sure you are," I said.

The cop asked, "Is what Mr. Carpenter said accurate?"

"I guess, maybe." Each word emerged at the speed of a molar being extracted.

"Why don't you tell us the story?"

"You heard it from him." If he snarled a bit more often in that tone, I might implicate him in the murder just for the hell of it.

71

"We'd rather hear it from you."

"I'm waiting for my mom and dad, and I'm not hiding behind them."

"Is there more you need to add?" Rohter asked.

Despite the detectives repeated proddings, Donny remained recalcitrant.

"They stole my clothes."

Scott said, "We found electronic equipment piled on its way out the door. He's run away from home at least once that we know of. We were afraid he'd try to bolt before his parents got here."

"They can't take my stuff," Donny stated.

Rohter said, "Chain him up and dangle him off the side of the building for all I care."

I said, "You must have teenagers of your own."

"Got that right."

Donny saw no sympathy coming from any quarter.

"When his parents get here," Rohter announced, "we'll want to see them and him. He doesn't leave town. I don't care how you keep him here."

Scott got up, left the room, and came back with socks, shoes, and a T-shirt. He tossed them to the boy. The young man went to finish dressing.

Rohter said, "I don't envy his mother and father."

"They should be here soon," Scott said.

"Call us."

We agreed to do that.

I asked, "What else can you tell us about what happened?"

Rohter said, "We discovered that Mr. Gahain had been robbed. There was no money or credit cards in his wallet. You sure you didn't see anyone else?"

"Absolutely. Could Donny have robbed him?"

Rohter said, "It wasn't part of the story he told you. Did

you find Mr. Gahain's credit cards when you looked through Donny's stuff?"

"No."

"Did he have a lot of money?"

"We found a thick wad of cash in Donny's backpack. No more than he could have stolen from his parents or taken out of his own savings account. How much money was Ethan supposed to have on him?"

"We don't know. His mother says she saw a few bills when he put the parking-garage ticket in his wallet before the event."

Scott said, "It would take somebody pretty cruel to rob a dying man and not help."

"We see it more than you think," Rohter said. "Traffic-accident victims lose their possessions all the time."

"Do you have any other notions on who might have done it?" I asked. "Have you checked on the protesters? There were a lot of crazy homophobes out there."

"And they did what?" Rohter asked. "Decided to murder one of the guests, snuck in, waited in an obscure bathroom, hoping someone would show up, and murdered him? To what benefit?"

I said, "To cause a sensation, besmirch the wedding. There's always someone who wants to wreck things."

Rohter said, "They could have called in a false fire alarm or bomb threat, done a whole lot less drastic and dramatic things than murdering a guest. Are you seriously suggesting someone would commit a capital felony simply to make you unhappy?"

"Not when you put it that way," I said.

Scott said, "We ran into a private detective named Jack Miller. He said he tried to talk to you guys."

"Trust me," Rohter said. "We do not rush to our nearest

private eye or amateur sleuth for assistance. We can handle this all on our own."

"Do you know him?" I asked.

"We checked him out. He's legitimate." Rohter's tone suggested being a legitimate private eye was tantamount to being a carrier of the black death.

"What happens next?" Scott asked.

"I have one or two things you might be able to help us with. When you got to the washroom, did you see signs of sexual activity?"

"No. Should I have?"

"We've got copious amounts of semen in his underwear and a bit more on his pants."

"His or the killer's?" I asked.

"We're having it examined. Maybe both."

Scott asked, "Are you saying he had an orgasm while he was being killed?"

Hoge said, "Maybe. More likely in the hour or so before he died. He could have been sitting at a table playing pocket pool and gotten out of control. He could have beat off in that john and used his shorts to wipe up, or he could have been having sex with another person and come before he could get his prick out because he was so turned on, or not taken his prick out because he got his jollies doing it in his pants whether alone or with someone else. I suppose there are a few other possible explanations of how they got stained that I haven't thought of."

I said, "I get the drift. I didn't see any stain."

"It was mixed with blood."

Scott said, "Maybe he was waiting until the cum residue dried before coming out of the john. A big wet stain on the front of your pants could be embarrassing."

74

Rohter asked, "Anybody at the party he might have had sex with?"

"I don't know if he was dating anyone who was at the party or not. I don't know if he picked someone up. He was unattached and not bad looking. He has four ex-wives, one in St. Louis and three here. I have no idea if they have a motive for killing him. Certainly they weren't invited to the wedding."

Hoge said, "We'll be talking to the ex-wives. I doubt if we're going to find they were all in town for a 'how to murder your ex-husband' convention. We definitely want to interrogate your nephew. Don't let him out of your sight."

Rohter and Hoge left.

We repaired to the kitchen. It was just after ten. Scott began frying bacon. I began chopping mushrooms, onions, sausage, and crumbling feta cheese for omelettes.

Scott said, "We could drive to St. Louis. It might be faster than flying."

It was about a five-hour drive. Flying would take an hour's trip to the airport, an hour's wait at the airport—I'm a get-there-plenty-early kind of guy—an hour or so of flight, an hour or so to pick up the luggage, rent a car, and get to downtown St. Louis. That would be assuming no delays. I reminded Scott of all this, then added, "Let's drive. I like to see the crops being harvested."

Some people like vast mountain vistas, or cold, deep-water lakes on remote plateaus, or cityscapes of breathtaking beauty. I like those, too, but the best of all are the flat plains of Illinois. From the grays, blacks, and browns of winter, to the golden harvest of fall, to the hot green of summer, they are the way the world should look, beautifully plain, stark, simple.

I said, "If we play our cards right, we could have dinner at Tony's." If you get a chance while in St. Louis, go to Tony's restaurant. It's near the Arch and definitely very pricey. Trust me. Just go. Take out a bank loan if you have to. It's worth every penny.

"I thought our goal was to look in Ethan's house."

"We have to eat," I responded.

We called Todd Bristol, our lawyer, and he agreed to talk to the authorities. The mayor had been at the damn reception after all. They couldn't very well tell everyone who had been there not to leave town. True, the mayor didn't find the body, but still. We asked about Jack Miller, the private eye. He'd heard of him.

"Jack Miller has quite a reputation. He has a very select clientele, charges astronomical prices, gets results nobody else can, and is totally gorgeous. Stunningly butch and reputedly extremely dangerous. He's got an international reputation. Sexual orientation unknown despite some of the best efforts of the most vicious old gossip queens in the city, myself included."

"I'll try not to be too impressed."

Scott finished frying the bacon. Over the years, he's gotten reasonably good at making omelettes. I figure my cooking is a success if I chop ingredients and don't slice off any parts of my anatomy. I'm still trying to boil an egg to his liking. To my liking, it's easy. Put the egg in water, turn the heat as high as it will go, wait twenty-two minutes, and the thing is edible. Add a little mustard, mayo, and pepper, and it's fabulous. Just because he took a class, does that give him a right to be finicky?

The kid strolled in.

"What would you like in your omelette?" Scott asked him.

Donny said, "If you cook me something, does that obligate me to anything?"

"Yes," I said. "If you don't eat what we put in front of you, we take you down to the hidden caves far below the sewers of Chicago, where to loud disco music from the midseventies, we torture you mercilessly, eventually beating you senseless with large baseball bats satisfying the primitive urges of the parents of every teenager on the planet. If you do eat, the same things happen."

"You're not funny," Donny said.

"I wasn't aware I was joking."

Scott said, "We've got Swiss cheese, cheddar, feta, onions, sausage, mushrooms, and probably a few more things in the refrigerator."

"Just cheddar cheese," Donny said.

Omelettes made, bacon distributed, juice poured, we sat down to eat. I said, "Donny, I'd like to make pleasant breakfast conversation with you, but I don't know what will set you off. Maybe you're too angry to talk to me or your uncle at all. If you'd like, I could leave the room, and you can talk with Scott alone."

The appraising look he gave me at this point seemed to be a trifle less hostile than usual.

After several moments he said, "I'm scared."

"Of what?" Scott asked.

The intercom phone rang. Donny's parents were downstairs.

9

Leaving Donny in the kitchen, Scott and I met them at the elevator. Hiram was taller than Scott's six foot four by at least five inches. He also weighed at least 100 to 150 pounds more than Scott. His wife, Cynthia, bulged out of her clothes. She had a high forehead with hair pulled back in a modified bun.

Hiram's first words were "Where's my son? I want to see him right now." He delivered the words with more snarl in his tone than his son had used in everything he'd said so far.

This was the first time Hiram and Cynthia had been to the penthouse. His words and the tone they were delivered in didn't strike me as an auspicious beginning. When Scott remained silent an uncomfortable amount of time, I said, "Welcome to our home. While you are here, you will observe the rudiments of civility. Nor will you make any demands outside the bounds of welcome guests."

Hiram turned red.

I continued, "Your son came to us. We're willing to help you and him, but we're not going to put up with any verbal abuse. I'm curious, though. In what way do you think being officious and demanding is going to help?"

Scott finally spoke. "Tom is right."

Cynthia put a hand on her husband's arm. "It's their home. You promised." She turned to us. "We'd like to speak with our son as soon as possible." Scott had always described her as a milquetoast, Baptist, obey-your-husband type.

Scott said, "There's a good chance if he's not supervised he may try to run again. He just got done telling us he was scared. He didn't have time to tell us of what."

Hiram and Cynthia exchanged confused looks, then stared at us. Cynthia asked, "What's he been saying?"

I said, "Why don't we listen to him?"

The four of us met the kid in the kitchen. Donny stood up as we entered the room. His mom hugged him, but Donny's hands remained slack at his sides. His dad approached, but Donny flinched back. Cynthia had a tearful reunion. Hiram glowered angrily. The boy did not look at his father. We all moved to the living room and sat down.

From running away, to blatant lies, to attempted theft—if the kid wanted attention from his parents, he'd certainly gotten it. Or maybe he was trying to gain power or assert independence, or a combination of all of the above? I didn't know what he wanted. Maybe he didn't know himself.

Hiram asked, "What the hell is going on?" He banged his fist on a glass-topped table. It rattled but didn't break.

Not a bad question, and I was close to feeling as frustrated as he sounded.

Cynthia gripped Hiram's arm. "Stop it! Now! How is pounding and demanding going to help!" She began to sob. Hiram sat with his mouth hanging open. Even Donny's eyes were misty.

I found some tissues and handed them to her. As Cynthia's tears subsided, Hiram reached out a hand to her. She brushed it away. Hiram frowned. I debated us leaving and letting the family resolve its own problems, but by his actions Donny had made us a part of his and their lives. And I didn't trust him to tell the truth, or even the same lies he had told us. I prefer teenagers who tell consistent lies. That's the kind of guy I am. And he was connected to the murder. That had to be dealt with.

I handed the parents Donny's wad of money, the stolen credit card, and the receipt from the plane ticket.

Cynthia Carpenter said, "Donny, why?"

"That's my money!" His voice squeaked. Donny pointed at us. "They took my stuff. They made me walk around in my underwear."

Very softly, Cynthia repeated her question.

Donny's eyes shifted from adult to adult. I sensed evasion tinged with guilt. He said, "You don't understand me."

I thought this was a weak countergambit. A universal teenage complaint, but hardly worth traipsing over a quarter of the continent for. He said nothing yet about being gay.

"What don't we understand?" his mother asked.

"Everything."

"That's not an answer," Hiram snapped.

"It's as good as your going to get," Donny snapped back.

Silence. Cynthia started crying again. Hiram softly beat the palm of his hand against the chair arm.

Scott said, "Here's what he told us."

At significant points in his narrative the parents reacted. It was Hiram who said, "We never caught him having sex." Cynthia said, "He's dated girls. They call him all the time." About abuse Hiram said, "We are strict, but we aren't animals. He hasn't even been spanked once since he was four or five."

Cynthia said, "I could count on one hand the times he was spanked." And even later Hiram said, "We never forced him to play sports. He loved being outdoors. He was a champion from the start. People said he could be as good as Scott." And later still, "We never found pot in his room." And finally, "We have no idea what he could be afraid of."

The mention of suicide stunned them.

"He's never said such a thing to us," Cynthia said. She reached out and touched her son. "We would never want to lose you."

The kid yanked his arm away. I wanted to belt him one.

Donny had squirmed during all these revelations, especially the bit about suicide. I couldn't tell if it was discomfort at the truth—unlikely as that seemed—or because of guilt for lying. Or because he didn't want his parents to know secrets about him. Or simple unease in the face of such raw emotion, or what. The kid was a liar and had told us some whoppers. It didn't take a team of psychiatrists to figure out something was seriously wrong here. With each new bit of information that Scott had revealed, the boy seemed to sink further into himself. I suppose the parents could have been lying, but at that moment I was in their corner.

Cynthia asked, "Donny, what are you afraid of?"

The kid was trapped in his lies, but his teenage defiance trumped any fear or common sense. He stood up and shouted, "Fuck you all!" and stormed from the room.

We four adults looked at each other for several moments.

Finally, Cynthia said, "I don't know why he would tell such lies."

"Why would he come to you?" Hiram asked.

Scott said, "If the gay stuff was true, it would make some sense."

"I swear," Cynthia said, "we never caught him having sex

with a girl or a boy. We have no reason to lie to you about that."

Scott said, "Then I'm not sure what's going on. Did he imagine we wouldn't talk to you about the accusations and claims he made? I guess based on how often we've talked in the past, maybe it wasn't an unreasonable assumption."

I said, "He may have convinced himself of anything. Teenagers have odd delusions about their powers of persuasion, their invulnerability, and the belief that the response of the universe to their often inept machinations will be benign."

Scott said, "Tom teaches teenagers. He knows them pretty well."

"There's more to the story than what Scott has told you. Things have happened up here." I told them about the murder at the wedding, and Donny's possible involvement. "The police want to talk to him. He refused to speak unless you were present. The police were waiting for you to get here."

"Murder!" Hiram exclaimed.

"They don't think he did it?" Cynthia asked.

Scott said, "You need to decide how truthful a kid you think he is. Certainly I can't think of any motivation for him to kill Ethan Gahain."

I said, "Maybe you should ask him without us present."

They decided to try having a conference with just the three of them. Scott and I returned to the kitchen. The kid had found time to wolf down the rest of his omelette and leave his dirty dish and utensils on the table. "Now what?" Scott asked.

I said, "We let them settle this themselves. They go talk to the cops. We go to St. Louis. Todd said he would talk to the cops. We're not suspects, and it's only a few hours down the road. I've already got the week off. We certainly can't go on our honeymoon with Ethan dead. I want to go to the wake and the funeral."

The intercom beeped again. Scott said, "This place is turning into Grand Central Station."

I said, "We've had one of the most reported murders since O.J.'s wife. It's gonna be nuts for a while." We hadn't been inundated with calls from reporters because we have an answering service screen all of our calls.

This time it was Jack Miller, the private investigator. We let him up. He wore the exact same outfit as yesterday. Today's T-shirt in full light looked newly ironed. We talked in the living room. His eyes roved over the view, the trophies, and the stuffed Eyores. The notion I got was that he wasn't being impressed, but that when he entered any room, he was always totally aware of his surroundings. He made no comment about what he saw.

Miller said, "My sources in the police department say you've got a kid who may know something about the murder."

"We only told them that around two hours ago. You must have good sources."

"They're excellent. I can give you some information if you're willing to share what the kid told you."

"If your sources are so good," I asked, "why didn't they tell you what he told us? For that matter, why didn't the police pay more attention to you?"

"I didn't say that I was best friends with people in the department. The regular detectives on this investigation would check me out, I'm sure, but otherwise they wouldn't have the faintest notion of who I am. I have connections that give me information. They know about the kid, but not what he said."

Scott said, "It's my nephew Donny. We're not sure how much of his story is true."

"I'll take my chances. I'm willing to give you what I've got. I talked to Josh Durst again. I told him about Ethan's death. He was pretty shook. He told me some more. He claimed he was Ethan Gahain's Web master and business partner. According to what he told me just a few minutes ago, Ethan Gahain was up to his neck in shady if not downright illegal activities. Mr. Durst says he was in charge of the naked-athletes jack-off tapes. Their main Web site hints about other sites, but there are no links. He claimed he didn't know about any others. The impression he left with me is that they must have had really kinky sexual stuff."

"Which isn't illegal," I said.

"It is in some jurisdictions depending on the kink."

I know in some jurisdictions anything but the missionary position is still illegal. Not enough people are aware of the number of states with those silly sodomy laws still on the books.

Scott said, "Legal or not, was it a motive for murder?"

Miller said, "Right now, I don't know. They could have been into all kinds of stuff: pirated books, tapes, and movies."

"Kiddie porn?" Scott asked.

"The Web site had none of that."

I asked, "Are you sure Cormac's not in Chicago? Maybe he followed Ethan and killed him. Maybe your source is the killer."

"At this point anything is possible," Miller said. "Cormac could also be in Tahiti on vacation."

I told him what Donny had told us.

When I finished, Miller asked, "You think he's lying?"

I shrugged. "It would be nice to assume he isn't, but I don't trust him."

Miller got up to leave. He said, "Let's keep in touch." We all agreed to do so. He left.

We went to pack for the trip to St. Louis. We only needed overnight bags so it took but a few minutes to throw a toothbrush, deodorant, and a change of clothes together. All this time we'd heard no sounds from the guest room where Hiram, Cynthia, and Donny were talking. I was nearly done packing when I heard slamming doors and shouts. In the hall I saw the results of fractured domestic tranquillity. Donny was kicking a wall, leaving scuff marks and at least one dent so far. His father stood five feet away and glowered. I heard sobs coming from inside the guest room.

The kid bashed the wall several more times.

I said, "Doesn't that hurt your foot?"

He gave one more extra-hard kick that produced another nasty dent. He squealed, "Ouch!" He tried to put weight on that foot. As toe touched the floor, he gave a loud yelp. He rested the foot on his heel. He spoke through clenched teeth. "I won't talk to the cops." He felt the need to repeat this numerous times.

Hiram strode over to us and said, "How do we get hold of the police?"

The detectives were called. Two uniformed cops showed up a few minutes later to escort the three of them to the nearest police station. Scott told his brother and sister-in-law that we would probably be leaving. He told them they were welcome to stay in the penthouse, but they refused our hospitality. They would stay at the Hotel Chicago.

Along with his limp, Donny managed a monumental sulk from living room to elevator. He had completely refused treatment for his foot. By the time they left, Hiram had turned less red, and Cynthia had stopped crying.

Before we left, our lawyer called. Todd said the police didn't care for the idea of our leaving town, but that they weren't going to stop us.

Downstairs in my SUV, I said, "Did you really trust them to stay in our home without us around?"

"Hiram's my brother. He may not like the fact that I'm gay, but he's still my brother. He and his family need help. He may or may not be grateful, but letting them stay would be the least I could do. Making the offer was the right thing to do."

We picked up the Sunday editions of the *Chicago Tribune* and the *Sun Times* before we hit the expressway. Each had an article about the murder, the *Sun Times* doing its best to be more lurid. The articles were long on gossip, sensation, and speculation but short on any information that would lead to an arrest.

We took Lake Shore Drive to the Stevenson Expressway at its beginning at McCormick Place and headed southwest to St. Louis.

. 10 .

The scenery was fantastic. I stayed awake on the drive far longer than usual to enjoy it. Ultimately, I grabbed my nap pillow and snuggled down to some serious snoozing.

I awoke around Springfield. As far as I'm concerned, two of the most important reasons for existence are chocolate and napping. I can devour enormous quantities of the first, and I excel at the second. Always go with your strength, I say. I work out diligently so I can continue to indulge the former. We even keep pillows in both cars so I can luxuriate in the latter.

I've napped through some of the most spectacular scenery in America. I figure the view is always pretty much going to be there, but a nap is a fleeting thing, needing to be nurtured and taken advantage of whenever the opportunity presents itself.

The only two things more important than chocolate and naps are Scott and sex. My love for him wins by a wide margin, but sex is right up there.

We arrived before six. We crossed the Mississippi River

on the Poplar Street Bridge and took US 40 West. The bridge and the upper level of this highway give a spectacular view of the Arch and the St. Louis skyline. We exited at Kingshighway and took it north to Lindell Boulevard. Forest Park on our left, scene of the 1904 World's Fair, rivals Central Park in New York as an ocean of green among urban sprawl. Our destination was Westmoreland Place, one of the gate-guarded streets between Kingshighway and Euclid, north of Lindell.

Ethan's parents had given us the key and the secret code to get past the security devices. Parking on St. Louis's west end can be difficult at best, but within the gated street there was plenty of space. Ethan's home was a three-story, brick, rectangular block. The sun was setting. Lights shone in a few homes. Ethan's was dark. The evergreen trees, two on each side of the path to the door, had seen at least fifty years of growth. The lawn was well tended. The shutters were painted brightly white.

I unlocked the front door, and we stepped inside. I flipped the light switch on the right-hand wall. A small lamp on an antique rolltop desk lit up. We were in an extensive foyer. Very pale pink rose wallpaper matched the wine-dark, rose-patterned square of carpet that covered the middle of the floor. A hat stand in one corner, a working fireplace in a wall to the right, a closed door painted black straight ahead of us. A horsehair sofa that looked brand-new. A stairway next to it leading up to the right and a landing and more stairs. To the left was a set of closed double doors.

Scott said, "It feels funny walking into a dead person's home." A collection of knickknacks sat on the fireplace mantel. A tiny brown, plastic football was among a bunch of other kids' things: toy trucks, a small rag doll, a pink Nerf ball, tiny plastic cars.

I walked over and touched the little football. I felt a small tear start down my cheek.

"What's wrong?" Scott asked.

"I remember this from the night he and I made love for the first time. It was on his dresser. It was the last thing I remember looking at before I closed my eyes as we kissed. It was the first time I kissed anybody."

"There's probably lots of little brown, plastic footballs. Are you sure it's this one?"

I turned it over and looked at the bottom. Ethan and I had scratched our initials into the bottom. They were still there. I held it out to Scott. "I'm surprised he kept this all these years. Him being dead is like losing a piece of childhood I can't get back again." I gently squeezed the small plastic ellipsoid. "It's not the value of the piece involved, it's the depth of the memory."

Scott took my hand and squeezed it. He murmured, "If you don't want to do this, we don't have to."

"I'll be okay. I'm not sure I hope we do or don't find something that explains why he was killed. A lot of me would rather have the memory of him from when we were in love with nothing in between. I'm afraid whatever we discover will tarnish his memory."

"I thought you were pretty much angry about what happened."

"It did end badly. That part couldn't have been worse, but the beginning couldn't have been better."

"Unfortunately, the murder is going to taint his memory forever," Scott said. "What we find could make it worse."

I sighed. "I guess I'd like to know what happened."

The entire house was as clean as if a hired maid service had gone through it within the past day or so: no dust and nothing out of place. A narrow hallway opened to a kitchen on the right. A toaster and a coffeemaker on the counter, no dirty dishes. The refrigerator was nearly full. The cupboards had plastic containers, pots, pans, and a large assortment of expensive dishes. A junk drawer crammed, not startlingly, with bits of junk. Under the sink, cleansers. Behind the kitchen, a study. In there on a large desk, from right to left, sat a charge-card machine, a computer keyboard, a monitor, a mouse pad, and a tower underneath with a built-in zip drive.

I turned on the computer. I'm far less intimidated by them than I used to be, which does not mean I now consider myself an expert. If there was time, I would look through all the programs on the hard drive and on the software. I wondered if we could just take it with us. We had his parents' permission, but did we need the cops'? The house was quiet as only the homes of the very rich can be. We heard the soft hum of electric appliances. The only movement came from the digital clocks counting minutes. In the study we examined every drawer and folder. We found a mountain of canceled checks, income tax records, family photos.

Leafing through the pictures, Scott found one of me in a football uniform. I glanced at it. Scott said, "You were very sexy then, too."

"That was probably senior year. After they did a team picture, they did individual shots for all the starters. I'm surprised he kept it, but more surprised he even had a copy."

"Why would you be surprised he had a copy of this one?"

"They only gave the photos to our families. The starting team got theirs in the yearbook." I touched the sides of the picture. "I don't think this is cut out."

In the pictures we looked through, I recognized many from our childhood. A few were from vacations his family and mine had taken together when we were kids.

We found nothing in the study that gave a clue to his murder or who Michael might have been. The master bedroom had a king-size bed and a matching set of walnut dressers. I found he wore white, cotton boxer shorts. There was no dirty laundry. In the closet, a rack of boring ties, simple suits, one each beige, blue, black, gray, plus slacks, winter coats, shoes, athletic clothes, jockstraps, running shoes, T-shirts.

We passed through three kids' rooms. Perhaps for when his various sets of children came to visit. One had twin beds and wallpaper filled with bunnies. The lampshades were all stark blues, whites, and pink. Another room was mounded with dolls, a third crammed with footballs and sports posters.

In the guest rooms we were more cursory with our inspection. We found only unfilled dressers and empty closets. Attic stairs led to a barren, dust-filled space. The basement yielded a washer and dryer, along with dank and mold and nothing else. Back at the computer I began calling up all the programs on the hard drive. Some I needed a password for and couldn't get into.

Scott began examining all the bills: "This year's seem to be kind of a jumble, but roughly chronological." We worked silently for an hour. Then Scott said, "I've got a series of monthly bills for a public storage facility."

"He was paying rent?"

"No. That would be fifty or a hundred bucks. These have to be mortgage payments."

I read over his shoulder. We examined the papers for fifteen minutes.

"Maybe it was just an investment," Scott said.

"I'm not sure. There are paid-for goods that were delivered there, and look." I held up part of the records. "There's a block of four of the largest bays in Building K that have no record of payments."

"It could mean anything."

The address was on Grand Avenue on the south side of the city. "Let's check this out next," I said. "I don't have the expertise to get around those passwords. Let's take a break and go see this storage space. He certainly didn't need to rent any more room. This place is immense."

⬛ 11 ⬛

Among the bills, Scott had found the key code to get into the storage facility. At the gate he got out and punched in the numbers. The rusted metal barrier jerked and rumbled open. The facility covered several acres. Building K, which, according to the receipts, was reserved for Ethan, was the last one before the property ended at the concrete wall of a vast warehouse. Building K consisted of four of the largest-size bays.

The weather was in the sixties with overnight temperatures expected in the low fifties. At one point I zipped up my leather jacket to keep out the creeping coolness.

One of the keys Mrs. Gahain had given us opened the lock. We rolled up the sliding door. A floor-to-ceiling wall of boxes met our view. On the left there were seven-foot-high towers of flat priority-mail video boxes. Next to these were flattened eighteen-by-twenty-four-inch boxes. We inched through a narrow aisle on the right. Behind the first neat piles were mounds of used boxes all jumbled together. I picked one up and looked inside. Empty. We began wading through the mess.

"This is nuts," Scott said. "Who saves empty boxes?"

"My grandmother does. You should see her collection. She's loath to throw out a box because she just might need one of exactly the size she's got on hand."

"Her grandson seems to have somewhat the same problem."

I admit I'm a pack rat. While I doubt it is a genetic defect, Scott has found need to mention this peccadillo on more occasions than I prefer him to.

Scott said, "But these are all the *same* size."

"I didn't say it was logical. Let's see how deep this thing goes." At the back we discovered someone had cut a doorway into the side of the wall to the next storage compartment. The lights from the front of the complex were dim back here.

Outside the door we listened intently, but heard no sound. The second of the two keys that Scott inserted fit this lock. We couldn't find a switch to illuminate the darkness. The light grew dimmer as we crept forward. We found flattened mailers in a variety of sizes as well as massive piles of plastic tape containers. In some larger and heavier boxes I discovered hundreds of blank cassettes.

We came to another door and used the same key to open it that had opened the second door. We listened again and moved cautiously into the third room. We were moving parallel to the drive outside.

This time we found a light switch. Scott flipped it on. The wall directly ahead of us, front to back, floor to ceiling, had shelves bolted to it. These were completely filled with VCRs. The display lights on all of them were set to the correct time. A three-foot-wide-by-nine-foot-long wooden workbench sat in the middle of the room. A computer and a printer nestled on the far end of it. The wall on either side of the door had rows and rows of tapes all labeled and dated. Each of the narrower perpendicular walls had five four-drawer filing cabinets.

I picked a tape at random and inserted it into a VCR that was connected to a small television. The first screen showed an opening disclaimer about the age of the people in the video, an FBI warning, and a date-of-production announcement. The film that followed was shot from one unvarying angle. It was a locker room. Guys were entering, taking off clothes, and putting on football uniforms. The men on-screen were obviously not performing erotically for the camera. It was a real locker room, with real guys, bantering, horsing around, and getting ready for a game. It was hard to guess exactly what year it might have been recorded. The hairstyles and clothing were from the midnineties. The quality of the film was a little grainy, but the images were clear. The logo on the uniforms said Iowa Teachers University.

I said, "We've found the storage facilities for their Internet pornography business." On one shelf the tapes were organized by month and date. Another had hundreds of them numbered consecutively. Others were alphabetized, many color-coded, some a mixture of these. I tried one of those dated thirty years before. The same warning labels appeared, but this time the guys' clothes and hairdos indicated it was from the early days of disco. It was still a locker room, but definitely not the same as the first one. There were fewer guys, and the angle was different. This time they were putting on wrestling singlets, and there were only a few men at a time. On this one the photographer had caught a portion of the showers. The film quality was much poorer than that of the other.

We spent nearly an hour looking through the materials. We opened numerous boxes from the previous room. Some contained hundreds of still shots, multiple copies of dozens of guys, sometimes the same guy in multiple poses. One box I found had movie underwear shots, different actors who'd appeared in films in Skivvies. I stuck in a tape I found in this box. Someone had frozen each frame from the start of the underwear-clad crotch's appearance to the end, then made a continuous videotape of the sequential frames. Another had stills of nude scenes from famous movies.

One of the most recent tapes had clips of male actors in movies or television. The video showed crotch shots of them either walking or sitting. For example, all the moments in *Dawson's Creek* or *White Squall* when the hunky young actors were moving, standing, or sitting in such a way as to reveal a detailed outline of dick and balls through their pants, or revealing a prominent bulge. Presumably that being where a guy's dick and balls must be. The scenes from *White Squall* included around thirty seconds of each frame of every instant of Ryan Phillippe appearing in his white briefs.

Another film had clips from baseball games. These emphasized players with prominent crotch bulges and/or guys groping themselves. In the filing cabinets the tapes and boxes were cross-indexed by type of sexual activity, by sport, by movie, by year, and so on.

One of the cabinets was filled with receipts in chronological order dating back over ten years.

"He's definitely been selling this stuff," Scott said. He'd been hunting through the receipts. For the most recent years we found computer printouts of orders. Thousands of them made from two Web sites: sexandnakedstars.com and naked-athletes.com.

Another drawer had a folder labeled PERSONAL. I found individual photos here. Many of these looked posed.

I flipped on the computer. The Internet connection came on instantly. I called up the sites. Each was basically a catalog with extensive listings combining pictures of stars along with text describing the action contained within videos. It also had lists of photo sets being offered. None of the names stood out prominently. We found no references that would indicate a specific Michael was more significant than any other. Nothing of me or anybody I knew. Scott was not listed in the sports section.

Where there had been blocks and codes at Ethan's home, I found none on this computer. Perhaps he felt no need to hide here. At home a kid or an ex-wife might have been able to stumble onto something unexpectedly. On the hard drive I found a master list of the cast members. It ran on for page after page. If it wasn't all of them, it had to be most of them. I printed it out. There were no names I recognized. I wasn't surprised. Porn stars didn't use real names. There were lots of variations of Rock Hard and Lance Thrust. They weren't going to be helpful. I did not find model release records. As far as I was aware, all legitimate porn operations kept or were required by law to have on file ID, date of production, and release forms for people who performed in their videos.

We found bank records. Ethan had at least four separate accounts. None had less than $50,000 on hand. In the last week alone $5,000 worth of orders had been filled.

"This business was that profitable?" Scott asked.

I said, "I'm obviously in the wrong profession."

Behind the last filing cabinet on the left near the back was another doorway. I asked, "Why was this one blocked with these filing cabinets? If the cops had a search warrant, wouldn't they move everything and find it? Maybe it was just to deter possible thefts, if the crooks were in a hurry."

"Is there a big market for stolen porn?" Scott asked. "For that matter, why steal it in the first place? All you have to do is buy one copy and start making your own."

We emptied several of the drawers then wrestled the cabinet out of its slot. Scott unlocked the door.

We entered the next storage space. From the soft, pale light dimly glowing behind us, we saw a room that seemed much deeper and narrower than the others. We groped for a hand's span along each wall trying to find a light switch. Nothing. Guided by the light from the room behind, we carefully stepped forward. A central set of bookcases contained tons of electronic equipment: still, digital, and video cameras galore; computers, monitors, and more VCRs stacked to the ceiling. The aisles between the shelving in the center and the walls were so narrow, we had to turn sideways to pass through.

Scott did say, "Isn't this the point in teenage slasher movies that someone says they should leave and they don't? Then a few seconds later someone dies?"

I said, "I thought we didn't admit to watching those."

"As long as we don't admit it publicly, we're okay."

We didn't even discuss splitting up and going down separate sides. Even somebody who never watched teenage slasher movies knew better than to split up.

The dark was nearly complete as we approached the far side of the room. The equipment in the center was on cheap, metallic, eight-foot-high, black bookcases. I could barely see my hand in front of my face. When the center shelving ended, we stepped into pitch-dark, empty space.

Scott let out a squawk, then said, "What the hell?"

"What?"

He sputtered and then whispered, "Something just brushed against my forehead." I felt his arm reach up. I heard a soft click. A dim bulb flashed on.

Six inches from my left hand an upturned face stared sightlessly at the ceiling.

˻ 12 ˻

Your average amateur sleuth might be able to trip happily through acres of bloody corpses, but at that moment I was unnerved. I don't care how many dead bodies anyone has seen before, finding one where and when you don't expect it is unnerving. I made some such noise as *ulp* or *erp*. I yanked my hand away and jerked back into the end of the center storage shelves, sending several video cameras crashing to the ground. Scott grabbed my elbow and steadied me. When I was stable again, Scott whispered the obvious: "He's dead."

The body had a bullet entry wound just in front of its ear on the right side of the head. The exit wound was obvious from the blood and gore caked over the papers to the side and behind him. He was slumped to his left against a desk. His right arm dangled down to a gun lying near his right hand. I didn't recognize whoever it was.

"Suicide?" Scott said.

"It looks that way or was made to look that way." I didn't see a note, but I wasn't prepared to move the blood and gore-encrusted papers to check for one. The blood was dry, but I saw no evidence of flies or bugs or maggots. I didn't think he'd been dead long.

I heard boxes being moved in the room behind us. It was too late to pretend we weren't here. We'd been speaking in low voices but anyone would have heard us. The crash of equipment moments before would certainly have given us away. I pulled the string and turned the light off.

A voice called, "I saw the light switch off. That's not very subtle. Who's there?"

I didn't recognize the voice. The tone sounded confident and sure, tough, as if a gun was behind it and someone who wasn't afraid to use it. A male voice—deep and threatening. A murderer? The person didn't identify himself as being from the police.

We were far enough back in the room to have chanced a game of hide-and-seek in the dark. Then again, all whoever it was had to do was stand in the original doorway and wait. And there could be more than one of them behind us.

With luck we could find the controls for the outside door opening, but we were extremely unlikely to find them in the darkness. If this person meant us harm, there wasn't much we could do. Certainly there wasn't any point to standing uselessly in the dark waiting for something to happen. If there were enough of them to be on guard outside as well, we were probably doomed anyway.

I pulled the switch back on. I frantically scanned the walls for buttons to open the outer doors. I spotted a series of switches obscured by papers stacked on top of stuffed in- and out-trays. Unhesitatingly, I flung aside the papers and plastic and flicked all of them. More lights blazed, and the garagelike outer door rumbled upward. Orange sodium light swept in. We shoved aside boxes and in a moment stood in an alleyway between buildings. No one appeared behind us with a gun, but I'm not sure we gained much by the move. The place was deserted. The manager's little shed where an indifferent teenager had been on duty was over half a mile away. Our car was at the opposite end of the building from where we were. At least we were no longer trapped. We ducked down the nearest side drive and peered cautiously back. A few seconds later Jack Miller appeared in the entrance to the first storage bay we'd entered.

I stepped out. He saw me and placed his gun in its holster under his armpit. He walked over.

"How'd you get in here?" I asked.

"A hefty bribe to the teenager out front, and you?"

"We had keys and an access code. I meant, how'd you know to come here?"

"I got word this afternoon from the guy I hired to go through Cormac's computer that this place existed. You were already gone. I hurried down. This has to be the heart of their operation."

I nodded toward the compartments. "We saw taping capability, hundreds, probably thousands of tapes and stills, and financial records."

"Have you seen Cormac?"

"There's a dead body in the fourth room."

Miller lost none of his suave, cool reserve. "You guys are hell on wheels." He strode past us into the fourth space. He came out a moment later seeming a little less confident. I guess dead bodies weren't on his daily menu. "It's Cormac Macintire. Sure looks like suicide."

"Could be faked," I said.

"We better call the cops," Scott said.

It was morbid to think of hunting through any more boxes or files with the dead body sitting there. It was also useless. It would take days to inventory the whole thing. The idea of running away and pretending we'd never been here was nonsensical. Miller used his cell phone to summon help. While we waited, we phoned Todd Bristol, our lawyer. He said we should remain calm and tell the truth. He gave us the name of a lawyer in St. Louis to call if we needed to.

While we waited, Miller asked, "How much of this stuff have you looked through?"

I said, "We spent about an hour before we found the fourth room. There's zillions of tape and photos. I'm wondering, how did these two get started? What was the original connection?"

Miller said, "Hard to know if how they met or how they got started means anything."

Scott suggested, "Maybe Macintire was in a sport Ethan filmed."

I asked, "How did you get permission to get into Cormac's office?"

"Ethan let me into Cormac's office when he hired me. Nothing I found in my first search indicated why he might be missing or in danger. I found a computer expert down here to continue cracking the codes on Cormac's hard drive. I tried and I couldn't. Before I came here, I went back to Cormac's to make a second search. There was no hint about who killed Ethan Gahain."

We explained to the beat cops. We gave details to the detectives. We spoke with higher officials. The son of Cecil Macintire dead in their city was going to rattle news cages across the country. The deceased scion being a mogul of a porn empire was going to make immense headlines. That one of the most famous baseball players in America had been among those who had found the body was only going to increase the furor.

The detective in charge, Jerry Berke, was tall and burly

and didn't seem to like us or anybody else for that matter. He maintained a stoical silence in front of his superiors. He snapped and barked at peers, subordinates, and possible witnesses/suspects.

"You were here because the parents asked you to come down?" he repeated for the third time. The sneer in his voice had an added note of warning and threat that it would take Scott's nephew years to master.

I certainly didn't think we needed our lawyer here, but I wasn't about to put up with an asshole cop. I said, "We've answered that question and all your others. We're leaving." I wasn't about to attempt an imitation of an amateur sleuth and start pushing this guy or suggesting how he should be investigating. I didn't sense a lovable, kindly interior behind his gruff exterior.

"I don't care for private investigators," the cop said, "and I dislike any kind of interference from anybody, whether disguised as help or not. Stay away." The detective turned to Scott. "I've got a gay son who would want your autograph. Would you mind?"

Scott's fame is immense. He's had tons of press coverage and media attention. One morning over my winter break last year, we were in Battle Mountain, Nevada, eating at Frieda's Diner. I couldn't imagine a spot we'd be less likely to be recognized. In minutes the place began to fill, people whispering and a few pointing. We were given breakfast on the house. It's an oddity. Fame can trump homophobia—sometimes. Or maybe the people of Battle Mountain are more enlightened and sophisticated than other members of the population. Or maybe they just like to gawk.

Scott signed the cop's notebook.

The last thing the cop said was "I don't advise you guys to leave town."

I said, "Neither Scott nor I killed anybody. Unless we're suspects, I don't think we need to deal with that kind of warning, but we'll have our lawyer call you." I didn't want to be stuck in St. Louis. I didn't want to deal with even one police jurisdiction hassling us, much less two.

It was late. It would take five hours to drive back to Chicago. I wasn't in the mood to back up my brave words and actually risk leaving town until I had spoken with Todd Bristol again.

Scott and I found a room at the renovated train station on the west edge of downtown St. Louis. Miller already had reservations at the Adams-Mark hotel. After we checked in, I called Todd. He said he'd deal with the police. My mother had left a message with our service to call her no matter what the time. She told me the funeral would be next Saturday. There would be a wake the night before. I didn't see any reason why I wouldn't be back for both of those things.

"Have you found anything out?" my mother asked.

I told her about Cormac's death and the porn empire. I was sure she'd be hearing about it soon enough. She could decide on the course she should take when the news broke to Ethan's parents. Sex and murder mixed would make the top of all the local newscasts as long as there wasn't a currently burning building to exploit.

Miller, Scott, and I stood in the barrel-ceilinged lobby of the Hyatt Regency Train Station and talked about the murders. Miller leaned his butt against the marble-tiled wall. Jeans, T-shirt, leather jacket, running shoes—a young track star in his prime.

I said, "The two murders are connected." They both nodded. "Is there a connection between their deaths and the porn? Were Cormac and Ethan lovers?"

"I've talked to people down here," Miller said. "Everybody

who knew Cormac said he was sweet, quiet, and unassuming. All of Cormac's neighbors confirmed this. Absolutely no one says they were lovers. I've already told you I learned nothing from Macintire's family. Cormac worked out of a shabby office just west of downtown. Using his address book, I made a lot of calls and visited a few people. They were mostly business connections. None of them claimed to know him well. Cormac didn't seem to be close to anyone. His wife certainly didn't seem to have a clue about his work. I was going to ask Ethan why they didn't have mutual acquaintances, but he'd gone to Chicago by then. The Web master, Josh Durst, the guy I told you I talked to, claimed he was never lovers with either man. Durst himself was hot enough looking to make it into the photos, but he didn't say anything about that."

Scott said, "With Cormac dead, we should talk to him."

"The three of us?" Miller asked.

"Did you mention him to the cops?" I asked.

"As part of the list of who I'd talked to. It was nearly fifty people. I didn't single out his name to them. I'm sure they'll talk to everybody on the list. If a whole parade of people show up—the cops, us, you—Durst might be inclined to stop talking."

"Or maybe he loves to blab," Scott said.

"We're going now," I said.

"As late as it is?" Scott asked.

"Ethan and Cormac are dead. The guy who knows of a connection between them needs to know that. He himself may be in trouble or in danger. I think he might be able to tell us a great deal more."

"We should report this to the police," Scott said.

"Share a bit of information with them?" I said. "Or look like we're trying to take an interest?"

The cops get suspicious of those who take too much

interest in a case, and of those who are trying to be too help-ful. In any reasonably competent jurisdiction, amateur sleuths would be questioned intensively.

"I think we need to talk to this guy tonight." I looked at my watch. "This morning."

"Us sharing information is one thing," Miller said. "Actively working together is another. He knows me, not you."

I said, "You told us yesterday he thought you were a fellow model. He might mistrust you when he finds out you're really a private eye. We should go with."

"He'll trust you?"

"At least we haven't lied to him," Scott said.

I said, "We'll be lucky to find him alive. I don't want to give, we have no right to give, a killer more time to get to him. There's no point in debating about going to talk to him. I'm not waiting."

"You are if I don't give you the address," Miller said.

"Is this a contest," I asked, "or a race? In fact, you found Cormac. Aren't you done? What's the problem? We're either working together or we're not. You either trust us or you don't. You decide. I do not choose to deal with another level of ambiguity."

"A little hostile tonight," Miller said.

"Well?" I asked.

Miller looked thoughtful for several moments. He glanced from me to Scott and back. Finally, he smiled. "Unpleasantly officious is not my idea of a good characteristic in a partner, but I'd be willing to figure out who killed them both."

I realized I'd been unreasonable. "Sorry," I said.

⌐ 13 ⌐

Josh Durst lived in Richmond Heights, just south of the Wash-
ington University campus, which is one of the most beautiful
I've ever been on. I'd driven down to St. Louis several times
while Scott and the team were in town. One June he spoke at
the university. We were given a guided tour on a beautiful
summer night. It had stormed the day before, and the usual
oppressive St. Louis summer heat had lifted. Scott spoke to
over five thousand people from the steps of the administra-
tion building. He faced east toward a double row of trees arch-
ing overhead, illumined by candles and torches and
flashlights and lighters. It was magical. I returned the day after
his speech to walk the campus in daylight. It was the site of
the 1904 Olympics. The campus looks the way a university
should look. Stately old trees, oceans of shade, dappled sun-
light, bright patches of sun-washed green, lots of old brick
and stonework, a Gothic chapel.

Josh lived in a house three blocks south of the university
and one block west of Skinker. The house was dark. The street
was quiet.

While sitting in the car, Scott asked, "Shouldn't we call first instead of just banging on the door in the middle of the night?"

Jack took out his cell phone and a small notebook. He turned on the dome light of the SUV, flipped several pages, found the number, and punched it in. After seven rings an answering machine picked up.

"That's his machine," Miller said. "I recognize his voice."

I said, "He's not home, he doesn't answer calls in the middle of the night, or he's dead. We can't take a chance that he's lying there hurt."

Scott said, "Maybe he's the killer." Miller took out his gun and clicked off the safety. He kept it out as we made our way to the door.

We rang the bell and knocked. No answer. "If we start banging and making all kinds of noise, we'll wake the neighbors," Scott said.

We walked around to the rear and up the back porch. "We won't need to break in," I said. We all saw the shattered square of glass in the door. Nothing gritted under our feet. The glass had been smashed inward.

Miller called the cops. Scott rang the bell, and I bashed my fist on the back door. We heard a loud boom from inside the house. We all ducked down and scrambled behind a gazebo in the middle of the yard. Seconds later a door slammed. I said, "That had to be the front." We began to inch back around in that direction. We heard a loud smash from inside followed by a series of smaller crashes. We were halfway to the corner of the house when the back door banged open.

A dim figure called, "Don't move. I've got a gun."

We didn't move. Miller said, "Josh?"

"Who's there?" called the voice. From where we were, I

could see he was crouched down in a cop-on-television shooter's stance.

"Josh, this is Jack Miller. The guy who talked to you last week. What's wrong?"

"Yeah, who's that with you?" The voice quavered.

"Two friends, Tom Mason and Scott Carpenter from Chicago."

"*The* Scott Carpenter, the baseball player and his lover?"

God bless fame.

Rotating lights from two cop cars filled the street. Durst walked down the stairs. His gun was at his side. He wore boxer shorts, but no shirt, socks, or shoes. Around five foot six, broad shoulders, a narrow waist; his boxers protruded slightly in front.

We heard banging on the front door.

I said, "We better talk to the cops."

"I can't," Durst said.

"Why the hell not?" I asked. "Are you involved in something illegal at this moment? Not unless you don't have a permit for that gun. You're standing here in your underwear. That isn't particularly illegal. It was a break-in. You can tell them that much. We have to tell them something. They've seen people in their underwear." Durst shivered in the night air. He jammed the gun into the middle of the dense foliage of a potted plant on the porch. He rubbed his hands on his shorts. Two dark figures appeared around the side of the house. One shone his flashlight on us. The other had his gun out. Both looked to be in their midtwenties. The one with the gun said, "Who the hell are you?"

I understand why cops who walk into dark backyards sound hostile and a bit frightened. Understanding didn't make me like that attitude at the moment. I hadn't done anything illegal. The presumption that I've done something wrong pisses me off. I swallowed my hostility for the moment. No matter how I felt, I was not about to piss the cops off unnecessarily.

I said, "My name is Tom Mason. We called the police because we found the glass broken in the back door. This is Josh Durst; he lives here." I gave him Scott's and Miller's names. We got no sign of recognition on Scott's name.

The cop shone the light in the middle of Durst's face. He panned it quickly from the guy's face down his shirtless torso to his naked feet.

"What happened?" The cop with the flashlight asked the questions.

Durst said, "I heard intruders. I couldn't get to a phone."

I said, "We must have scared them when we knocked on the front door."

"Awful late to be visiting," the cop said. As each of us spoke, the flashlight got turned on us.

I couldn't keep all the sharpness out of my voice as I said, "I didn't know hours for visiting people were regulated by statute."

"They are if you're disturbing the peace."

Miller said, "The three of us just got here. We can't tell you anything about the intruders. We'd like to be helpful. I know Mr. Durst here, and Tom and Scott are my friends."

Durst said with more confidence, "Whoever broke in ran out the front. I heard noises so I came back here."

"What did the intruders look like?" the cop asked.

Durst said, "I don't know. I never got a good look at them."

The cop said, "Mr. Durst, you sure you're all right? You're not in danger from these guys? You can come with us. We'll protect you."

"It's okay, really," Durst said. "Thanks for coming."

In a few short minutes the police took down a sufficient

110

amount of information for their report and left.

Durst ushered us into the house. He turned on the lights. In the kitchen the toaster and the microwave were lying upside down on the floor. A few pots and pans still dangled over the stove, but most were strewn about the room. Smashed dishes littered the floor. We helped him pick up the mess.

"What happened in here?" I asked.

"I tripped as I came into the room. I didn't want to turn the light on. I'm lucky I didn't brain myself."

You could cross to the door opposite in five steps. Heavy blue curtains covered the window that looked out on the backyard. Refrigerator magnets of naked men in passionate embraces were placed square to the sides of the machine. Durst sank into one of the four kitchen chairs. We all took seats. Durst propped his elbows on the table and put one hand on each side of his head.

In the better light of the kitchen I could see he was a handsome man in his early twenties. He had blond, brush-cut hair, and pale, smooth skin. Well-developed pecs and six-pack abs; he had better need to work out to have muscles that developed. If they came naturally, he was a genuine menace.

"Gosh," he said, "this is so weird." He looked from Scott to me. "You guys are like heroes to me." Durst looked into Scott's eyes. He prattled, "You're so beautiful. I tape you whenever I can catch a game that you pitch. I've never met someone so famous." Now, I'm not saying all gay men are shallow, but this seemed an odd time even for such an obvious twinky to be drooling over a hot man. Then again, I've seen the straight guys at work, in some odd situations being pretty crude about women's looks.

When I tuned back in, Durst was continuing to blather: "We're so lucky to have such normal guys as gay spokespersons. It was so cool that you got married so publicly. That was the best yet. Stick it in the faces of those bigoted right-wing pigs."

Scott patted Durst's hand. "At the moment we're more worried about you."

At the touch Josh Durst smiled, blushed, and continued to burble and gush. After a few minutes, when he finally looked able to respond intelligently, I asked, "What happened tonight?"

"I just got in on a late flight from the West Coast. Then I had a cup of coffee with a friend at the airport. I'd only been home a couple of minutes. I started to get undressed for bed. When I thought I heard a noise downstairs, I reached for my gun. I guess I should have grabbed for the phone. I turned out the lights. I went to the top of the front stairs. I realized whoever it was had come up the back stairs and was behind me. Then I heard the front doorbell and loud knocking. That must have been you guys. I rushed down the front stairs, not thinking about the possibility of there being two intruders. I practically ran down a guy who was at the bottom. I was almost past him when he grabbed my throat and my gun hand. With my free hand, I grabbed his dick and balls and pulled. He screamed and let go. I tried to keep hold, but he was stumbling backward and managed to twist away. Then I heard footsteps behind me, and I knew for sure there were two of them. I couldn't move my gun fast enough to aim it. I fired anyway. I heard two sets of footsteps running. Then I heard banging on the back door. There was silence for a few seconds and then somebody ran out the front of the house. I stumbled through the kitchen and came out the back door."

"Brave but stupid," Miller said.

Durst said, "Easy to criticize when you weren't the one feeling the fear, making instant decisions."

"There could have been more of them," Miller said. "We

112

may have startled them, but we could've been out to hurt you as well."

"They didn't knock. You did."

Miller said, "You moved outside where we could have killed you in a second. You hunched down, but I would have had a clear shot. As is generally true for a nonprofessional, a gun is much more likely to make you do something stupid than give you protection. You bought the gun, but probably took no classes—"

I interrupted, "Is immediately after a traumatic experience a good time to give lessons in under-attack etiquette?"

Miller said, "He could have gotten himself killed."

"It's over," Durst said. "I certainly don't want to hear you guys arguing." Everyone paused for a beat or two.

"Who were they?" I asked.

"I don't know."

"Why didn't you want to talk to the cops?" Miller asked.

"You wouldn't understand."

I've always found that to be a monumentally fatuous thing for someone to say, which is perhaps why they use that phrase so much on television. They resort to it in any show whenever the writers don't know how to come up with plausible resolutions to plot problems and rational dialogue for characters to speak to each other.

I said, "Do you mean, you would be embarrassed? Or perhaps the explanation would be in a nonterran language or at least one that we don't know? Or that you've suddenly forgotten how to speak English? Or the explanation involves or implicates you in something illegal? What?" Neither Scott nor Miller interrupted my tirade.

"Hey, come on. I was just nearly killed."

I said, "And if you want to stay undead, you probably need to begin to trust somebody."

"I only know you're famous. Maybe you're dangerous. Why are you guys here in the first place?"

Miller said, "That's the first sensible question you've asked. If the three of us wanted to kill you, you'd be dead by now. If we wanted to hurt you, we wouldn't need to sit here talking."

"Maybe you'll hurt me to get information out of me."

Scott gently placed the palm of his hand on Durst's left arm. Using his deepest voice with its most sonorous thrum, he said, "We mean you no harm. If you want us to leave, we will go, now. We won't bother you again." He paused a moment. "I can't make the same promise about the men who broke in here earlier."

Durst gazed at him carefully. "Maybe they were just burglars."

Scott said, "You're afraid of something."

"Yes."

Scott said, "You have good reason to be. You know Ethan Gahain is dead, but did you know Cormac Macintire is also dead?"

Durst turned very pale. "You sure?"

The three of us nodded.

"Why?" Durst wiped his hands across his face. He looked at us. "What the hell is going on?"

I said, "We found the warehouse/factory with the computers, boxes, work space, master tapes, and photo sets. When the cops look, they're going to find your picture, aren't they?"

"They won't find my name."

Miller said, "I gave them your name among the list of people I've talked to connected with looking for Cormac Macintire. I'm a private detective. I'm sorry I lied."

Durst glared. "You lied to me. I knew I shouldn't have talked to you. I knew it. I knew it."

"I don't lie to the police," Miller said. "Did you kill either one of them?"

"No!"

I asked, "Then what's the problem with the police?"

Silence.

Scott did the hand-on-arm, thrumming-voice thing again. "Everything's going to be okay," he soothed. "Don't you think it's better to trust us than the police?"

Durst asked, "Are you going to find out who killed Ethan and Cormac?"

I said, "I've known Ethan and his parents since I was a kid. His mom and dad asked me to find out why he was killed."

"They were both great guys," Durst said.

"How'd you meet them?" I asked.

Durst sighed. "On the Internet. If you saw the tapes, you know Ethan was into porn, but a unique niche. He didn't specialize in hiring models and videotaping them fucking, at least not when I first started working for him. He'd go to college athletic events, get to the gym early, and set up hidden cameras. After a while he moved into getting individual athletes beating off or pissing. Later on he started making more traditional ones."

"What kind of videos did you do?"

"He did tape me naked in a locker room. He caught me making a move on a guy. Afterward he approached me and offered me a job. He said he needed an assistant. Mostly I did camera work. I helped the guys in the videos be more comfortable."

"You were a fluffer?" Scott asked.

A fluffer is a person on a pornography set who supposedly does a lot of hands-on work keeping performers aroused. I've read where numerous people in the porn industry deny that such people exist. For some reason I don't believe that. If fluffers are such a persistent myth, perhaps it is because it is such a believable myth.

I asked, "How'd he get into the locker rooms?"

"It's real easy. He was a fairly well known coach, but there's always a zillion people hanging around. It's not like professional sports teams. Small-time college programs are easy to infiltrate. So are big wrestling or swim meets that have lots of different athletes and coaches from lots of different teams. Sometimes I'd pose as an athlete to get in. It's easy to fake it. After a while Ethan had other guys do that, too.

"Sometimes he'd pay members of teams to videotape teammates. Other times he'd simply go to a college baseball or football game, or wrestling meet or whatever. He'd video-tape the athletes in action and edit it down to extended crotch shots, or athletes hugging each other, or grabbing them-selves. Those singlets the wrestlers wear can be very reveal-ing. Once in a while he'd go to small towns and tape the games in men's baseball leagues. He'd say he was a scout. Nobody questioned him much. He'd compile images that were similar and put descriptions of a tape's contents out on the Internet or take out small ads in the back of a few gay magazines."

"How long has he been doing this?"

"I never asked. I got the impression he was taking pictures in college, but he didn't start selling them until after he grad-uated. I also think he bought older tapes from guys who had their own private collections of the same kind of thing. I think he'd been making or selling his own for at least ten years."

"His wives didn't suspect?" Scott asked.

Durst shrugged. "I never met his wives. He didn't talk much about being married, at least not to me."

"What happened recently?" I asked. "Why did he come to

our wedding? His parents told me he wanted to talk to me. He told me the same thing himself. What was so important?"

"I know we'd been getting threats lately. I don't know from who. We never tried to blackmail anyone. What was to blackmail? The ones who weren't willing participants didn't know they were participating. The willing ones got paid. We used to keep all the stuff in a big warehouse way in the south suburbs. A few weeks ago we moved the operation to the warehouse he owned. The day after we left, the place in the suburbs burned."

I asked, "Was he planning to get out of the business?"

"Ethan never said anything like that to me. Cormac never mentioned it. Jesus, they're both dead. This is terrible. What do I do?"

I said, "You obviously need protection. You'll need to talk to the cops. If you don't know a lawyer, I'd hire one. We can give you our lawyer's name."

"Yeah, I better do all that. All this porn shit is coming home to roost. That's why I didn't want to talk to the police. We always had to be careful of them. We had to take all kind of precautions, make sure we were complying with all the laws."

I asked, "Who else knew about the business?"

"Well, everybody who ordered stuff, but it was mostly us three who ran the operation. Sometimes we'd hire temps to do the shipping if we were really busy. Usually I answered phones or filled orders. Cormac would create the sites, and I would maintain them, keep them up-to-date. Cormac and Ethan would plan new venues for taking pictures. Cormac was a whiz at editing. He was teaching me the software program for doing it. The software was real expensive."

"Any fights with the temps?"

"Naw. They were mostly elderly illegals. No green cards. They were never a problem."

"Who would have the model release and ID records?" I asked.

"They never told me where they were kept. I suppose in the warehouse."

We'd never get a chance to go back and look for them now.

I asked, "Was there anyone named Michael connected with this whole thing?"

"Who?"

I said, "Ethan's last words were, 'I love you, Mike.' "

"You were with him when he died?"

"Yeah."

"Wow." Durst shuddered, then clutched his arms around his torso as if to keep himself from shivering although the house was warm. "I've never been there when somebody actually died." He shook his head.

"Anybody named Michael?" I reiterated.

"Do you know a last name?"

"No."

"I suppose there were all kinds of Michaels over the years. We used lots of fake names. For the hidden videos there weren't any names. He thought you were Michael?"

"I don't know what he was thinking. I'm just trying to figure out who Michael was and if he was connected to the murder. Maybe Ethan was hallucinating. I don't know."

Durst said, "Like in the movie *Citizen Kane* when the guy says 'Rosebud' as he dies."

"I guess," I said.

Durst asked, "What am I going to do now? This morning? Even if I call a lawyer, he won't be able to stop me from being in danger. He'll only be able to help me with the police."

Miller said, "After the police talk to you, I can take you with me. If necessary, you can come to Chicago. I have someone who can protect you and hide you. Did Cormac go missing because of the threats?"

"Neither one of them ever said anything to me. I just went to work, and Cormac wasn't there. I left messages for Cormac. He never called back. Sometimes they were both gone for days, but they always called in. I was the one who told Ethan that Cormac was missing. Something was sure wrong. Maybe they were scared. They were really rotten not to tell me what was going on."

I agreed. "You did know Cormac's dad was Cecil Macintire?"

"Oh, yeah. He talked about him once in a while. I figured they'd hate each other, you know with Cormac doing porn and his dad being a big right-winger, but from what Cormac said his dad never knew what he did. Who would tell their parents they had a career in porn? Cormac never said a whole lot about anything."

Scott said, "So another child of a right-wing ranter is gay?"

"I always assumed Cormac was, but he never talked about it. I don't know if Ethan and him were lovers now or ever. They didn't act like it or talk like they were."

Miller asked, "Did you ever have sex with Ethan or Cormac?"

"No. Gosh, no. They were older." So much for the visions of youth.

I asked Miller, "Did you talk to people at Ethan's regular job?"

"Not about this."

Durst said, "I think Ethan kept his job because it was an entry into the world of locker rooms at the college level. He didn't need it for the money. I think Cormac did legitimate

Internet work but kept his porn career separate. I think Ethan's job was sort of a cover to fool his wives, but I also think he really enjoyed coaching young athletes. He was very good at it."

"Did he ever take pictures of his own athletes or in the locker room at his college?"

"He talked about that. If he ever got caught at his college or on the road, he didn't think it would make any difference. They'd fire his ass."

I asked, "How did they meet and start working together?"

"Ethan was videotaping the Olympic swimming tryouts eight years ago. Cormac was trying out. Cormac never got beyond the first round. Somehow they hooked up there. I never got the whole story."

Scott said, "Cormac must have been pretty good to even get that far."

"Yep. I never learned the specifics of their relationship. I was mostly just a clerk."

Miller agreed to take Durst to the police and then keep him safe. We decided to go to Lafayette University together the next morning.

Back at our hotel, we found our room had been broken into. Scott and I had each packed only an overnight bag: clean underwear, socks, and a shirt, along with deodorant, toothpaste, and toothbrushes. There was nothing valuable.

"Was this random or deliberate?" Scott asked.

"If it was deliberate, how would they know we were staying here?" I asked.

"Someone called every hotel in St. Louis until they found Tom Mason registered."

"That takes a lot of energy. I suppose they'd start with the best and work down." We usually registered under my less-famous-than-his name, although we sometimes registered under his agent's name. There is certainly more than one Scott Carpenter or Tom Mason in this world, but if someone had a notion of where we were, and we used our real names, and they were nuts enough, they could track us down.

We didn't find anything missing. We called the front desk. The hotel manager was effusively apologetic. He offered us the best room they had available for free. We took it. I wasn't about to stay the night in a room someone knew how to get into. Even with the dead bolt and a chain, I didn't want to take chances.

$\llcorner 14 \lrcorner$

First thing Monday morning, we called Scott's parents. Our hotel room had two phones. Scott suggested we both listen. Hiram was out. His mother gave the phone to Cynthia. She sounded awful. "Donny's missing," she said.

"What happened?" Scott asked.

She sounded as if she was crying. "He walked out of the interview room and never came back. We didn't call a lawyer like you said. We should have."

Scott asked, "What had the police been asking just before he left?"

"The police had just asked him about why he had left instead of calling for help. I'm embarrassed about that. He knows better than that. He was brought up to know what's right. Donny just seems to get more hostile and sullen every day. He wouldn't listen to me, or Hiram, or the detectives. We're not sure what to do. Hiram's afraid that because Donny left, the police might think he had something to do with the murder."

Scott said, "Call our lawyer. He'll be able to give you good advice." He gave her the number.

The news of Cormac's death filled the morning news shows. Cecil was reported to be too emotionally upset to meet the press. Unusual in a press glutton, but a very understandable reaction, in my opinion. We flipped through several newscasts. Our names came up. They dwelled on the possible illegal activity and the pornography connection. The news of Ethan's Internet business was not going to make his death any easier for the Gahains. At a newspaper stand, the headlines on all the papers were about the murder.

The night before, we'd agreed to meet Miller for breakfast. In the lobby we discovered Miller had left Josh in his hotel room.

"Is that safe?" Scott asked. We explained about the break-in in our room.

Miller shrugged. "If the police are giving out our names, there's nothing we can do. No one else would know my name was connected with this."

"Sure people would," Scott said. "You've been investigating one of them for several days. People would remember your name."

"But not connected with the murder investigation," Miller said. "I think the chances are pretty remote. Who did you guys tell you were coming to St. Louis? Only my secretary knows, and I trust him implicitly."

"It wasn't a secret," I said, "but we didn't publish it. Ethan's and my parents, my sister and brother-in-law knew. Scott's brother, sister-in-law, and his nephew. Not a lot."

"It's enough," Miller said.

"Someone's onto us," Scott averred.

"Or it was random chance," I said.

We decided to speak with a few of the people in St. Louis whom Miller had talked to already. They might have some hint about what had led to the murders. Maybe someone would know who Michael was.

I said, "If there were two intruders last night in Durst's home, don't we have to consider the fact that we very possibly have two killers?"

Miller said, "It's possible. If they weren't simply there to rob the guy."

Scott added, "And if Durst is reporting accurately. None of us saw anybody run out of his house. We only heard doors slamming."

We returned to Miller's hotel and took the elevator to his room.

On the way up I said, "With all these dotcom businesses failing, why couldn't Ethan go broke like all the rest of them?"

Scott said, "I'm not sure an initial public offering for porn would sell a lot."

"I bet it would sell a bundle," I said. "I think people would be lining up."

Josh Durst was gone. Looking out the window at the Arch, I said, "Another revolting development. This is turning into an epidemic. If we keep this up, all we have to do is wait until everybody's gone missing and arrest the last person who's still here."

Scott said, "As long as it isn't one of us."

"Do we know anything helpful from the tapes you did see?" Miller asked.

I said, "They'll be able to interview the athletes from the colleges because of the names on the uniforms. Will they get much? Those guys didn't know they were being videotaped."

We called Durst's home. No answer.

Miller said, "I told him to stay put. Maybe he just ran down to get coffee."

"Why'd you leave him alone?" I asked.

"We aren't the enemy," Miller said. "He isn't our prisoner. He must have run for a good reason."

Miller said he would try to talk to Cormac Macintire's wife. We figured his going by himself made more sense than all three of us showing up at once. As the grieving widow, she would undoubtedly be upset. It wouldn't be right to add to the mob who were probably traipsing to her door. Miller also agreed to keep hunting for Josh Durst. Meanwhile we would drive to Ladue to interview Ethan's fourth wife.

Ladue is one of the wealthiest suburbs of St. Louis. A maid answered the door. We explained the reason for our visit. She left and returned in a few moments and ushered us down a wainscoted hallway to a room filled with nearly as much sports equipment as we had at the penthouse. A woman in a bright red spandex bodysuit finished hefting a fifty-pound weight and sat up and stretched extravagantly. She had a svelte figure with muscles and mammary glands protruding significantly. I'm not inclined to notice a woman in a sexual way, but it was hard to miss this woman's endowments and attractiveness. The maid left. We introduced ourselves. The woman shook our hands.

"You're the fabled Tom Mason."

"I beg your pardon?"

"You must have had some kind of mystical hold on my ex-husband. He talked about you. Not often, but enough that I knew he had some kind of feeling for you, trusted you. The last time I saw him he kept saying he had to go see you. He wouldn't tell me what about. Is he in some kind of trouble?"

"I'm sorry," I said. "I have bad news. Ethan is dead. He was murdered in Chicago on Saturday."

She looked from one to the other of us, touched her hair, drew a deep breath, and finally said, "Wow."

We wound up sitting at a kitchen table. She put on an automatic coffeemaker, set out cups, spoons, sugar, cream, and sat down. "Wow," she said again. "I hadn't heard. I don't listen to the news."

I gave her a brief outline of recent events.

"Wow. Did they catch who did it?"

"Not yet."

"They'll be here to question me, won't they?" She shrugged. "I'm not going to have much to tell them."

"The divorce was amicable?" I asked.

She smiled. "Very. I do have money of my own. I got a few hundred thousand and this house from him. Plus my kids' college educations are paid for."

"Did you have children with him?"

"No. My son and daughter are from a previous marriage. He was very good to them. They got along well. He cared what they did."

"Will they miss him?"

"They didn't know him all that long, but I'm sure they will."

I asked, "Did you know he was rich when you married him?"

"While we were dating, I knew he was well-off. I got to know the details after we were married."

I asked, "You knew he was more than a college PE coach?"

"Did I know about the porn? Sure. He made a fabulous income from it. We had an excellent lifestyle. I didn't mind how he made his money. As someone once said, never let your morals get in the way of having a good time."

126

"Why did you break up?"

"Ethan is gay. He may still not want to admit it, but I figured it out. He wasn't anywhere near as interested in sex with me as a straight guy would be."

"Maybe he just didn't have much of a sex drive," Scott said.

I didn't believe that. We'd been pretty randy teenagers. Multiple-orgasm sessions with him when we were fifteen and sixteen had been the rule, not the exception. Still, I wasn't prepared to reveal this to them. My general rule is that only under extreme duress should one reveal one's sexual exploits with previous lovers to current lovers. Extreme duress in this case being the moment just before the final yank with a rusty pair of pliers would pull your tongue out of your head.

"I need sex," Brenda Gahain said. "The rare times we made love after we were married, he was a fantastic lover. I needed more than he was willing or able to give. We were both very civilized over the divorce."

"How did you find out about the porn?"

"He told me. It wasn't some dastardly secret that he could be blackmailed about."

"Did they know at the college he taught at?" I asked.

"Well, no. I guess they'd have been upset."

"Did he have any enemies," I asked, "or any major fights with anyone while you knew him?"

"He was always fighting with wife number one. She was certifiable, a raving loony."

"How so?"

"She'd call at all hours. Make demands on his time that made no sense."

I'd met Dana, the first wife. She'd struck me as reasonably sensible. Maybe we had different definitions of what *raving loony* meant. I asked, "Didn't he have kids with her?"

127

"Yes. He took care of them financially. He was a real good guy, but he wasn't great with adult relationships. He was always great with his kids. He had custody of the ones he had from his second wife. They got along great with my kids. There were issues with her about custody while we were married. His first wife lives in Chicago. He would see the kids whenever he was there. They would visit for a month every summer, but she was nuts. She'd demand he'd come over to fix things, as if he was to drive from here to there to repair a leaky toilet. What was even more laughable was that he had difficulty telling which end of a screwdriver was which."

"Any enemies, fights, or arguments with people outside the immediate family?"

"Some in-fighting at the college. He never seemed to be able to keep his mouth shut at opportune times."

"What was the fighting about at the college?"

"Heavens, I'm not really sure. I only half listened to that crap. I'm afraid I was as interested in the details of internal faculty politics as he was in having sex."

"Do you know why he was back in Chicago?"

"I didn't know precisely where he was. I do know he was determined to attend your wedding. He said he had to talk to you. I don't know what about. I told that private investigator the same thing. Like I said, we had very little contact. As part of the divorce, I got a lovely little trust fund, from which I get a lovely little check once a month."

"What happens to that now that he's dead?"

"Nothing. It goes on. I made sure of that when we set it up. I wasn't going to have my old age show up and half my income disappear. I had nothing to gain or lose from him alive or dead."

"Why did you marry him?" Scott asked.

"I was in love."

I asked, "I realize you said you didn't see him much, but do you know if he was in any kind of trouble lately, scared or frightened about anything?"

"Nope. Sorry. You might try wife number three. I think she kept up with him."

"You were never in any of the videos?" Scott asked.

She smiled. "Thank you for the compliment, but no."

"Did you know Cormac Macintire?"

"I know he was a business partner. I met him once, but other than that, no."

"How about a Josh Durst?"

"Nope, sorry."

I asked, "Did Ethan ever mention someone named Michael?" I told her what he'd said as he was dying.

She thought a moment or two then said, "He certainly never mentioned anyone named Michael in any significant way. He may have had several relationships with men while we were married, but I never knew for sure. I don't think I wanted to know. I was more comfortably off than I'd ever been in my life. I didn't care much what he did." With that, we said our good-byes and we left.

In the car Scott said, "She didn't come across to me as very loving and caring toward him."

"Yeah," I said. "But I find it hard to believe she would take him having affairs so calmly."

I tuned the radio to an all-news station. The announcer dwelled at length about all the pornography associated with Cormac's murder. A sexually explosive connection with one of the biggest right-wing talk show hosts was great grist for the media. I couldn't wait to see the ranters deal with this one. The most blatant ranters on the air are on the Fox News Network. There are no real news correspondents or reporters on any of the Fox News Network shows. There is no pretense of objectivity. Most of the hosts on all the programs are right-wing hacks, delivering milder or harsher forms of rants depending on the show. If there is a token liberal, he or she is always presented as ugly and inarticulate, while the right-winger is always clean-cut, all-American, and aggressively obtuse.

I'm not sure we'd done a lot of good with our investigation. So far we would be able to go back to Chicago with salacious connections, but not any insights about why Ethan was killed or who did it. What we'd done was find information that would add to Ethan's parents' misery. I didn't imagine uncovering the fact that their son was a pornographer was going to be good news. I was not looking forward to facing his parents.

We heard a live interview from a reporter in Chicago with Barney Natlik, who'd been told he'd been taped. This had to be awful quick for the cops to look at the tapes and begin contacting people. Barney Natlik had gone on to win a gold medal at the Olympics after having been coached by Ethan. Natlik had been recognized quickly because his being caught naked in the locker room had been spliced with shots of him accepting his gold medal.

Natlik was furious: "I trusted this guy, and he repays me by taking pictures of me naked. That's disgusting and it's sick. What kind of guy is it that does this kind of thing? I was a kid."

I said, "I thought he coached him in college."

Scott said, "I didn't see any evidence of kiddie porn. Barney probably means when he was younger, not specifically underage. We'll have to check to be sure. Underage stuff would add a whole other dimension to this. We should try talking to the guys in the videos."

"The cops are going to be interviewing a zillion people. We haven't got the time or the resources to talk to that many.

Remember, a lot of them were secretly taped."

"I didn't mean all of them," Scott said. "Maybe just one or two. If some of them found out what had happened, they might have been really pissed. I bet it wouldn't take that long to figure out the venues, dates, and names even from the ones where it isn't clear which university the players were from."

"We don't even have access to the tapes anymore. It's hopeless thinking we're going to get some kind of insight from them. We won't have access to that information, if at all, until long after the fact. They're going to have a lot of people to interview."

"If we knew somebody on the police department," Scott said. "Miller knew cops in Chicago. Maybe he has a contact in St. Louis."

"We can ask."

"What if somebody who was at the reception was on the tapes?"

I said, "That would raise more than a few questions."

⌄ 15 ⌄

We drove to Lafayette University, where Ethan had taught. It was off Interstate 70 just west of the airport. We found the athletic department. The secretary told us the head of the department could see us. Scott's fame helped open that door. Gay or not, win as many MVP trophies as he has and make as much money, and certain doors will open up to you.

Larry Weiser, the head of the department, was broad-shouldered, at least six feet six, and three hundred pounds. He looked like one of today's professional-football linemen ten years after retirement. He had black, buzz-cut hair and spoke with a hint of a Canadian accent.

He shook hands enthusiastically and said, "In all the time I've been an athlete and a coach, I've never met a player at the pro level. This is great. What's it like playing in the pros?"

Scott's also heard that question several million times. He's used to it and doesn't mind answering, especially if a kid is asking or it will ease someone into talking to us.

Scott said, "You train Olympic athletes here. It's a lot more like real work than anyone ever imagines. Playing professional sports, I'm sure, is very much like being an Olympic athlete. It helps to have innate gifts, but everybody at that level has extraordinary natural talents. To be the best among those, you've got to work your butt off and have a bit of luck. The skill level is higher, but the amount of work and emotional commitment for me isn't that much different from the sports at the levels you must have played."

"I'm not talking about the amount of work involved. I'm talking about the name recognition and fame and cash. Except for a select few, Olympic champions' names are usually quickly forgotten. I guess it's gotta be different and the same all at once."

Scott nodded.

I said, "We came to try and find out more about Ethan Gahain. We're trying to figure out why he died." I explained about my familial connection with Ethan. I included the part about us being lovers. I wasn't going to sugarcoat Ethan's life to a stranger.

Weiser said, "I can't believe this—him being gay, murder, pornography." He shook his head. "Ethan was a great guy. I thought he was a great guy. He was one coach who could really motivate a young athlete. We were truly lucky to get him away from Carl Sandburg University. There is so much rivalry between our schools. It was quite a coup. For the size of our programs, they and we send proportionally more athletes to the Olympics than any other colleges."

Scott asked, "How does a private university afford an Olympic program?"

"We'd never be able to do it without massive donations. The university has been interested in this since the Olympics were held here in St. Louis in 1904. The alumni established a fund back then. Today we have a huge endowment for it plus private donors and public sponsorship. The university gets first-class physical education facilities and a lot more prestige as part of the bargain."

Scott asked, "Isn't it a little odd for a well-established, tenured coach such as Ethan to leave his previous university?"

"A little. We were just so glad to get him. He brought four first-class athletes with him. The son of one of their coaches, Shawn Ranklin, switched. The big coup was Barney Natlik joining our program. Everyone is predicting for him to win as many gold medals in the next Olympics as he did in the last. We also got Henry Diamond and Billy McConnel, who almost certainly will qualify for the next games. Ethan has been a dream of a recruiter for the past couple years. Kids and their parents loved him."

Ethan always was a charmer to anyone he wasn't done fucking.

Weiser said, "As a coach he was the exact opposite of a Bobby Knight. There were never any emotional outbursts. He could talk to an athlete quietly, sincerely, with maybe just the slightest physical touch, and half an hour later the kid would shave seconds off his best time, or have more stamina, or come closer to or even break a record. I saw that over and over. Ethan was great to work with. Now I find out he's a perv. How can you take pornographic pictures of guys like that?"

"Money," Scott said.

"There's lots of ways to make money," Weiser said.

"Actually I think it wasn't illegal," I said. "At least it wasn't as of a few years ago when a scandal about taking hidden photos of athletes broke. Ethan's name was never in the articles I read about it at that time."

Weiser said, "If it had been, we'd have never hired his ass. No, when I ask why, I guess I mean what motivates him to make money that way? Everybody's saying he must have been gay. I don't know if I believe that. He sure didn't act gay."

"And how would that be?" Scott asked.

"Sorry," Weiser said, "you know what I mean."

"I'm not sure I do," Scott said.

There are times, such as this moment, when I can tell Scott is irritated with someone. Usually he's the calmer of the two of us. If we're finding out information, normally he's willing to skip the blunders of the unenlightened. Not at the moment, obviously. Weiser must know we were gay. He may not watch talk shows, but that someone involved in sports wouldn't know Scott was gay would be rare. It'd be as big a sensation if Michael Jordan announced he was gay.

"You know," Weiser said. "He wasn't effeminate or any of that crap."

Before Scott could begin a debate, I asked, "How was he as a colleague?"

"Funny and hardworking. A great sense of humor, but you could count on him to get something done. He was always volunteering to help out with any out-of-town trips."

"That wasn't suspicious?" I asked.

"Not until this moment. If somebody had a scheduling conflict, Ethan was always willing to step in. He was always eager to go on overnight trips. Damn. I never dreamed he'd want to go to make pornographic videos. Who would? He was a very committed coach. He really cared about his athletes. Now I know the real reason. It's disgusting."

"How many out-of-town trips were there a year?"

"Not as many as at a Big Ten university, but enough. If a kid was good enough to go to a state or national competition, his or her coach usually went. Most of the time the regular coach would accompany the athlete. There were a few exceptions, but Ethan was an assistant for three sports. While we've got a great reputation and a great program, still, we're not a big university. Everybody has to kind of pitch in and help out. He was on the periphery of everything we offered, as is most everybody."

"Did you know anything about his photo operation?"

"Hell no. What kind of question is that? Besides, I talked to the police earlier. I wasn't in most of those cities at the times they're supposed to have made the videos. I'm head of the department. I don't coach a lot. I don't get involved in the kids' lives much anymore. It's kind of a shame. I miss it."

"You never heard any of the athletes or coaches talking about pictures or videos?"

"Never."

"Anybody express any reservations about working with Ethan? Maybe they quit because they didn't want to work with him? Or quit without any explanation?"

"Not since Ethan's been here."

I asked, "Did you ever hear Ethan talk about someone named Michael?"

"We've had kids in the program named Michael. At least one or two every year. We've got lots of kids in different programs."

"Anybody that he seemed especially close to?"

"No. The cops asked that."

"St. Louis cops or Chicago cops?"

"St. Louis."

If the St. Louis cops knew to ask about Michael, the two jurisdictions had to be communicating.

"Anybody suggest he tried to make it with any of the athletes on out-of-town trips?" I asked.

Weiser said, "I would never have thought of Ethan as the type to try to have sex with one of the athletes he coached. He didn't invite students to his house, at least not that I knew of. The coaches who do get close to the kids and become involved in their private lives are all very up-front about it. This is the college level. It's not like high school where they're underage. Nobody here is going to countenance having sex with the kids, but it's nowhere near as big a scandal as it would be if they were in high school."

Scott said, "Are you equating being gay with being a child molester?"

"There isn't a connection?"

"No," Scott said. "There isn't, no matter how many times the right wing tells that lie."

"Oh."

"How difficult would it have been to hide all of this from you?"

"Not as hard as it should have been. I never suspected anything. I'm just an average guy. Sure, there are probably gay coaches around, but I don't know any, or at least they don't come out to me. I don't care if a guy is gay or not. I heard there were guys on my football team in college who were gay. Nobody said much about it."

I asked, "Did you know Cormac Macintire?"

"The other guy who's dead? Nah. I never heard of him."

"How about Josh Durst?"

"Josh went to school here a few years back. He worked really hard. He wanted to be a baseball player in the worst way, but finally had to admit he wasn't going to even make the minor leagues or the Olympic baseball team. Realizing he wasn't going to the Olympics or into professional baseball was tough on him, but he wasn't the first we've seen who needed to come to that realization. A nice kid, great work habits, lots of self-discipline."

"We think he might have been working for Ethan and intimately involved in the porn business."

"What! I just don't believe this shit. For the past couple

years after he graduated, Josh did help a lot with the training here at the college. He was great at giving the guys massages." Weiser shook his head. "I must be the most naive dope on the planet."

I asked, "Do you know if Ethan was frightened of anything or worried about something recently?"

"I'm not sure about fear, but for the past few weeks, Ethan talked to me about moving on."

"Quitting his job here?"

"I don't know about quitting, but kind of like starting new. He talked about selling his house. He talked about having a big garage sale to get rid of a lot of stuff. He talked about taking real vacations for the first time in his life, which I thought was kind of funny. He always had plenty of money. He could go anywhere he wanted, but he never really let up at work. The only trips I ever knew him to take were with the teams."

I said, "Maybe he was planning to get rid of all of his porn stuff?"

"Could be. I wouldn't know."

"He came to Chicago, supposedly he needed to talk to me. Do you know anything about that?"

"Ethan never mentioned either of your names that I remember. I knew about Scott as a player, but I never watched any shows when he was interviewed. I read the sport pages every day, but that's about it."

I said, "If Ethan wanted to talk to me, something must have been going on that was unusual."

"Maybe it was just old-friends shit. You said you knew him as a kid."

"Who were the people closest to Ethan here?"

"I think Salvatore Fariniti, the wrestling coach, was probably closest."

"Is he here today?"

Larry Weiser took us to a group of offices across from a gymnasium. The room had eight cubicles spaced around a room the size of my classroom at the high school. Six-foot-high, felt-covered partitions and cabinets created visual barriers.

Fariniti looked like a wrestler somewhere in the 150- to 160-pound weight class. Weiser left us with him. Fariniti had a black mustache. It is only a slight exaggeration to say that he had thick hair on every exposed bit of flesh except his fingertips and his eyeballs. He must have to shave several times a day. He wore a baggy T-shirt, gold polyester shorts that hung below his knees, white socks, and gym shoes.

Fariniti smiled at us. "Wow! Scott Carpenter. How can you be gay and be so good at sports?"

"A genetic defect," Scott snapped.

Fariniti's smile disappeared. "I didn't mean to give offense. I just don't know a lot of gay guys. I just know about drag queens."

"You've never wrestled against gay guys?" Scott asked.

"I never hung around with anybody who wasn't an athlete. Even my wife is a swimmer. Nobody I knew growing up admitted to being gay. I was Missouri state wrestling champion in my weight class when I was in high school. As far as I know, all the guys were straight. Nobody got a hard-on while I was wrestling with them. I went to the national finals in college my junior year. You always hear somebody making fun of wrestlers because we touch other guys. You get a few shrinks who insist we're gay. You get a few guys from the football team who've had a little too much testosterone with their Wheaties and they rag you once in a while." He held out his hands palm up. "You get used to it real young. You get on with your life. If you've got a temper, you fight."

139

"Believe me," Scott said, "there are gay athletes and we have lots of skills. Frankly, I find it hard to believe you don't know more gay athletes."

"How many other gay major league baseball players do you know who are out of the closet like you are?"

Touché, I thought. Sad but true.

After a moment's pause Fariniti said, "I guess I was a little insulting. You're good though. I seen you pitch even after you came out as gay. That took balls."

I said, "We were wondering if you could give us some information about Ethan Gahain."

"I don't know nothing about any of that photography shit. Ethan was fucking nuts to be doing that crap. Taking pictures of naked guys. He must have been gay. Maybe if he was taking pictures of women, it would make sense."

"How could he keep it secret that he was doing it?" I asked. "You'd think somebody would notice."

"If they did, they never told me. Ethan was a good guy to work with. He was really funny. He was always willing to help out the kids and the coaches. He was always volunteering to do extra work. He saved my butt a couple times. He took over my coaching duties when my wife almost died after our first baby was born. When I heard he was dead, I was devastated. Then I heard about this porn shit. That pissed me off. How can somebody do that? That's really sick."

Scott asked, "You've never looked at a porn video?"

"Well, sure."

"Somebody's got to make them."

"Well, yeah, but with women in them."

Scott said, "It's all sex, and it's all money."

Fariniti said, "I guess it's more the betrayal of trust that's the worst."

"That's true," Scott agreed.

I said, "Do you know who he was close to outside the university? Did you ever meet Cormac Macintire?"

"I know the whole story with Cormac. He was a creep. He was always over at Ethan's house. Cormac was at parties where both of them were at. He was always kind of a sleaze. He was married, but he would try to pick up women. He wasn't very good at it. You'd notice him getting turned down. Women would clutch on to their husbands when he was around."

"You mean he was obviously obnoxious or blatantly violent?"

"More just kind of creepy."

"He wasn't bad looking," Scott said.

Fariniti said, "He had bullshit for a personality."

"But he was interested in women?" I asked.

"I see where you're going with that. I'm sure Ethan and him were never boyfriends or did any of that dating shit. I'm not sure why they were such good friends. Ethan always seemed to have more class than Macintire. Not that I understood what was going on. I think maybe it was more Cormac had something that Ethan needed rather than a real friendship. I think Cormac was a user."

I bit my tongue on saying so was Ethan.

"Did you ever meet Ethan's wives?" I asked.

"I met wife number four a few times. She was nice. I don't know about the others."

"Did Cormac's father ever come around?"

"Not that I know of. Cormac never talked about his dad. I never really thought about a connection until somebody pointed it out to me."

"Was Ethan close to anyone named Michael?" I explained about his final words.

"We had a few kids with that name. I sure don't remember

141

Ethan being particularly close to any of them."

We thanked him for his time and left.

As we walked to the car, I said, "You let your irritation show when those guys were homophobic."

"I'm not in the mood for a lot of crap. Jocks feeling the need to act superstraight is not new. I hate to criticize, but maybe you didn't have a really clear picture of Ethan."

"What do you mean?"

"You always say Ethan was a user, but he sure seemed to go out of his way to help these kids and the adults he worked with."

"When you are nice to people just to get them to like you or, in this case, just to deceive them, that's not helpful, that's a user and someone who has desperate self-esteem needs."

Scott said, "There's one thing I don't get. With all those kids and all those marriages, was Ethan gay or not?"

"I've never been able to figure that out. Maybe he thought siring kids proved he was hetero. Maybe he was straight. You certainly couldn't prove it by me."

"We found out about the porn, but nobody beyond Josh Durst knows anything. Let's go back to Chicago. I've got to find out what happened to my nephew. I tried calling my mom and dad at the Hotel Chicago to find out what's going on, but no one answers. We need to get home."

As we approached the parking lot, we heard a loud car alarm. At first I wondered who'd had the ill luck to have their car broken into or more likely whose alarm accidentally started blasting for whatever reason inanimate objects have for annoying humans. Then we saw a Lafayette University cop car parked perpendicular to ours. We rushed forward. Someone had smashed the rear window of my SUV. Nothing inside

142

the SUV was disturbed. The cops said, and we agreed, that whoever had broken the window was probably frightened away by the noise before they could take anything. I didn't like the coincidence of our car being the one broken into.

The cops said, "Weren't you the guys who found the dead body yesterday?"

"Yeah," I said.

"Jerry Berke, the detective, wants to talk to you."

We called him from the cell phone.

"You guys seen Josh Durst?" he asked.

"Not since last night," I said.

"We went to his place. It's been ransacked. We wanted to ask him a few questions."

"He stayed with Jack Miller last night. He left without telling us where he was going."

"Odd."

"I sure thought so." I figured I might as well agree. Berke could just as easily think we had something to do with Durst's disappearance.

We went back to the hotel. As far as we could tell, this room had not been tampered with. We checked out, called our lawyer, who called the cops to tell them we were leaving town, and we left.

The only thing I missed from our visit was not having dinner at Tony's.

Between naps on the way back to Chicago, I listened to the all-news stations. We heard more athletes from Lafayette and Carl Sandburg Universities were holding press conferences and being interviewed. Copies of the tapes of athletes were surfacing. Names of athletes and university identification on the uniforms were easing the spread of who was on and where the tapes had been made. A few of the athletes were smirking and pushing themselves as total studs. Most were taking Barney Natlik's approach and were pissed and threatening to sue.

I used the SUV's speakerphone to call Jack Miller. He was still in St. Louis but planning to leave soon. He said, "I didn't find Josh Durst, but I do have one interesting item. No one can find the model-release paperwork or videos."

"That's what the murder was about?" I asked.

"Until they're found, it's really suspicious."

"Would Josh Durst know any of the models they took pictures of?"

"I was planning to ask him that question. It'll be the first topic of discussion after we find him."

"Do we know anybody into doing porn?" I asked. "Even more, do we know anybody into porn who we also invited to the wedding?"

"Your mother and I didn't look over everyone's job résumé," Scott said. "We didn't require biographical submissions to get into the wedding. Nor did we ask for data on their sexual practices."

"Maybe you should have," Miller added.

"Whose side are you on?" I asked.

"Nobody's. I'll try to find somebody to give us porn information."

"Did Cormac's wife know anything?" I asked.

"She was upset, genuinely grieving that he was dead, but, no, she didn't seem to know anything."

Scott asked, "Do you know any St. Louis cops who could get us access to what was in that warehouse?"

"Sorry, no."

After agreeing to keep in touch, I hung up.

We listened to call-in sports shows for as long as we could take it. Talk radio in general may be the stupid leading the stupider, but sports talk radio is the epitome of useless drivel

144

designed to increase the level of moronicness in the universe. Who cares if Joe Nobody thinks the entire Chicago Bears team should be traded for a set of orphan koala bears? What's the point? And why should these people be encouraged to express their opinions? Far better, they be talked to in soothing voices while being given heavy doses of medication. The hosts and callers were obsessing about the murders and their connection to pornography.

Near Pontiac, Scott turned off the radio. "I need to not listen to that for a while." He drove in silence for a few miles. The weather was pleasant, sunny. We'd borrowed a piece of clear plastic and some duct tape from the hotel and fixed up a barrier to prevent the wind whistling out the rear window. "Do we know anybody who worked with Ethan at Carl Sandburg?"

"My old high school football coach, Frank Ranklin, is head of the department. I think Ethan helped one or two of the guys from my high school team land jobs. Ethan was always very loyal to those he wasn't sexually involved with."

"No bitterness there."

"Not a bit."

"Do you want to call Ranklin?"

"He was at the wedding. Remember, he lived in my old neighborhood. I baby-sat for his kids when I was in eighth grade." I used the cell phone to set up an appointment.

◣ 16 ◢

We drove straight to Carl Sandburg University. We arrived just before six. Frank Ranklin had a tiny office near the locker room. Ranklin was a tall, muscular man with hair slightly graying at the temples. He had a deep, sonorous voice. He looked as fit as he did when he was our coach. Back then he worked out for an hour and a half every day. He obviously had not altered his regimen. He sat in his office in black spandex shorts, a gray Carl Sandburg University sweatshirt, white socks, and black-and-silver running shoes. He'd been my coach when our high school had won the state football championship. It had been his first year coaching. Younger teachers sometimes have closer relationships to students. Ranklin was lucky enough to be able to mix closeness with discipline. It didn't hurt that we won every single game.

Weiser had mentioned Ranklin's oldest son, Shawn. Besides being an Olympic hopeful, he had several minor athletic-gear endorsement contracts in the offing. The boy had come in eighth in the marathon in the last Olympics. He had every hope of winning a medal in the next.

Coach Ranklin said, "Sorry the wedding didn't end the way you wanted. The police were around asking questions already." He pointed to me. "You aren't going to be a suspect?"

"No. We're reasonably sure my nephew can provide me with an alibi. He may be able to recognize the killer. If we can figure out who killed these guys, I'll feel a lot better. We're trying to uncover more about Ethan's life. We learned some stuff in St. Louis. We'd like to find out more."

"Ethan was tremendous. He helped a lot of people. Always went out of his way."

I asked, "Did you have any inkling about any pornographic activity?"

"I've been thinking about that," Ranklin said. "At the time I had no notion, but you know how you look back and rearrange what happened in light of new information?"

We nodded.

"I've been doing that. He always attended almost every sports event he could. Even those he didn't coach. You'd hardly think he was married with kids. He didn't seem to take much time for them. Sometimes he'd bring the little ones to sports events he wasn't coaching, but even that he didn't do too often. Dedication and overenthusiasm aren't crimes. He sure fooled everybody."

"Do you know if he got pictures of your son?" I asked.

"I sure doubt it. Shawn is a marathon runner. As far as we've been able to figure, Ethan wasn't on any of the trips Shawn took. Shawn doesn't remember him being there."

"What about these athletes who are planning to hold the big news conference?" I asked. "Are you going to join them?"

"If I'm there, it would look like the university is involved. As an institution, we want to stay as far away from this as possible. We're afraid of lawsuits ourselves. Personally, I think the kids have got a legitimate beef."

I asked, "Did he have any fights here at all? Anybody who might wish him harm?"

"No infighting beyond a few petty jealousies. Mostly he kept out of that."

"Why did he leave?"

"Big push from Lafayette that we couldn't match. Our programs are similar, but theirs is much older, much better funded. If they'd made me an offer, I'd have been tempted to go. I was likely to be the new head of the department here so they probably believed I wouldn't have been interested in the first place."

"If you're head of the department here, why'd your son go there?"

"Lafayette has the best marathon program in the country. They got Alex Panko, the best marathon coach in the world. And like most kids he wanted to get away from home."

"Did you know Ethan's wives?"

"I knew two and three from here. Number four is from St. Louis. I didn't know her or his first. The ones I met seemed nice enough."

"Did he cheat on his wives?" I asked.

"I saw him with the women who became wives two and three before he divorced wives one and two."

I said, "So far I've got no indication that any of the wives would want to kill him."

"There's one or two guys around from the old days," Ranklin said. "You should talk to them. Robert Murphy is here part-time. He teaches a couple of night classes."

．　．　．

Robert had been the star middle linebacker on our championship football team. His college career had ended under a pile of Georgia Tech linemen one rainy Saturday afternoon.

Robert was in his office. "Hey, Tom!" His greeting was effusive. He shook hands with both of us. "I only know you from the talk shows these days. It's a damn shame about Ethan. I liked him. He wasn't always the best friend, but he was a good guy."

"How wasn't he a best friend?" I asked.

"Well, he was kind of a slut in high school."

"You're gay?"

"No, but I heard about how he kept trying to seduce all the guys on the different sports teams."

"I never heard about this," I said.

"Everybody thought Ethan was gay. Nobody thought you were. He would try and get the guys on the teams to let him give them blow jobs."

"He didn't!"

"Sure. I was told he was successful more than once. Just rumors, I suppose. I figured you knew. You were buddies with him."

"We were lovers. I thought he was faithful."

"Well, this would have been during your late sophomore and early junior years. It was probably before you guys were lovers. Were you really lovers with him in high school?"

"I was for my part." I was still reeling from his news. Ethan had been cheating on me back then. I felt soiled. He was a slut extraordinaire. My anger of old was rekindled anew.

"Sure," Robert said. "How often he succeeded, I don't know." He shrugged. "Everybody kind of forgot about it. He got married and I figured it must have been a phase. When I applied for a job here, he put in a good word for me. I was grateful."

"Did you have any notion about all the porn Ethan was into?"

"Not a clue."

"How about academic infighting?"

"We aren't like a regular college department. We've got real goals that connect with the real world."

"You didn't know if he was frightened about anything recently?"

"I haven't seen him."

Back in the car I said, "I am stunned."

"I'm sorry," Scott said.

"You didn't do anything wrong."

"I'm sorry that your memory is no longer what it once was."

"He fucked his way through high school and probably college. Besides the substitute teacher, he probably fucked half the faculty, half the football team, the coaches, and the opposing players." I ranted for several more minutes.

After I ran down, Scott said, "There's nothing you can do about it now."

"I can be angry for a while longer."

After a few minutes of silence I took several deep breaths.

Scott said, "We need to decide who we're going to talk to next."

"Can we try and talk to Barney Natlik, the Olympic guy?"

"I can call a reporter I know from the *Chicago Tribune*. He might have an in. He'll want something in return."

I said, "You can promise him we'll give him an exclusive interview if we get anything."

This time in the parking lot we found the plastic from the rear window on the ground along with most of the contents from the interior of the car. The contents of our overnight bags lay scattered over ten square feet. In the light from the interior of the SUV and the headlights of the cops who showed up after we called them, nothing seemed to be missing.

We sat in the car. "Somebody's looking for something," I said.

"I'm getting more than a little nervous about this," Scott said. "We might want to have protection with us."

"We don't seem to be the object of the violence. Somebody thinks we have something. Do we?"

"We don't have anything more with us than when we left Chicago."

Scott called the reporter and spoke for several minutes. Ten minutes later he called back. After they finished this conversation, Scott said, "They've got press conference stuff going on down at the Athletic Center across from Michael Jordan Auditorium tomorrow morning. He can get us in."

.17.

First thing the next morning, we drove to the Athletic Center. We took the damaged SUV to be fixed and used Scott's Porsche for transportation. The still incomplete center was on the south side of the Michael Jordan sports palace just west of the Chicago River on Grand Avenue. A crowd of reporters milled around the Grand Concourse. The entrance lobby of the Athletic Center was two stories high with pictures of Ernie Banks, Ryne Sandberg, Frank Chance, George Halas, and other Chicago sports heroes of the past blown up large on the walls.

We met Scott's reporter contact, Doug Clangborn, in a quiet corner near the as-yet-unfinished gift shop. Clangborn was in his fifties, short, bald, and overweight. He rolled an unlit, expensive cigar between his fingers. After Scott introduced me, he said, "I get anything you guys find, right?"

We nodded.

Clangborn said, "The sports guys in this town would go nuts if they knew I was talking to you."

Scott said, "They're an okay bunch of guys."

Clangborn pointed the cigar at me. "You found the bodies in both places."

"Yeah."

"What's the connection between the two guys? Strictly business? Lovers?"

"We're not sure."

"What do you hope to accomplish talking to Natlik?"

Scott said, "Doug, you know the ground rules. We want to talk to him to find out some information. Until we find out something substantial, we aren't doing an interview."

"I can get you an intro, but I can't guarantee much more than that."

Scott said, "See if my name makes a difference."

"You being gay could just turn him off," Clangborn said.

"We've got to try something," Scott said. "Sometimes athletes will open up to other athletes faster than they will to reporters."

We watched Clangborn shuffle through the distant mass of people. My lover and I had our hats pulled low over our eyes. We were past masters of blending in. All it normally took was a baseball hat and perhaps sunglasses. It's surprising how many people don't notice you when they don't expect it to be you. No one paid us any mind. They were mostly harassing the detectives we'd met Saturday night. A few minutes later Clangborn returned.

"I've seen it a million times," the reporter said. "Fame reaches to fame. I don't get how celebrities glom on to celebrities."

"Sure you do," I said. "You've hung around them long enough. It's the same for reporters, cops, teachers. Those in the group all speak the same language. For athletes the experience of being in a group together is extremely intense because of the fame and money. These men and women have had unique experiences all their lives. They are probably the star athlete of their hometowns. Did you see the movie *Varsity Blues* or read the book it was based on, *Friday Night Lights*? These men and women have been treated differently all their lives. It takes a strong or special person to come out of such a background even remotely normal. Often they feel that only someone with their experience will understand them."

"So how does it work for you two guys?"

"We're in love," Scott said.

"Sounds sappy," Clangborn said.

"Works for me," Scott said.

The noise from the crowd grew. For a moment I thought we'd been recognized. The podium was filled with the dynamic presence and entourage of Cecil Macintire. He had to be over his spotlight-shy grief. Or maybe he wanted to make a spectacle of his sorrow. Cecil looked a whole lot like Charlton Heston after graduating to the role of God on a particularly wrathful day, and he wasn't happy about it. Cecil had a mane of gray hair that he kept swept back from his forehead.

Cecil leaned into the microphone. "I have a statement to make." He glanced at a thin sheaf of papers. He looked to be near tears, although I'm told he managed to do this in his radio show studio nearly every day. To what point with an unseen audience, I'm not sure. I was willing to be lenient in these circumstances. The man's son had died. He said, "My son was dearer than life itself to me. I do not believe any of these ridiculous charges against him. I believe it is a smear designed by my enemies, you know who you are, to destroy me."

On his shows, he seldom actually named specific groups that he considered enemies. I was told he'd make sly innuendos, roll his eyes, make faces, nothing designed to further rational discourse. All this with a live audience of less than ten people.

Scott said, "Let's get out of here before I lose what little sympathy I have for the man."

Outside the sports complex we split with Doug Clangborn.

Half an hour later Scott and I met Natlik in a tiny little restaurant on Orleans Street across from the Merchandise Mart. Natlik looked like a wrestler. He was maybe five eight and 160 pounds. His muscles bulged under his shirt. His neck looked thick and strong. His shoulders massive, his abs taut, his butt slender. He wore a black T-shirt, faded jeans, and a leather jacket.

We sat in a back booth. The place was dim and quiet. It looked as if they'd carpeted the walls and the floor. After we ordered—coffee for Scott, mineral water for Natlik, and diet soda for me—we talked.

Natlik said, "Doug Clangborn said it might be important to talk to you guys. You were in St. Louis and might know stuff. You found the bodies."

I said, "Ethan and I went to high school together. Scott and I went to St. Louis at the request of his parents to try and find out why Ethan was killed."

Natlik said, "This is all crazy. I never wanted this kind of publicity. What is someone going to think of me being naked all over the world? I've got a mother and father."

"It wasn't your fault, was it?" I asked.

"I certainly didn't consent to it if that's what you mean. I had no idea he was videotaping me. I looked up to him."

"How was he as a coach?"

"I wouldn't have gotten to the Olympics without him. He

was great. The best coach I ever had. He was excellent at maximizing a guy's talents and desires. He didn't yell or scream. Very quiet and fatherly, soft-spoken. I liked it. My own dad thought berating me constantly would motivate me. Bullshit. I really liked Coach Ethan. That makes me even more pissed off. Why would he do this?"

I asked, "How did you find out he had tapes of you?"

"I heard the first media reports of porn. Then friends began to call with rumors. My dad is a Chicago cop. He has connections in St. Louis. One of his buddies was part of the group that started looking through the pictures. The guy saw mine and called my dad, who has gone nuts about these pictures. He thinks I posed for them. When it comes to porn, people think the worst. Plus a lot of people presume that if you're a wrestler, you must be gay. Like wrestling is just an excuse for touching guys. You didn't go out for the football team so you're not as tough as you should be. You know how they talk about soccer fags or band fags."

I knew. "Does it make a difference?"

"To my dad it does. I admire you guys for being honest. It's tough being in the spotlight. Even the little I've been in it is rotten. The pressure on you guys must be immense."

"But you're not gay?" Scott asked.

"I've got a wife and a little boy."

A classic evasion to a too personal question.

"Did you meet Cormac Macintire?" I asked.

"No."

"How about Josh Durst?"

"Oh, yeah. Lots of times. He was kind of an assistant at Lafayette. He'd help out as kind of a trainer. He was great at folk remedies for injuries. You know like when the guy in the *Karate Kid* slapped his hands together and then 'healed' the kid's leg."

156

"Ethan and Josh were close?"

"They worked together. I never figured either one was gay. Now I think they both must have been. What would be the point of a straight guy taking pictures of naked guys?"

Scott said, "You mean it would be better if they were straight taking pictures of naked guys than if they were gay taking pictures of naked guys?"

"Well, yeah. Then they'd just be in it for the money."

Isn't capitalism special.

Scott said, "Isn't that like a call boy saying that he isn't gay because he only lets guys blow him?"

"Well, yeah, but isn't that true?"

I may have realized the futility of debating, but Scott seems to enjoy engaging in rational discourse with everyone from the simplistically illogical to the willfully stupid and crazed right-wingers. I keep telling him rational discourse when connected to the religious right is an oxymoron. He refuses to give up. The man believes in the triumph of reason. I wish I did more than I do.

Before Scott could get in a rejoinder, I asked, "Do you have any notion of when they took pictures of you?"

"I haven't seen them, but I think it must have been in Chicago at the national college wrestling tournament five years ago."

"But you're not sure?"

"I heard from some other guys. That's when Ethan took pictures of them."

He pointed to Scott. "He didn't have pictures of you, did he?"

"No," Scott said.

Natlik turned to me, "Did you know he was a pornographer?"

"No."

"Doesn't it make a difference to you?"

"Not particularly."

"Why not?"

"Pornography in and of itself doesn't offend me. His parents and my parents are exceptionally close. He's an old friend. We care that he died. We'd like to find out why. Can we talk to some of your other friends he took pictures of? Especially to anybody who knew about what was going on."

"I'm not sure who knew at the time. Nobody ever said anything. A bunch of the guys are going to get together secretly without the press being there. I guess I could invite you guys. You're not reporters."

.18.

We followed Barney Natlik out US 90 to a sports bar in Schaumburg across from Woodfield Mall. The place had the usual red leather, brass, and ferns surrounded by memorabilia-covered walls. Photos of the 1985 Bears, the 1908 Cubs, the 1917 White Sox. There were also nineteenth-century pictures and scenes of downtown Chicago pre– and post–Great Fire.

Seven guys were gathered at a table in the back of the bar. Two were in their early thirties, muscles gone to seed with potbellies drooping over too tight pants. Two were slender, in their early twenties. Another was a tall redhead. The sixth was muscular, in his late twenties with short, blond hair. He wore construction boots, faded jeans, and a flannel shirt. He looked as if he'd just walked off a building site. Turned out he had. His name was Derrick Kaufman.

The seventh was Shawn Ranklin. We greeted each other warmly. I had not seen him in many years. I remembered him mostly as a redheaded moppet when I'd baby-sat for him when he was five. Now he was tall, thin, and lanky.

After we were all seated, we did a round of "You're the famous ballplayer," "You're the gay guys."

I call this the *Notting Hill* effect. In that movie Hugh Grant brings Julia Roberts, as the famous actress, to his sister's birthday party. All of Hugh Grant's friends and/or relatives are strongly affected by the star's presence. Imagine if Mark McGwire walked in as your daughter's or son's date. All that out of the way, we asked about the pictures.

Instead of answering, Kaufman asked, "Did you guys really find the body? What was it like?"

I was annoyed. It wasn't that my stint in the marines had made it easy to deal with death, but I was a little less likely than the average person to become upset by coming upon it unexpectedly. I just wasn't all that eager to get into gross and disgusting. I said shortly, "Cold and bloody."

"Here and in St. Louis?" Kaufman asked.

I said, "Both places, cold and bloody." Several of them shivered.

Natlik said, "I don't want to talk about dead bodies. I want to find out what the hell Ethan Gahain was up to."

They had all been coached by or at least known Ethan. The older ones, Derrick Kaufman, Ranger Fresten, and Benny Mydans had known Ethan at Carl Sandburg University. The younger ones, Cass Manguel, Floyd Nelis, and Pavel Voronezh, had known Ethan in St. Louis. Only Shawn had known him in both places. They were small enough schools that all the coaches and players from the different sports pretty much knew each other. Only Voronezh was actively being coached by Ethan. Ranklin, Manguel, Nelis, and Voronezh had come to Chicago at Natlik's urging.

"I don't know what all the fuss is about," Kaufman said. "I think it's cool. I'd like to see what pictures they have of me. I might want a few. I think I'm a stud. I think I still look good naked. If any of them are hot, I'd like to blow it up and put it in my living room."

"Wouldn't you feel odd when your mother came over?" Voronezh, the redhead, asked.

"She's seen me naked."

"Not as an adult, I hope."

Kaufman shrugged.

One of the overweight ones, Benny Mydans, agreed with Kaufman. "I looked good back then. I was a runner. I liked wearing the tight shorts. I liked thinking that people could see my prick bulging out. I'm an exhibitionist."

"We know," Kaufman said.

There was obviously a story there. "We know what a stud you were with all the girls," the other overweight one said. He was Ranger Fresten. "We heard enough times about how big your feet were. How they made you a great runner. How their size meant you had a big prick. And how all the women were impressed with your endowment. I heard it more than most because I went to high school with you, too. None of the guys cared then. I doubt if anybody cares now."

"Coach Gahain obviously cared," Kaufman said.

"Yeah, well, he was gay," Fresten said.

I asked, "Was he known as a gay coach? He was married four times to women."

Fresten said, "Well, I didn't think he was gay until this picture thing came out. If you're taking pictures of naked guys, it stands to reason that you've got to be gay, doesn't it? Why else do it? Although, I did meet one or two of his wives. They were nice. Maybe he was like one of those transsexuals or something."

Kaufman said, "Transsexuals have that sex change operation."

Fresten said, "No, I think that's transvestites."

I wasn't going to start correcting their sexual misinformation yet.

"Did any of you think he was gay?" I asked.

"What difference does that make now?" Kaufman asked.

"I don't know about Coach Gahain," Voronezh said, "but that buddy of his he brought around to help out, that Durst guy. He had to be gay. He always managed to be around the locker room when it was time to shower."

"There must have been other gay guys on the teams," Scott said.

"There might have been," Voronezh said, "but they never told us about it. Durst wasn't exactly on the team. He was a good athlete. He sure knew how to do a massage to ease sore muscles."

"Maybe he knew how to massage athletes for another reason," Kaufman said.

Voronezh looked as if this were a brand-new thought to him.

Cass Manguel, one of the younger ones, said, "I don't care if he was gay or straight. I'm pissed about this whole thing. I've still got sports to play. I could still get to the Olympics. Gahain only coached me my first year out of high school. How can I show up at events with everybody knowing my body's been plastered all over the Internet? How are you ever going to get any kind of endorsement contracts? Sponsors hate any kind of negative publicity. Nobody says let's hire the guy who used to be in porn pictures. I love athletics, but I'd also like it to make me rich."

"You always get so hyper," Kaufman said. "You were never going to get endorsement contracts. Your ego was always bigger than your common sense. You always get sick before every track meet. You're always in the john barfing your guts out for half an hour before any competition. How would you being naked on the Internet make a difference in your chances of winning?"

Manguel gripped his bottle of beer. "I'm talking about pride and dignity, two things you obviously don't understand."

Fresten said, "You're a shit, Derrick. You never did win anything. How would you know how it felt?"

"I won plenty."

"Not when it counted."

Manguel said, "I think at the very least this must be some kind of sexual harassment."

"Don't be dense," Kaufman said.

Natlik held up a hand. "We didn't get together to fight."

"Why did you get together?" I asked.

"We wanted to find out if anybody knew anything," Natlik said. "Who else there were pictures of. Maybe discuss a class-action lawsuit."

Ranklin said, "I wanted to be supportive. I don't think he got anything of me, but if he did, I want to know about it. I think we have good reason to be outraged."

Manguel said, "I wanted to find out if any of this was mob-connected. Maybe we're in some kind of danger."

"Why would we be?" Kaufman asked.

"Are you too stupid?" Manguel asked. "Everybody knows the porn industry is mob-connected."

Several nods around the table.

"I guess I heard that," Kaufman said, "but I never associated anything about Coach Gahain with the mob."

"How would you know?" Manguel asked.

Kaufman said, "I don't suppose those guys advertised themselves as being mob-connected on their Web site."

Manguel said, "It's not funny."

"Get a grip," Kaufman ordered.

Natlik said, "I think presuming we're in some kind of danger because of what we did is irrational. I'm pissed about it, but it's just pictures."

Voronezh asked, "Has anybody tried the Internet sites to see what's actually on them?"

"I did," Manguel said. "I thought I might have recognized a couple guys from a few of the teams we had meets with, but I didn't recognize anybody from our program. As the cops go through them, they'll be able to notify the colleges by the uniforms. I guess we'll find out soon enough."

"We've got to try and look at every picture they took," Voronezh said.

"We found a huge storage facility full of possible porn," Scott said. "The police are never going to let you look through it."

Natlik said, "My lawyer said we might be able to get some kind of court order. The cops said all that stuff might be evidence in a murder case."

"Nobody's going to care about whether we were naked or not," Kaufman said. "A year from now, no one's even going to remember our names connected with this."

"None of you knew or were suspicious about this beforehand?" I realized as soon as I asked it that this was a fatuous question. Why would anybody admit this in front of witnesses? Then again, maybe somebody secretly knew and had been afraid to tell until now. So I quickly added, "Or heard a rumor or got a notion about what Ethan was up to?"

They all shook their heads.

I asked, "Did he ever try and seduce any of you?"

Head shakes no.

I said, "We heard he asked people to make some videos."

Except for Kaufman, this didn't seem to be the kind of crowd that would be willing to discuss voluntary participation in pornographic videos. They'd have to be talked to individually, and they would have to trust us far more than they did now.

"I would have made them," Kaufman offered. "I've always wanted to be in a pornographic video."

"Why?" Natlik asked.

"Why not?" Kaufman responded immediately. "It would be fun. I'd get to fuck women without worrying about commitments or entanglements. I wouldn't have to talk to them. Maybe I'd get to fuck two or three at the same time. Maybe even do twins. I've always fantasized about doing that. I like fucking. I enjoy coming. I'm not afraid of sex. Maybe doing a video would lead to some great sex, new things. Plus getting paid for screwing, why not? You guys are overreacting. It's just naked pictures."

The others denied being offered roles in videos or being willing to make them.

Floyd Nelis spoke up for the first time. "It's just not right. It's a violation of who we are. We're amateur athletes. We were just kids. He took a bit of our childhood away from us."

"We're not really kids," Natlik said. "We know what the world's like."

"You really think it's that bad?" Kaufman asked.

"Good and bad aren't the real issues," Voronezh said. "He took away my choices. I don't like it. If there are pictures of me, I want them. I want all the copies I can get my hands on. Then I'm going to destroy them."

Kaufman said, "If they're on the Internet, anyone can get them."

"We could get an injunction," Fresten began, "like with that Napster company."

Kaufman said, "Logistically tough to shut down an operation set up in the Internet ozone."

Fresten said, "I think part of the problem is that people are going to think we did this willingly. They'll presume it was with our consent. Maybe people will think we're gay. No offense to you guys, but still, you know what I mean."

Kaufman said, "You were changing clothes, for Christ's sake. What's the big fucking deal?"

"Some rumors say they caught guys pissing," Natlik said.

"So fucking what?" Kaufman demanded.

Natlik said, "You may want to be a porn star. I don't. You could never understand how the rest of us feel."

"Now it's feelings," Kaufman sneered. "Bullshit!"

Natlik said, "I'm going to sue. Coach Gahain had to support all those ex-wives and kids, and he sure lived a rich lifestyle. I'm going to make him pay."

"It'll be his estate that pays," Scott pointed out. "The only people who will be out money will be those ex-wives and kids."

Natlik looked as if he hadn't thought of this. The other seven of them grumbled for a while about the unfairness of the world and getting even in some vague way. Other than suing somebody, they didn't have much of a plan. I wasn't sure there was much of a plan they could have or needed to have.

I asked, "Did Ethan ever mention somebody named Mike? The last words he said were 'I love you, Mike.' I'd like to find out who that was, and if he has any connection to the murder."

They all looked thoughtful. Natlik said, "I think maybe one of the starting basketball players at Lafayette last year was named Mike."

Kaufman said, "Wasn't one of the pitchers on the baseball team named Mike?"

Voronezh said, "Maybe it was a kid from one of his classes. There had to be lots of Mikes."

Fresten said, "If his last words were those, he must have been gay."

Natlik asked, "Do you really think there's any significance to him saying that?"

"It means for sure he was gay," Kaufman said.

"I'm not sure exactly what it means," I said. "I just want to find this guy."

No one knew anything else. After fifteen more minutes, they began to leave. When they were all gone, Scott and I decided to eat. This restaurant was as good a place as any. We were just finishing when Floyd Nelis returned. He was nearly as tall as Voronezh and thinner than the others. He was a swimmer. He came up to our table.

"Can I sit down?" he asked.

We moved a chair over for him. He clenched and unclenched long, thin fingers together. Finally, he hunched over the table close to us and said, "I need help. You guys are part of this. You seem to know what you're doing. You knew this Ethan Gahain better than I did. He wasn't really my coach. I was in the swimming program. Maybe you can help me."

We leaned closer.

Nelis announced in a voice barely above a whisper, "I made a video for him." His face flamed scarlet. "I really fucked up."

Perhaps literally, I thought. I asked, "How did you happen to do that?"

"It started when I accidentally found out about his secret tapings. I walked back into the locker room unexpectedly before a meet last year at the University of Iowa. He didn't seem real upset at what I saw."

"What did you see, exactly?" I asked.

"I saw him setting up a bunch of gym bags and equipment with a camera hidden in the middle of all of it."

Scott asked, "What did he say?"

"He was real calm about the whole thing. I don't think it was the first time he'd been caught. I was flabbergasted. He began talking to me, real fast and low. He always spoke in this soft, deep voice, you know, kind of fatherly and comforting. He sat next to me on the team bus on the way home. He offered to put me in videos. You know how it is with amateur athletes. Nobody has any money. If you want real coaching and good facilities, you've got to pay. It cost one hell of a lot. It was a lot of cash. I agreed not to tell anybody what I saw."

"Why didn't you just blackmail him?" I asked. "What he was doing was clearly out of bounds."

"I could never do that. Blackmail's illegal. I'm a decent guy. I saw a chance to make some money. It was like working for a living, a little. I was getting paid for doing something, not trying to do something against the law. It might be immoral, but I know it's not illegal to be in a porn movie."

"What exactly did you do?" I asked.

"I didn't have sex with anyone. No offense, you guys, but I'm not gay. He kept promising he'd set me up in videos with women. He never did. He kept trying to talk me into making videos with guys. I think that Josh Durst was the one he used a lot for making it with straight guys."

"Josh made videos?"

"Sure. He worked the cameras some, starred in a few, and acted as, you know, one of those guys on porn sets who helps keep the guys turned on."

I wanted Josh Durst found fast.

Scott asked, "How did the operation work?"

"When I was there, they used two cameras. Coach Gahain held one, and Josh had the other. The production took a whole lot more time than I thought. I did it twice in his house in St. Louis and once in some condo in Chicago. I remember most two things. That the rooms were cold and that it was pretty boring. They took forever to make sure the light settings were perfect, getting the camera angles right. Coach Gahain never really said a whole lot. Josh hardly stopped talking. I think he was trying to make me comfortable, put me at ease while I sat around naked or in my underwear. He did help. Once they took a video of me mostly with my clothes on sitting on a couch. Josh asked me questions about sex, like details about my first time beating off. I never talk about that kind of stuff, that's sick, but they were paying me money, and Josh told some stories, too. Maybe they were true. So, then I got undressed. Mostly they taped me beating off while I watched a straight porn video. They were actually pretty nice, pretty patient. He paid me a thousand dollars for about six hours' work each time."

Hell of a scale to pay on.

"That was it?" I asked.

"Yeah. We could never agree on the details for making movies with more people. I got my money. I figured if I needed more, I could press them to put me in a straight video. They said I'd be more likely to be used in videos if I was willing to make them with men and women." Nelis shrugged. "I wasn't."

"Where was the condo in Chicago?"

"I'm not sure. I'm not from here. I remember it wasn't far from the lake."

"Did any of the other guys in the group that was here make a video?" Scott asked.

"I sure didn't hear them ever say anything," Nelis said. "Derrick would have been the one I would have picked to try it."

I said, "I would have picked all the others before you."

Nelis grinned. "You gotta watch out for us quiet types."

I asked, "Did you know anybody else who was ever taped?"

"No."

I asked, "Did you ever know any of the business aspects of the operation? How the tapes were packaged, sold, or distributed?"

"Nah. I didn't care anything about that. I figured my parents would never see me or know about it, so it made no difference to me. Now, I'm really worried. Me being caught naked has probably been all over the Internet, but maybe it hasn't. If it's possible, I don't want what I did to get out. I guess some of my buddies would be envious if I did straight porn, but simply beating off isn't going to convince anyone I'm less than a fool."

"When did you do this?" I asked.

"I did the first tape about a year ago, the last a few months ago."

"Do you have any idea of what Ethan or Cormac or Josh might have been afraid of recently?"

"Not really. Coach has been pretty much the same at practice. He was never a real emotional guy. He'd go all fatherly on you. His method helped me a lot."

I asked, "You ever see him argue with anybody either at the school or with strangers at meets?"

"He used to feud with some of the other coaches on the opposing teams, but that was normal. People are competitive, but nobody really takes most of that rivalry stuff seriously. At least not seriously enough to kill somebody over it."

Scott said, "When you came back, you said you wanted advice. What can we do for you?"

"I guess I really just wanted to talk to someone about it,

and . . ." Nelis shook his head. "I don't know what to do about those videos existing."

"There's not much you can do," Scott said. "Chalk it up to experience, and get on with your life."

"What if people find out?"

"You have no control over that," Scott said. "You made a decision back then. You make decisions now."

Nelis left.

19

On the way back to the Loop I called our answering service. My mother had left a message asking me to give her a call.

She said, "Ernie Gahain wants to talk to you. Caroline said it was important. Ethan's parents found out this morning that Ethan owned a condo on the north side. Ernie and Caroline went there at Perry and Rachel's request. I think Ernie and Caroline found something they want to talk to you about."

"I learned about the condo just a few minutes ago. I wonder what they found."

"Your sister wouldn't tell me, so I suspect it's more about the pornography connection."

I agreed with her about that. I didn't blame Caroline for not telling my mother. I hadn't been tremendously eager to discuss porn with her either. She gave me the address on Buckingham, a half block west of Broadway.

As we cruised down the Kennedy Expressway, I called the police to see if they would give me their version of the meeting with Donny and his parents. After I dialed, I pushed the speakerphone button. We had one of those sets where you didn't have to hold the phone to talk.

Detective Rohter answered our call: "I heard you found another dead body in St. Louis."

"You heard correctly," I said.

"What happened?"

I tried to eliminate all rancor from my voice as I said, "I have no doubt that you talked to the police in St. Louis. I'm sure they told you what they know, certainly everything they know about us and our involvement. I'm sure you shared all the information you had about us from up here. If you really want to make an issue of our involvement or try to turn us into suspects, why don't you simply say that instead of playing some kind of gotcha game with us."

I figured he'd simply hang up on me. He didn't. Maybe he was working under the assumption that if you've got a suspect irritated and talking, you're on the side of the angels.

"Who needs help from who?" Rohter asked.

I drew a deep breath and backed off: "Perhaps we should share information." It was pretty clear we were at least on the periphery on any suspect list. How could we not be? Your average amateur sleuth seldom had a heap of bodies piling up such as we were beginning to accumulate. I figured maybe if I unbent a little, the cop would be a little more forthcoming. So I gave Rohter a brief version of finding Cormac's body.

When I finished, he said, "Two bodies in twenty-four hours. Most people don't find one dead body in their lifetime."

"What can I say? Neither Scott nor I killed anybody, although for my money, I'd be suspicious of any amateur sleuth. I think it would be great if in the very last two-hour episode of your ordinary detective television series, it turned out the amateur sleuth committed all the murders, and he or she is the greatest serial killer in history." He didn't seem to be even the slightest bit amused by my observation. "Scott and I are just trying to look out for my parents' best friends' interests."

Rohter harrumphed at this.

"What happened with my nephew?" Scott asked.

"They were quarreling when they walked into the station. Father and son yelled at each other intermittently. Mother kept trying to calm them down. During the intervals when we finally got them settled down, we didn't get much information."

"What were they fighting about?" Scott asked.

"The boy kept accusing them of not trusting him. The father kept talking about how he kept running away proved their need to keep a tight rein on him."

"But they calmed down?" Scott asked.

"More like they had an outside group to focus their anger on for a little while. Even with his parents around, the kid was not cooperative. Hiram Carpenter seemed like he hated us as much as he hated his kid. He kept telling Donny to talk to us and then piling on what sure sounded like right-wing militia paranoia. Like, trust the cops, but hate the government. Weird."

Scott said, "I don't think he actually hates his own son. He is right-wing, but I don't think he's in any nut group."

"His kid could be," Rohter said. "Their crap is all over the Internet. If the kid was hearing a version of a nut group's pitch from his dad, why wouldn't he be susceptible to it when he found it on the Internet?"

As the cop spoke, we exited the expressway at Addison just after the junction. Scott drove east on Addison.

Scott said, "The kid did not come all the way from Georgia to kill somebody he never met."

Rohter said, "I'm still waiting to decide on that. I sure think the kid has a tendency to violence."

"Why do you say that?" Scott asked.

"They didn't tell you what happened?" Rohter asked.

"No," Scott said.

Rohter said, "He hit his mother. He didn't just slap her or accidentally bump her, he hauled off and belted her."

Stunned silence on our end.

"We'd just asked him why he hadn't called for help, mentioning that maybe if he had, medical assistance might have arrived in time. Mrs. Carpenter began to chide him about what he should have done. I thought she was being pretty gentle in what she was saying. If he'd of been my kid, I'd've been ready to beat the shit out of him. He just shut his eyes one second. The next he was on his feet with a closed fist. The blow glanced off her ear. He cursed and spat at her and ran."

"What did Hiram do?" Scott asked.

"He ran after the kid. He's big, but his son weighs maybe half as much and was much quicker."

"The police didn't stop Donny?" I asked.

"He was gone too fast. Nobody expected the kid to run. He wasn't in cuffs."

"He hit his mother?" Scott said. I don't think his question was prompted by doubt about the veracity of what Rohter had just told us, but by astonishment that it had happened at all.

"Yep," Rohter said.

"There's got to be a history of violence in the family," I said. "This can't be the first incident." I also figured that the son was simply emulating the father.

Rohter said, "We checked into the boy's background. He's got an older brother who had some trouble with the law."

Scott said, "I never heard anything about that."

"Father and son got into it about Donny trying to take after his older brother, Darrell. At that moment Mr. Carpenter looked like he was ready to belt the kid a good one. The mother screamed at the two of them. Things calmed down for a while. Then, like I said, the kid clocked his mom and bolted out of here before anyone could stop him. We'd like to see the kid again."

Scott said, "He must have been feeling guilt about not doing what he should have done. He could have saved a life. He should have felt guilt."

Rohter said, "For whatever reason, he wouldn't answer the questions. Your nephew was more recalcitrant than the most hardened gangbanger. Maybe the kid had something to do with pornography. He could also be the killer. That would explain his reluctance. Runaway kids often get involved in all kinds of seedy or illegal activities they wouldn't normally."

I said, "He's hardly been gone long enough to hook up with anything shady. Although, I know deadly can happen in an instant."

"Doesn't take long," Rohter confirmed. "Maybe this wasn't his first time running. Maybe he was involved in something before he ran. Pornography—"

I cut Rohter off. "Nobody has mentioned anywhere that Ethan was connected in any way with child pornography. We found only consensual adult stuff."

"Not so consensual if they didn't know they were being photographed."

"We didn't see any pictures of kids," I said.

"But you don't know there weren't any?"

"Did the St. Louis police say they found any?" I countered.

"No."

I'm not sure why it was so important to me that Ethan be

176

thought of as an adult pornographer and not a peddler of kiddie porn. Adult stuff was okay. Kid stuff would be a major stumbling block. Somehow thinking of Ethan as exploiting kids turned my few good memories into something soiled and dirty.

"Are you close to finding out who killed Ethan?" I asked.

"I think a kid who hears someone being murdered, but who doesn't report it, needs to be talked to at great length. I think we should be very suspicious of people who find bodies, especially in two different jurisdictions."

I said "Would it have made you feel any better if we found both bodies in the same jurisdiction?"

I got a frozen silence in response to that crack. I knew I didn't kill anybody. I doubted if Donny had, but I didn't know him all that well. I said good-bye to the cop.

Neither Scott nor I could think of a thing to do about his nephew for the moment. We agreed to stop at the Hotel Chicago later.

We drove over to Buckingham to see what Ernie Gahain wanted. Ethan's condo was in a building on the north side of the street almost in the middle of the block between Broadway and Halsted. The brick was pinkish red, the shutters and fixtures bright white. It was three stories high with two condos on each of the first two floors and one penthouse on top. Ethan owned the penthouse. We rang the buzzer. Caroline's voice asked who it was.

We took the elevator up. When we entered, Caroline was at the front window looking out on the trees below. Ernie was in his wheelchair. Half the living room ceiling was a skylight. For furniture the room had a pole lamp and nothing else. The windows did not have curtains.

After greetings I asked, "Did he actually live here?"

Caroline said, "The bedroom has a little more furniture than this, but not much. About a quarter of the place looks like a movie set."

The northeast corner of the penthouse had movie lights, cameras, props, and VHS tapes still in plastic wrap. "It's a porn studio," Ernie said. "I came over here because my parents asked me to. They found keys and an address in his luggage." Ernie handed me a package that had been sitting in his lap. "We found this in a briefcase behind a stack of videos." It was a twenty-one-inch-by-fifteen-inch manila envelope at least two inches thick.

Ernie said, "I opened it. It's pictures of naked men. We heard about what Ethan was doing in St. Louis."

"Did you know about the pornography before this?" I asked.

"No. All I knew was my younger brother was a college coach. I never knew about and most certainly never had anything to do with anything illicit, immoral, or illegal."

Caroline nodded. "The Gahains are just devastated by all the news. They aren't angry at you for uncovering Ethan's connection to pornography. Rachel said that whatever he was doing would have been discovered somehow. It isn't your fault he was doing it."

"My brother was always a shit to them," Ernie said. "I'm glad you uncovered it. He was always the sainted younger brother. He was twelve years my junior, but he got more privileges than I ever did and at earlier ages. He always got away with everything."

"You're not kids anymore," Scott said. "Why still be angry?"

Ernie glared.

Caroline said, "You don't know how difficult it has been for Ernie. He's covered for Ethan for years."

"Covered what?" I asked.

Ernie said, "When Ethan refused to come home for holidays, anniversaries, or other family celebrations, I was always the one who made excuses for him."

"Why?" Scott asked. "He was an adult making decisions. Why did you have to get involved?"

"I didn't want my parents hurt."

"Weren't they hurt anyway?" Scott asked.

"Not in the same way. He never remembered their birthdays. He hasn't sent them a Christmas present for years."

"Is that why you guys didn't get along?" Scott asked. "Because you felt you had to make excuses for him all these years?"

"It was his attitude more than anything. He just didn't seem to give a shit. He didn't really seem to care for people. He was a user and it extended into his family worst of all. He dropped out of I don't know how many different colleges before he finally graduated. He'd borrow money and not pay it back. My guess is he used my parents' money to start his porn empire."

Caroline added, "He's really very hurtful."

I knew exactly how hurtful he could be.

Ernie continued, "As I got each new bit of bad medical news, he seemed to care even less about me. My parents won't say it, but they always worried about him the most. Now we find out he's involved in all this porn. It's like he's reaching out from beyond the grave to give my parents even more grief."

"Porn by itself isn't illegal," I said.

Caroline said, "Let's not split hairs, Thomas. It's scandalous. Sure, it wasn't Mr. and Mrs. Gahain making movies, but it was their kid. Worse, there's no chance to make it better or talk about it or resolve it."

"I don't get it," I said. "What's to talk about or resolve about this issue that is so different from all the things he hasn't talked about or resolved for years?"

"Thomas! People are hurting."

"I know that," I said. "I don't see what you're annoyed at me about."

Only family members who are extremely annoyed with me call me Thomas. My mother adds my middle name, Peter, when she's really pissed. Once in a great while, Scott will murmur my full name in the throws of passion, but that's different.

"Why don't you just look inside the package," Scott said.

So, I did.

The top pictures were of Ethan in the throes of passion with himself including a shot of moments from a rather spectacular orgasm. The next ones were of Cormac Macintire also naked and masturbating. I didn't recognize anyone in the other photos.

"Do you know who these people are?" I asked.

Ernie and Caroline shook their heads.

"Why did you need to show me these now?" I asked. "Maybe these were just his favorite porn pictures to beat off to."

"Keep looking," Ernie said.

At the bottom of the pile I found an eight-and-a-half-by-eleven manila envelope. Inside were several pictures of me. There were sports or action photos taken in high school. The last one was of me naked, standing next to a swimming pool.

"How'd he get that picture?" Caroline asked.

I said, "I know exactly when this was taken. At Randall Bergeron's birthday party just before our junior year in high school. Everybody decided to go skinny-dipping. I didn't know anybody was taking pictures."

"You're not shocked he had these?" Ernie asked.

"I'm not elated that these might be on the Internet. I can't believe he'd sell pictures of me naked."

"Maybe he didn't," Scott said.

"If he did, maybe he was into kiddie porn."

"So far yours is the only one with somebody that young, that we know of."

I said, "I don't want him to have been into underage sex pictures. I don't want to deal with that. Yes, I know I may not have a choice."

I riffled through the other pictures in the folder. Most of the pictures seemed quite old. I found a few others of my teammates. The starting quarterback on the football team my senior year had a big smile on his face. He was in full uniform, a football clutched in his left hand, his right hand grasping his hard prick, which was jutting out of the front of his football uniform pants. The background was the shower area of the boys' locker room at my high school. I showed Scott.

"The quarterback was gay?" Scott asked.

"I think he was more of a big goof. He was nineteen our senior year. He'd flunked first grade twice. He never offered to make mad, passionate love to me. He married some college cheerleader after a dismal career at a third-division college. I could see him posing for this. He'd do just about anything if he thought it was funny. What I can't see is Ethan working up the nerve to ask him to pose for this."

"Maybe you didn't know either of them as well as you thought."

"I guess not."

Scott said, "Or it was a moment of passionate silliness, which is not a crime."

Ernie said, "It is if the silliness goes terribly wrong."

I said, "Then it isn't silliness anymore."

"I guess not," Scott said.

Ernie held out a white, business-size envelope. "This was inside as well."

I took the envelope and pulled out the sheet of paper inside. On it was printed a single sentence all in caps: YOU'VE GOT THE PICTURES AND DISCS AND WE WANT THEM.

Ernie said, "There may or may not have been something illegal about the porn, but there was something dangerous and lethal going on."

"There're no discs?" I asked.

"We didn't find any."

Scott said, "I hate to belabor the obvious, but there is now no doubt that Ethan was using the pictures for blackmail."

I said, "Gotta be. There has to be a reason these pictures were separate from all the rest. I wonder if it's possible to find out who these people are? Only our former star quarterback is in a uniform with a recognizable logo."

Scott said, "Since we've got pictures of Cormac, maybe we should take them to his father. After seeing these he might be more willing to open up to us than he was to Miller."

"If he even knows anything," I said.

"Will it hurt to ask?" Scott inquired.

From the penthouse Scott called his agent to get him to phone Cecil Macintire's people. Fame calling to fame to set up a meeting. He would get back to us.

20

We had gotten Ethan's second wife's address from Jack Miller.
She lived in Evanston. We took Sheridan Road. Wife number
two lived in a small frame house. Surveying the modest struc-
ture, I said, "I don't think she got as much in her divorce as
wife number four did."

It turned out she was eager to speak with us. Mabel Gahain Yancey née Bradford introduced us to her husband, Roy
Yancey. He wore a hat with a Peterbilt truck logo on the front.
He had skinny shoulders and legs and a protruding gut. She
was short, slender, blond, freckled, and mean. He was
meaner. No burbling about fame here.

I began, "We're concerned about who might have wanted
to harm Ethan Gahain."

She pointed a skinny finger at her chest. "I certainly didn't
want to. I am not a violent person. Why do you care about
him now that he's dead? I don't imagine any of his ex-wives
would care."

"I'd have killed him if I had the chance," Roy Yancey said.
"Don't worry, I have an airtight alibi."

Figured.

Mabel said, "He was an evil man." So much for not speaking ill of the dead. "I know that isn't Christian of me."

I said, "I heard you're seeking custody of the children you and he had together."

"Of course we were fighting for custody," Yancey said. "We found out how he was making money."

"Why didn't you have custody in the first place?" Scott asked.

Mabel said, "I was young, foolish, and stupid. A year ago, I called Dr. Laura. She told me to go do the right thing. I knew what she meant. I was supposed to fight for my child." A three-year-old scampered into the room, saw us, and retreated to Mabel's side.

Dr. Laura does have a constitutional right to free speech. She does not have a constitutional right to a television show. Hypocritical bitch.

Roy Yancey said, "I supported Mabel completely. How could we let the boy stay in that environment?"

"What environment was that?"

"A single, gay man is not an appropriate environment to bring up a child."

"He was married to his fourth wife up until a couple of months ago."

"We know he's gay," Mabel said.

"Yes," Roy Yancey added, "when we found out about the pornography, that was the last straw."

"How did you find out about that?" I asked.

"That information was difficult to uncover. Christian people are infiltrating the Internet and pornographic sites. We're going to the addresses or staking out the post office boxes listed and following people back to their homes and offices. We're alerting neighbors, husbands, wives, and children to

184

the lewd, disgusting, and immoral behavior of their neighbors."

I asked, "You're telling children about pornography?"

"We have informed child-custody judges and social work-
ers. Anyone connected with a child has no right to be engaged
in such activity."

I asked, "Is there a lot of hunting down of pornographers
or is this right-wing rhetorical excess?"

"Oh, yes," Yancey said. "It's the newest tactic. The group
we belong to KID, Keep It Decent, has as a goal to expose
every pornographer."

Scott said, "Making pornographic movies is not unconsti-
tutional."

"It should be," Yancey snapped. "Look how it's led to the
rise in crime and abortions."

He had managed to combine in one statement the three
debating gambits I hear the right-wing use: if someone's making sense, change the subject; get the statistics wrong; or say
something totally illogical.

I said, "The organization has that many members with
that much time to find all these folks?"

"Enough for them to have tracked down my former husband," Mabel said.

"Why didn't you just ask wife number four?" I asked.

Mabel said, "Once we had the report, she needed to know
the kind of man he was. The kind of danger he posed to her
children. She laughed at us and called us hicks."

"Where are your and Ethan's children now?"

"They're with the third wife. Now that Ethan's dead we
fully expect to get full custody without much quarrel."

"Had you made threats recently?" I asked.

"Threats?" Mabel said. "I don't call them that. We'd gotten
the information almost two weeks ago. We've had several

meetings with our lawyer. Last Thursday he was served with legal papers, and I visited him. I told him what we knew and what we were going to do. I told him he could kiss his career and his kids good-bye. I had no reason to murder him. He might have had reason to murder me because I was giving him information he didn't like, but God is on my side. I wasn't worried."

Yancey said, "He was going to lose those kids. He was petrified."

We left.

In the Porsche I asked, "Is that what he wanted to talk to me about? The threats from his second wife? What good would it do to tell me?"

"Maybe it wasn't logical," Scott said. "Maybe he remembered the love and friendship you shared."

"It would be like him to forget everything in between."

"We're all guilty of selective memory."

"Ethan was the kind of guy who could completely misperceive something that happened."

After a few minutes driving in silence, Scott said, "Since we've been driving my car, nobody's tried to break in. Is that significant? Or did whoever it is find we didn't have anything in Sandburg University's parking lot?"

"I don't know if we should be less worried or not." I didn't feel safe yet.

Getting in to see Cecil Macintire was easier than I thought it would be. When Scott phoned our service, we had a message from his press agent. He had set up a meeting for late that afternoon. We met in Macintire's luxury building in Evanston.

Cecil Macintire's radio program was the most popular in the country. He was overtly homophobic, barely contained his racism and anti-Semitism, and indulged in every right-wing paranoia panic there was. I had actually spent time listening to his program one summer as I drove to different cities to be with Scott on a road trip. The reason I listened was simple. I hate people who try to ban books, especially those who haven't read the books they want to ban. I figured it was sort of the same for Cecil Macintire. Certainly I could read about the awful things he said. It was very different listening to him. I no longer had to take anybody's word for how hateful he was. I knew for myself. I've always known that much hatred exists in this world, but at least when it's not shoved in my face, I can believe that things are getting better. Cecil Macintire sowed hatred, and he made millions doing it.

Macintire's show was a mixture of call-in vilification and extended rants by Macintire himself. There was no pretense of objectivity. If a left-wing caller was put on the air, it was always the most inarticulate or boneheaded representative of such views. And Cecil kept the cutoff button handy. If someone began to get logical or rational with him, they'd be silenced instantly. Of course, I think people who call these talk shows have to be pretty pathetic to begin with. Cecil would often permit an abusive caller to be on the air. I assumed this was done deliberately to set up Macintire as a sympathetic, put-upon victim. Such calls gave him a chance to launch into a wounded tirade. Frankly, sometimes I assumed they were all using a script, with fake callers and Macintire delivering hatred on cue.

As we drove, I reflected that, over the years, a number of the right-wing nuts I've run into have had more than their fair share of troubles. While it is certainly not my fault these people had connections to right-wing political views, they did seem to keep dropping dead at my feet with disturbing regularity. If this trend was true, maybe I should think about visiting all the right-wing congregations and conventions around the country. Instead of "typhoid Mary," I'd be "toxic Tommy." I could change the course of history by just showing up. A tempting thought, but one not terribly well grounded in reality. Besides, I didn't want all the right-wing people to die horrible deaths; just plain dying would be plenty good enough.

At the radio station we met in Macintire's office on the top floor, which had a spectacular view of the Lake Michigan shoreline. His secretary was a blond who might have been out of her teens. If the material from the clothes she was wearing was flattened out and stretched to its limits, it might have made a washcloth. I marvel at the right-wing moralizers who indulge in the hypocrisy of flaunting the sexuality of those near and dear to them or more likely those over whom they exercise control.

Cecil Macintire stood stooped over behind his desk. On the wall behind him were a series of pictures. They looked like candid family photos. One showed Cormac in a pair of Speedo swimming trunks. He was surrounded by Cecil and a number of people I didn't know. They were at the edge of a swimming pool. Cormac held a trophy high in his right hand. He'd obviously just won something.

Cecil's hands rested palm down on his desktop. His hair lay flat to his skull. His eyebrows were thicker, fuller, and bulged out farther than many people's full beards. He gazed at us malevolently.

"We're sorry for your loss," I said.

"Thank you," he mumbled.

I continued, "We know there probably isn't anything we can say or do to make your loss easier, but we are sympathetic to your pain. We want to find the killer of these two men because of our friend."

Macintire said, "My child is dead. I just wish there was something I could do. No prayer to my God is going to change the grief I feel." He sighed deeply. "You asked for this meeting. What is it you want? I need to begin making preparations for my son's funeral."

"We know this is a difficult time," I said. "We just had a few questions. Were you aware that Ethan and your son had been receiving threats lately."

"The police told me so. My son and I were estranged."

"We found a picture," I said. "It's intense for a parent to see. If you'd like . . ." I held out the envelope.

He nodded wearily. He only glanced at the picture for an instant, then dropped it as if it were a live coal. He put his face in his hands and moaned. When he finally looked up, he said, "I didn't want to believe it was true."

"You had no idea?"

"No. If I had, I would have been furious, but I am not so irrational that I would have him killed or murdered him myself over this. I am not a monster. Before yesterday I didn't know of or care about Ethan Gahain. I still don't."

Macintire's heavy frame seemed to deflate as he lowered himself into the plush leather chair behind his desk. He rubbed his hands across his face. He whispered, "I did not want my own son to be dead. This is the worst thing that could happen to anyone. Losing a child is devastating. It hurts too much. I don't expect you to understand. That's something you and your kind will never understand for which I am grateful."

Scott said, "I don't understand how you can go from grief for your son to a diatribe against us in the next instant. I would think the death of a child would pale when compared to politics. Gay people have children."

"Pah. That's a sad imitation of what real people do."

"Gay people aren't real?" Scott asked.

"You know what I mean."

"Actually, I don't."

"It's easier for me to make up conspiracy theories than to face my own failures. I'd rather try to believe that liberals tried to kill my son to cause me pain." Macintire gulped. "I'd rather think about anything else than about the loss of my son. I'd rather have fantasy than reality." He sighed. "I didn't kill my son. Tell me why I shouldn't think you did it? You found both of the bodies."

"You're free to think whatever you wish," I said. "How does hating us help your grief?"

"I'd rather think about hating you than the fact that my son is dead."

I held any hostile responses in check. His child was dead and I'd rather get answers than trade pointed and probably useless barbs. I asked, "Did you have any contact with your son?"

"No. I did not know he was a pornographer. Nor did I know of any problems he was having nor did I know of any enemies he might have had. I didn't know enough about my son. I didn't know how to raise a son. I had no father myself. I had no model to follow. I was lost. I wish we had been closer. I suppose I'm not much different from many fathers that way."

"Why did you agree to see us?" I asked.

"Because you found his body. Because you saw him. Because I want to know everything about my son. If you actually had useful information, it might let me feel more connected with my son. If I learn more about his life, maybe I'll feel a little less guilt."

"Why do you feel guilt?" Scott asked.

"It was the great tragedy of my life to be estranged from him." Macintire wasn't ranting, and I didn't detect a false note in this admission. "We will never be able to reconcile. We have no future. Can you or anyone give me that back?" He shook his head. I saw a tear on his face.

I said, "We didn't know him. I'm sorry. If you want to know what we found, we'd be happy to tell you."

"Yes, please," he murmured.

I told him about the circumstances of the death as I knew them. I finished, "The police can probably tell you more."

"The police won't tell me anything. I've tried using my fame to get me answers. It hasn't helped. What was the connection between this Gahain person and my son?"

"All we know is that they were business partners. I don't think they were lovers. I don't know if your son was gay. Is that why you were estranged?"

"Cormac never told me that he was a homosexual. When he was a teenager, he dated women. For God sakes, he was married to a woman. All the media are saying that he was a homosexual. That's what all the homosexuals are saying, too. That my son hung around locker rooms taking pictures of men, so what else could he have been?" Macintire shuddered. "Where did I go wrong?"

I said, "I suspect every parent asks that at some point in their lives no matter what their child's sexual orientation."

"But few of them ask it after their child has been murdered, or after they learn their child was a pornographer." Macintire sighed. "I knew nothing of my son's life. I knew none of his friends."

"Would your wife have known?" I asked.

"I'm divorcing my third wife. Cormac's mother died ten years ago of breast cancer. They were reasonably close. He barely knew any of my other wives. The last time I saw Cormac was at my first wife's funeral." Macintire gave another big sigh. "I'm sorry. My lack of closeness with my son is going to be a great burden to me for the rest of my days."

"How did the estrangement start?" I asked.

"When he was growing up, we disagreed about politics and religion. He thought I was a lousy father. I thought he was a terrible son. He didn't think I was attentive enough during his mother's final illness. He would never listen to me just as I would never listen to him. Now it's too late." Macintire bowed his head and stared at the top of his desk.

After several moments of silence, Scott asked, "If we find anything out, would you like us to call you?"

Macintire met Scott's gaze. "You would be willing to do that?"

Scott said, "I understand the difficulties between fathers and sons. Yes, I'd be willing to do that."

"Thank you," Macintire whispered.

.21.

We drove out to Barrington to meet with Ethan's parents. To avoid the media, they were staying with one of Ethan's uncles. My parents were there when we arrived. We met in an elegantly appointed living room. Mr. and Mrs. Gahain looked awful.

Mr. Gahain asked, "Is all that we're hearing in the media true?"

"I don't know what you heard," I said. "Let me tell you what we found." I told them everything. What was the point in lying or holding back? They might hear much worse. Better the appalling truth than the awfulness of wild rumors and media speculation.

They listened to my recitation stoically. When I was done, Mrs. Gahain said, "Why would he do that? Why would he take pictures?"

"I don't know." I wasn't about to speculate in front of the Gahains or make flippant comments about making money. "Do you have any idea how long Ethan had the condo on the lakefront?"

"Ernie called a few minutes ago," Mr. Gahain said. "It seems like he bought the condo a while ago. I think maybe he was making trips to Chicago and stayed there. Trips he didn't tell us about. Obviously we didn't know our son as well as we think we did. We didn't know anything about it. He just came to town Friday and asked if he could go to the wedding."

"He knew about the wedding already?"

"Yes. We'd mentioned it to him," Mrs. Gahain said. "We were a little surprised he hadn't been invited. I know you weren't as close as you once were. I hope there hadn't been a quarrel."

I gave as neutral a response as I could. "We weren't as close as we had been as kids."

"Who killed him?" Mr. Gahain asked. "Did this Cormac Macintire lead our son astray?"

I didn't say I thought their kid was plenty old enough to be making decisions of his own without having to rely on the old falling-into-bad-company defense.

We talked about Ethan for a little longer and then left. In the car I phoned the answering service.

Detective Rohter had left a message for us to call. He said, "One of the fingerprints we found in that bathroom stall was your nephew's."

"How'd you know it was his?" I asked.

"He had his hands all over the top of the table when we interviewed him. It might not stand up in court, but he was in that rest room. He told you he didn't go in, but we figured we'd better be as sure as we could. Turns out he had."

Scott said, "Maybe he used it before the murder."

"The print was on top of the blood. The print smeared the blood. The print happened after the killing. It was Ethan Gahain's blood. We want to find this kid, and we want to find him now."

"I think everybody does," I said.

"Have you talked to Donny's parents?" Rohter asked.

"Not today. The kid can't have gone far. We have his money. He doesn't know anyone in town."

Rohter said, "None of Mr. Carpenter's relatives at the hotel admitted seeing him. I want to talk to them again, especially the cousins near his age. One of them could be harboring him."

Made sense. We'd put everyone up at the Hotel Chicago. We set up a time to meet at the hotel the next morning.

Back home we called Scott's sister Mary. We spoke with her over the speakerphone. She was closest to Scott of all his siblings. We filled her in on what had been happening and Donny's possible role in the murder.

Her first reaction centered on Donny hitting his mother: "My God, I don't believe it. A child hitting his mother. That is an outrage."

"Has he done that kind of thing before?" I asked.

"Not that I know of."

Scott asked, "Does Hiram hit Cynthia?"

Mary paused to think for several moments. "I have no proof that he does. Daddy was never violent with us. He was gentle. I don't know where Hiram would have gotten it. Aren't abusers simply repeating what happened to them? Daddy never raised a hand to me."

"Me either," Scott said.

"Yes, but you were always the Goody Two-shoes in the family."

"Sometimes I just can't help myself."

Mary said, "I'm not aware that Hiram ever did such a thing. Cynthia never mentioned Donny being violent. My kids went to school with him. They never reported him being the class bully or anything, although he did run with a rough crowd."

I asked, "Do you think Donny could kill someone?"

"I can't imagine why he would. The family dynamic must have been far worse than anyone ever let on. Hiram always was close-mouthed."

Scott asked, "What the hell is going on in that family?"

"We get together for holidays. They don't seem to fight any more or less than anyone else. I kind of like Cynthia. She's very much in that Baptist adore-and-obey-the-husband tradition, but she's got a good sense of proportion. She knows what is best for her kids. She fights for it. She's no fool. She recognizes Hiram for exactly what he is. The Carpenter men from Georgia can be a stubborn lot."

I knew this to be true.

"When our kids were younger, she was always willing to sit for them, especially on short notice. I did that for her as well. My husband and Hiram don't get along much, but who does get along much with Hiram, except Cynthia? I'm not sure Hiram gets along with Hiram. Donny's older brother, Darrell, is another story. He has been in all kinds of trouble. I would believe any report of violence done by him. Hiram and Cynthia have had to go to court several times about Darrell."

"How come I didn't know this?" Scott asked.

"They didn't talk about it much. Cynthia would confide in me sometimes. I don't think she's got a lot of friends outside of the house. She goes to church a lot, but that's about it. She's usually so quiet."

"We've seen her near raving," Scott said.

"It's her child. Her youngest. Undoubtedly she's got powerful feelings. Maybe she believes Hiram has ruled the roost long enough, and she's finally willing to put her foot down."

"What kind of kid was Donny?" I asked.

"He was always very polite to me, very Southern gentleman. Then again, maybe he knew I wouldn't put up with his crap. He used to sit for my kids. We came back early one time and found him talking to some girl on our porch. It didn't seem important at the time. It wasn't like he was trying to have a mad, wild party."

Scott said, "But Donny and the older brother were close?"

"I'm not sure *close* is the right word. The younger brother adored the older. He emulated him. Wore the same kinds of clothes. Tried to hang around with the same friends. In fairly typical sibling fashion, the older boy sometimes permitted the closeness, sometimes pushed him away. Those two boys had some horrible fights."

"You mean physical confrontations."

"Knock-down-drag-out. Darrell sent Donny to the emergency room after several fights."

"Isn't that abuse?" I asked.

"By my definition it is, but nobody stepped in to stop it. I tried to talk to Donny about it, but he denied Darrell ever hurt him."

"How do you know it happened?" I asked.

"My boys talk to him. They're about the same age. They told me."

"When was all this?" Scott asked.

"A couple years ago. Then Darrell got sent to that work-farm program for an accumulation of offenses."

"Work farm?" Scott asked.

"It was the juvenile home when we were kids. Now it's a 'work-farm program.' It's kind of a boot-camp version of juvenile hall. You've heard of those."

"Was either one of them involved in drugs or pornography?" I asked.

"I have no hints of anything like that. I think my kids might have told me that kind of thing, but I'm not sure."

"Where's the older brother now?" I asked.

"As far as I know, serving another term at the work farm."

"I don't get a lot of family information," Scott said.

"You moved away. You were never close to Hiram. He's been jealous of you since he was in first grade. You were older. You were always better than him athletically. He didn't like that. You always got so much attention. He felt slighted. Even when he got older and got physically bigger than you, it didn't help. Your coordination was better, your reactions faster. Your muscles might not have been bigger, but they were stronger or you were able to use them more effectively."

"But we never had fistfights," Scott said. "He never sent me to the emergency room."

"Was that pure luck or just never getting caught?" Mary asked.

"It didn't happen," Scott averred, then asked, "Why would Donny have run away to us?"

"I don't know. The logical explanation would be that he was a gay kid running to somewhere that he thought would be supportive."

"He told us that," Scott said, "but I think he may have been lying."

"I sure have no indication that the kid is gay. Certainly, Cynthia never said anything to me about his sexual orientation. I never caught him naked with another boy."

I asked, "Do you think Donny would have the wherewithal to get himself up here on his own, or would he have had some help?"

"I suppose in this day and age it isn't that tough to get tickets, especially with the Internet. I think he's a resourceful kid. He has an exaggerated sense of his own cleverness, but he's not stupid."

198

We called his parents at the Hotel Chicago. I left the room to let Scott talk to them. I nuked a few leftovers in the microwave for us to have a bite to eat. Scott joined me about ten minutes later.

He flung himself onto a kitchen chair. "They warned me about seven times to be careful. They suggested several times that we just go on our honeymoon."

"That sounds kind of liberal of them."

"I don't think it means they approve of what I'm sure they don't think about. It's more, if we were out of town, nobody would try to harm us."

"I couldn't possibly leave before the funeral."

"I reminded them about the familial connection. I think they kind of understood, but their concern for me, their kid, outweighed that."

"But we haven't been in particular danger."

"Somebody broke into our hotel room in St. Louis and into our car in the parking lot of both universities."

I asked, "Have they seen Donny or your brother and sister-in-law?"

"Hiram and Cynthia were there earlier. They were out hiring a private security firm that specializes in looking for missing kids. Nobody thinks Donny was kidnapped, so nobody's worried about him being molested and killed. He ran. No one knows why."

"Did you tell them about the bloody fingerprint?"

"Yep. They were real quiet after I told them that. I don't think they wanted to believe it. That fact changes a lot of things."

"Where the hell could the kid go?" I asked. "You can't survive in this town by random chance. He's got to be sleeping somewhere. How could he find those places he could afford? Why isn't he afraid of being in those kinds of places? He grew up in rural Georgia, but very comfortable and safe rural Georgia. There can't be a lot of crime down there."

"As long as you were a white, male Protestant, it was generally very safe."

"Yeah. You know we're starting to turn into our own little crime wave."

"Don't start that amateur-sleuth crap again. I'm tired of hearing about how the Miss Marples of the world are one-person death squads."

22

First thing Wednesday morning, we were off to visit wife number three. We'd gotten her address from the Gahains the night before. She was the current repository of several of Ethan's children. She lived in a narrow, wood-frame home on Beldon Avenue just west of Sheffield. Terra Summa answered the door. She held a nursing child in her arms. She wore what used to be called a granny dress and gold-rimmed spectacles. When she was older, I could picture her being the perfect grandmother. Her bright pink face looked well scrubbed, open, and honest. We told her why we'd come.

She invited us in. We sat in overstuffed armchairs in the living room under the boughs of a live tree framed by the picture window. The container that held it was bigger than two bathtubs. The plants in the room were well trimmed and very green. The exterior might have been from pre-1900, but the interior was modern earth-mother. The floors were new and well polished. The walls were well scrubbed and recently painted. I could smell new-sawn wood, next to the smell of burning leaves, one of the great olfactory experiences. Every doorway and window was framed in dark-stained oak. The six oil paintings on the walls depicted children at play or staring raptly at some splendor of nature. Terra Summa had not taken Ethan's last name, not even a hyphenate.

After we sat down, I said, "We're trying to find out details about Ethan's life. We're trying to figure out why anyone would want to kill him."

She smiled. "He could be a trial to live with. He could be arrogant and a know-it-all. He wasn't good at being domestic. I love being domestic. I love rearing children. I don't think in terms of hatred. I think in terms of how we can help each other."

Fine. I tried a different tack. "Who would be least likely to want to help Ethan?"

She smiled. "I don't have a clue."

I agreed with that. I asked, "How many of Ethan's children do you have here?"

"We had one together. One from his first marriage is here. I have temporary custody of two others from wife number two."

"Those are the ones Mabel Yancey is after."

"Yes. Ethan brought the two of them to me Friday night and asked if I would look after them. He had a court order giving me temporary custody."

"He must have told you he was coming and that he would have such a document."

"He would know he could trust me. He would know he would need protection from his second wife. He would take any necessary precautions. I would help him out no matter what."

A stunningly attractive woman entered the room. We stood up. I stared for a moment. I hadn't seen her in at least ten years. It was Ethan's first wife, Dana. She was as attractive as I remembered. She was dressed in a gray suit jacket and matching skirt. She walked up to us and held out her hand. "Hello, Tom, and you must be Scott Carpenter."

I said, "Dana, good to see you."

"Congratulations," she said. "I read about the wedding. Ethan managed to upstage it. That's the kind of man he was. If you were doing something, he did it better or greater or had more toys than you did."

"He was a taker," I said.

"So true." She offered us coffee. Dana had never struck me as a raving loony. She and Terra sat opposite. The affectionate looks they exchanged, the tenderness in looking at the child, the nearness with which they sat, certainly indicated to me that they were a couple.

"Who would want to kill him?" I asked.

"Mabel Yancey is an angry woman," Dana said. "I hated Ethan for a few years." She shrugged. "I got over it. Wife four made a lot of money out of the marriage."

"The two of you didn't have custody issues?"

"It was very complicated. Terra and I each had a child with Ethan. We have custody of them."

"Ethan knew you were a couple."

"Oh, yes."

"Did you know he was gay?"

"He was never terribly demanding as a lover," Dana said. "I thought my lack of sexual interest in him was my fault. Turns out I wasn't interested, but for fundamentally different reasons." She and Terra clasped hands briefly. "As for who would want to kill him, I certainly don't know anyone specific. Wife two and her husband are nutcases, but that doesn't mean they're killers."

"We were told you were always after him for things."

"I'm sure someone described me as a 'raving loony.' "

Since she already seemed to know this, I didn't feel a need to confirm it.

She continued, "For a long time I guess I was. Back then my ego was caught up in what a man, what men think of me. I've gone through a lot of therapy. I've finally met someone I love." She patted Terra's hand. "I'm much better now. I don't need some man to validate me."

"What's going to happen with custody now?" I asked.

"I don't know," Dana said. "I'm a lawyer, but my specialty is corporate law. We have an appointment with a family lawyer. I'm sure we're safe with our biological children, but the ones Ethan had with wife number two, I don't know."

23

We drove to the Hotel Chicago. It was nine-thirty and the meeting with the police and Scott's family was set for ten. We wanted to get there early to talk to his parents. The suite we'd rented on the top floor for Scott's parents was immense.

We got there before the cops, Hiram, or Cynthia arrived. We sat down with Scott's mom and dad. He said, "Has anyone heard from Donny?"

They hadn't.

"Did you hear that Donny hit Cynthia?"

They shook their heads.

"He attacked her when they were being questioned by the police."

Mrs. Carpenter said, "We didn't bring you kids up to do that kind of thing."

Scott asked, "Does Hiram have a history of abusing Cynthia? Has he hit her before? Maybe Donny's simply acting out what his father does."

"Hiram isn't that kind of man," Mr. Carpenter said. "Donny's older brother, Darrell, has been violent. He's always been in fights. Hiram's been angry since he was a kid, but he's never shown violence toward us, and he's never been violent in front of us."

"This is terrible," Mrs. Carpenter said. "Hiram is a good father, but his kids have been a handful. I don't think he tells us much of what happens. I suppose he thinks he's sheltering us. It's a small town we live in so people know each other's business, but we never heard anything this bad. Mostly the violence was connected with Darrell. He got picked up for drunk-and-disorderly conduct several times before he even got his driver's license. He got drunk and crashed a car when he was fourteen."

Mr. Carpenter said, "Donny sure did admire his older brother. We tried to tell him he shouldn't. He wouldn't listen to us."

Scott said, "Finding Donny's fingerprint inside the bathroom stall in the hotel is very bad. It also means it is possible that if Donny had called for help, they might have been able to save Mr. Gahain."

Mrs. Carpenter put her hand to her mouth. "Oh, dear. That's terrible."

Mr. Carpenter shook his head and tsk-tsked.

The cops arrived a few minutes before Donny's parents. When Hiram walked in the door, he was in full tirade: "I want to know what the hell is going on."

Cynthia looked ready either for tears or a tantrum or maybe both. Her left ear was bright red.

Scott said, "Hiram, you're not in charge. I'm not sure why you continue to think angry blustering is going to get us closer to finding Donny. I suppose it must accomplish something in your daily life in Georgia. You're here now. You're not in charge. He ran to us. He didn't contact you. Doesn't that tell you something? We don't know where he is. Your continued anger is a very poor cliché, a senseless way of dealing with the world. I suggest you give rationality and logic a chance."

"You done?" Hiram demanded.

"I'm done speaking directly to you. What I want to do now is figure out where your kid is. My hunch is that the kid has been staying with one of his cousins right here in this hotel. It's the only logical assumption."

Scott's dad said, "We figured that, too. We've checked with all of our grandkids. They say they haven't seen him."

"Can you believe all of them?" I asked.

Mrs. Carpenter said, "I think there are several of the older ones who might be inclined to help him out. I'm not sure which ones."

Detective Rohter said, "We'll question all of them again."

Scott said, "Maybe someone from the family talking to them would be more likely to get information out of them."

"Believe me, they'll talk to me," Hiram said.

"I already tried," Mrs. Carpenter said. "If they won't be honest with their grandmother, I'm not sure they'd be honest with anyone."

"Mama," Scott said, "I'd sure like to believe they wouldn't lie to you, but you're two generations from their age. I don't know who they'd tell the truth to."

Hiram said, "Why isn't the killer one of these men this Ethan person took pictures of?"

Rohter said, "The real question here is about the kid. He's involved in a murder investigation. I want to talk to everybody who is in town connected with the family."

"We'll get the truth," Scott's dad said.

I asked, "Is there any significance to the scorpion tattoo just below Donny's navel?"

"What?" Cynthia Carpenter asked.

"He doesn't have a tattoo," Hiram said.

"We weren't hallucinating," Scott said.

"I've never seen it," Hiram said. "How did you?"

Scott said, "We hid his clothes to try to get him to talk to us. It didn't work."

"He was naked?" Hiram asked.

"He paraded around for a few minutes in his boxer shorts," Scott said. "He was not traumatized. The police were there at almost exactly the same time."

Cynthia said, "I don't know of any significance to such a tattoo. Isn't it illegal to get a tattoo if you're under twenty-one?"

I had no idea if that was true.

Scott and I stayed in the background as the Carpenters assembled all of the clan who'd come up for the wedding. Only three of Donny's cousins were left in town. The rest had had to get back to various commitments in Georgia. The three cousins were in their late teens. One was a junior in college in Michigan, the other was spending an extra week in Chicago to check on job possibilities in construction. A third was staying with her parents for a vacation. None admitted to having seen Donny.

I conveniently found my way to the hallway while Scott's nephews were being interviewed by the police. I asked Scott's favorite niece, Connie, "Did you ever see Donny hit his mother?"

She was young and blond and pretty. I remembered her as being vivacious and smart. Mary's kid. She said, "I never saw him hit her."

"Did you hear about it?"

She took a quick look around to make sure no one was in hearing distance. She leaned close and whispered, "When we were younger, he used to play mean tricks on all of us. He never really got violent. He tried to tie me up once when we were about ten. I was bigger than him so I just walked away. Many times he's boasted that if either of his parents tried to stop him, he'd hurt them."

"Stop him doing what?"

"He was never very specific. It's the influence of that older brother of his. That Darrell. He's very violent. He always wanted to pinch, punch, or pulverize."

"How angry or frightened would Donny have to be to hit his mother?"

"I don't think anyone is ever angry or frightened enough to be justified in hitting their mother. Uncle Hiram is kind of a Neanderthal, but Aunt Cynthia's actually pretty nice. We all like her. Nobody likes Donny except Darrell, and I don't think Darrell likes him all that much. I think he tolerates him. Donny is a wanna-be. He's the inept one in that bunch. He tries to imitate someone really being mean, and he always flubs it. I think he'd try anything to get his way. Tell any lie. Darrell's the violent one. Two black churches burned in our county. If it wasn't Darrell who lit the match, it was his crowd. At least that's what everyone believes. Donny's the kind of kid who would follow any leader."

"Why wouldn't he run away closer to home?"

"This was probably the biggest, most public family event ever likely to happen. Maybe he didn't want to miss it. His grandparents were here, some cousins, uncles, and aunts. It wasn't that daring. I doubt if he planned much beyond that. He isn't all that bright. He made attempts at deviousness. In school he would make homophobic comments behind a teacher's back. You know after they pass in the hallway."

"A coward and a prick."

"He wasn't very nice. Maybe he went to you guys because he thought you would be easy marks."

24

We asked to meet with the detectives in a coffee shop down the street. After we settled in, we showed them what Ernie Gahain had found in Ethan's place in Chicago.

Rohter said, "We didn't know he had a condo here."

"Neither did we," I said. "The parents found evidence of its existence in his luggage."

"We should have been notified," Rohter said.

"Gee," I said. "Here's a possible thought process. Their son has just been murdered. They've gone through his luggage to try and find something for him to wear to be buried in. They find a key and some record of a place he's been staying in Chicago. Their first thought is to call the police. I don't think so. We called you as soon as we found out."

"We'll have to go over the place."

I handed him the envelope.

Rohter opened it. He and Hoge perused the photos briefly. "This is the first we've seen of the porn empire."

"I think the question has to be why were these separated from the rest of the collection?"

"Gotta be a reason," Rohter said. "I appreciate you giving this to us." He held up the picture of me skinny-dipping. "He had one of you."

"I didn't need to kill him to get that. I didn't even know it existed. I wouldn't be embarrassed because of it. I wouldn't lose my job over a picture that old. There was no way he was blackmailing me with it."

Rohter said, "We also understand there's a history of violence in the Carpenter family. That your sister was convicted of murdering the sheriff in your little town down in Georgia."

"Yes," Scott said. "And that means?"

"It's a piece of the puzzle," Rohter said.

"What else have you learned?" I asked.

"Right now we're stuck on your nephew as the prime suspect," Rohter said. "The bloody fingerprint is gonna get him a trip to the station for serious questioning. It won't take much more evidence to get him arrested."

I asked, "How often do you do frivolous questioning?"

Nobody laughed. Sometimes my sense of humor isn't as appropriate as I think it is.

"He's not a killer," Scott said.

"Doting uncle declares nephew's innocence," Rohter said. "As an avowal it has a certain headline appeal."

Detective Hoge asked, "How well do you actually know your nephew? He lives in Georgia. You're here. Does he visit you often?"

"No," Scott said.

Rohter said, "We want to talk to the nephew and draw our own conclusions. If he didn't kill him, there's got to be a damn good reason why his bloody fingerprint is on that john wall. Donny Carpenter was certainly there before Ethan Gahain died, and we didn't get any call until we got yours. We've checked all the 911 tapes and all other emergency calls. Nothing. The kid might have saved a life."

Scott said, "I think that's the worst part of this. Even if it wouldn't have saved him, walking out on an injured person was an awful thing to do."

"Donny couldn't have killed Macintire in St. Louis. His plane ticket stub said Atlanta to Chicago one-way. He'd have had to go to St. Louis and back to Georgia. He's only fifteen. That's a heck of a lot of running around for a kid."

"But not impossible," Hoge said.

Rohter said, "The St. Louis police believe there are some key parts of the operation missing. These photos might be part of that. Some financial records are missing. They can't find the model releases."

"Were they going to have lots of those?" I asked.

"Not for the athlete stuff, but for the videos they made, yeah. Not having the names of who was in the videos sure makes it look like somebody took them. The killer might have wanted to cover up something."

"Are you sure they even had them?" I asked.

"A couple people have come forward. They've confirmed signing them and making statements for the camera that they were making the film of their own free will."

Hoge said, "Trying to figure out who they all are by their pictures is going to take forever. Some may never be identified."

"Whose gun was it that was used on Cormac?" Scott asked.

"The police say Cormac had a permit for the same type of gun they found."

"Was it definitely murder or did he commit suicide?" I asked.

"They found powder residue on his hand. It looks like

suicide, except they also found bits of skin under two of his fingernails. He fought back against somebody. When we get a suspect, we'll be able to match DNA. It makes sense that whoever he fought against would be the killer."

I said, "This had to have been blackmail."

"Yeah," Scott agreed, "but why? Everything in St. Louis sure looked profitable enough."

I said, "For some people there's never enough profit."

"Maybe they wanted something else," Scott said.

"But what?" Rohter asked. "We haven't been able to find any connecting motive."

"I know you're going to look in the condo here," I said, "but you won't find any clues there. We sure didn't see anything."

"Unless you were busy covering up for yourselves," Rohter said.

"Am I really a suspect?" I asked.

"We don't rule anybody out, ever," Rohter said. "I'm not putting you on the top of any suspect list, but I wouldn't suggest finding any more bodies for a few days at least. I tend to get testy the more bodies somebody finds."

I said, "I'll do my best to keep clear of falling corpses."

Everybody left.

⊾ 25 ⊿

We had a message at the service from Scott's reporter friend, Doug Clangborn. We called him on the speakerphone.

"Have you guys heard anything about a live Internet Web site Ethan Gahain was supposedly running?"

I told him the two we knew about.

"Neither of those," he said. "This was supposedly all masturbation all the time."

"You're kidding," Scott said.

"Nope. It's supposed to be a real Web site. Everybody here's been trying to find it. We've looked under all kinds of key words starting with masturbation and every synonym we can think of for that word. We've looked under Ethan's name and anyone's name connected with the case. Nothing so far."

"Where'd you get the rumor from?" I asked.

"Sources."

Weren't amateur sleuths traditionally good friends with reporters? Didn't everybody cheerfully reveal their secret sources to them? There's got to be a union to complain to about this kind of treatment.

"What good does it do to find the Web site?" Scott asked.

"It's another part of the whole," Clangborn said.

"Don't some people have cameras on themselves all the time?"

"Twenty-four seven," Clangborn said.

I'd vowed to beat into insensibility the next person I heard say that. Unfortunately, reaching through the phone was not an option.

"Huge numbers of those people who put themselves on the web must have sex and masturbate," I said. "How many of them are involved in a murder investigation? The people who he got to appear on the site wouldn't have much reason to kill them. Assumedly if they're appearing live, it's a choice. Porn is always a good thing to mix in with murder, and a blackmail angle makes sense. Hell, simple embarrassment at doing something stupid and wanting to cover it up could be a reason."

Scott said, "Didn't that kid in the movie *American Pie* have a camera set up?"

"Yeah," I said. "It wouldn't be all that complicated." I called the cops and left a message about what we'd just heard.

We went to the electronics room and turned on the computer. We surfed the Net looking for the masturbation site. We found Ethan's basic Web sites easily enough. There were a lot of links to a lot of pornographic things, kinky and unkinky. Nothing about all masturbation all the time.

After half an hour of some fairly salacious viewing, Scott said, "You'd think they'd want people to find the site."

"They must. If it exists."

We called Jack Miller's pager number. He'd managed to set up a meeting with a porn expert.

He told us, "Somebody's got hold of a bunch of the tapes and is putting them on the Internet."

He gave us that URL. We punched it in while we talked. Miller said, "They take a while to download and for some of them you've got to have a pretty sophisticated computer. The universities involved have that. You've got some angry young jocks coming out of the woodwork."

"I still don't get that," Scott said. "I wouldn't want somebody to see me naked changing clothes, but I'm not sure I'd be pissed off about somebody seeing me naked changing clothes. There's nothing I did to plan it. There's nothing I can do to stop it now. Why fight it? Why get angry? Why even care? Even if I was running for some public office and somebody saw me naked in pictures taken without my consent, who is going to give a rat's ass?"

Miller agreed and added, "I've got the URL number for that all-masturbation Web site."

"Everybody up here has been frantically searching for it."

"My guy in St. Louis found it." He gave us that URL. Scott called it up while we talked.

I said, "This had to be an awful big operation to have it run continuously. It couldn't just be three guys."

Miller said, "Do you have it there?"

"Yeah."

"You can see that it wasn't quite as continuously live as rumors claimed it to be. They did lots of live things in the past. They ran a whole lot of ads for their other stuff interspersed with printed interviews, pictures, older videos, clips from upcoming productions. They didn't have a new person doing some kind of sexual thing every minute. They didn't go from live orgasm to live orgasm, although they did that sometimes. Most often they'd tape folks. You've got people using the Internet for porn the way they used to use magazines. It's just more uncomfortable sitting up in a chair whacking off than it is lying down in bed with a magazine."

"Porn Positions 101," I said. "A required course for technology sexuality."

"They did a lot of those solo jack-off things where the guys beat off. Before the guys would undress, they'd talk to them about sexual activity. A lot of the athletes have tuned in to the site. They've got herds of lawyers trying to get it shut down. The actual physical broadcast site could be anywhere on the planet."

I said, "They've got to be able to track it down. There's got to be a provider like AOL or something."

"Ain't necessarily so," Miller said. "For whatever reason, it hasn't been shut down yet and the world is tuning in to watch masturbation. The kinkiest stuff I've seen advertised is for several sets of twins, both genders, making love with themselves and others."

I asked, "Do you have reason to believe something kinky led to the murder?"

"No."

I asked, "Does this fourth site use the athlete videos?"

"There seem to be several separate sets of materials. So far on the first two sites they've found video of four professional and seven amateur athletes who in their college days changed clothes. We're getting some of the same reactions as you did from those guys you talked to earlier. Some want residuals for showing their studly selves. Some want to sue. Some are outraged, or at least they think the public wants them to be outraged."

"Who are the most outraged?" I asked.

"There's a few guys who are talking about going to Mr. Gahain's wake and having a protest."

"I doubt if anything will come of that," I said. "Most athletes talk big about doing brave things, but they really aren't very political."

"Think Steve Largent," Scott suggested.

"Think moronic twit," I suggested.

Miller said, "I've got a contact in the porn world for you to interview. He wouldn't talk to me. I mentioned your name. I guess I shouldn't have been surprised that Scott's name got you an interview. Unfortunately, along with the name, it's going to require an in-person appearance. You're not afraid the guy would use this to blackmail you?"

"Star baseball player meets with prominent porn person," I said. "I can see the headlines." I told Miller to set it up.

We explored all the Web sites. They seemed to be filled with a whole lot more glossy ads for themselves, but there were certainly links that you could reach for a credit card number and a fee. We checked a few of them out. In one of the video clips I thought I recognized the fixtures at the condo. After several minutes in several different sites, I said, "I've seen naked men before." Nothing on the sites gave us clues to the murderer.

26

We drove to Caribou Coffee on Broadway to meet with Jack Miller's porn connection. We found him waiting outside the door. As so often is true, all the tables were filled in the coffee shop, so we walked up to Windy City Sweets several doors north. This is perhaps the warmest, friendliest, and best-stocked candy store in town. They also have a few seats inside. We settled down to single-dip ice cream cones on the high wooden chairs.

Marty Burnes, the porn prima donna in Chicago, reviewed videos for several gay publications under different pseudonyms. I'd read a rumor in the gay press that the last reviewer, a closeted kindergarten teacher, had married a porn star and retired with him to Australia. Burnes had added the gig at the *Gay Tribune* at that time. The previous writer had also written several sexual-fantasy columns. Burnes was slender and a head shorter than Scott and I. He had skin the color of mocha coffee, heavy on the cream. Not a blemish on it. His hair was thick and black with a slight upsweep in front that was dyed a dark shade of brown. He looked to be in his midtwenties, lean with taut muscles. He had heavy, black eyebrows and white teeth. He smiled at us. He said, "I've always wanted to meet a baseball player who was gay. I think every gay guy on the planet wants to meet you."

"We're here for information," Scott said.

Burnes looked thoughtful. "I will supply it. It's just so cool being with a gay icon who is an athlete."

"You must have played sports," I hazarded.

"Yep, but it's not the same. I was a soccer fag. Went with my university team to the national championships. We lost, but you, you're a star." We did a few more minutes of star-jock-sniffing before we got Burnes onto the track we wanted.

"Pictures, pictures, pictures," he said. "Did he have any of you?"

I said, "We found two of me from back in high school. One with me in my football uniform. The other from a pool party when a bunch of kids went skinny-dipping."

"That sounds like Ethan."

I asked, "What can you tell us?"

"I know everything there is to know about porn in this city."

"What was the deal with Ethan? How did he get started in the business?"

"Innocently enough. When Ethan was a kid, he let older guys take pictures of him."

"Kid? How young?"

"Certainly high school." Burnes held up a hand. "Don't get hyper. Ethan did not take pictures of kids. He told me numerous times he didn't. Believe me, kiddie porn is dangerous business. I won't have anything to do with it. No self-respecting pornographer will. That's a fast way to go to prison. However, being a subject of the pictures is another thing. Ethan told me how he used to love to turn older guys on, said he made tons of money doing it."

Thinking back on it now, I didn't remember Ethan ever having money problems as a teenager.

"While Ethan was in college, one of the guys who took pictures of him was retiring from the business. He set up Ethan. Ethan started with his few little videos and an ad or two in some sleazy gay-porn rags. He made a lot of money very quickly, a surprising amount. He just kept taking pictures of stud athletes. Then he found a few guys who were willing to beat off for cash, and the rest, as they say, is history."

"If he was making so much money, why did Ethan coach at all?"

"Respectability? The desire to be among young, muscular, hot men? The chance of seeing gorgeous guys naked up close and personal? He was stupid? He enjoyed coaching? Could be any number of reasons."

"Were he and Cormac ever lovers?" Scott asked.

"Not that I know of. Supposedly, Cormac was not gay. He was hot, a former swimmer who kept in shape. Ethan said his partner was only in it for the money."

"Did they have any rivals in the business, fights that you know of?"

"Not in the porn business. He had problems at Carl Sandburg University with Robert Murphy. That was a classic rivalry."

"I knew him slightly from when we were kids. He said he got along fine with Ethan."

Burnes gave an unpleasant little laugh. "Robert is a shit. They hated each other. He's betrayed more people in this town than anyone else. Robert was rich, young, and hot. He and Ethan were bitter rivals in the department."

"What was the problem?" I asked.

"Robert Murphy is the kind of guy who is gay, but who avoids other people who are. He's the kind who is afraid people will think you are gay if you have a friend who is homosexual."

Scott said, "You catch being gay by being in close proximity to someone who is gay?"

"I think it's a little more subtle than that for those who are severely closeted, which Robert is. He hated Ethan. If you're looking for a killer, he'd be a great one to start with, or end with, as the case may be. Ethan found the ins and outs of university politics easy. He was a charmer. Kids in the program liked Ethan better. Ethan was better at recruiting. Robert was the Bobby Knight of Carl Sandburg's athletic program in all of the negative aspects of that comparison."

"Murphy wasn't invited to the wedding," I said. "He may have a perfectly legitimate alibi."

"You're sure the killer was invited to the wedding?" Burnes asked.

"It would make sense logistically."

"But are you sure?"

"Well, no."

"You should check Murphy out," Burnes said.

"They were rivals," I said. "What else?"

"Bitter rivals. The severely closeted are often a big problem. Ethan wasn't about to tell everyone that Murphy was gay, but Murphy found out about the porn. He threatened to expose Ethan if he didn't quit teaching. Ethan barely batted an eye. He got an offer from Lafayette and took it. Although that turned out to be kind of a hoot itself."

"Why?"

"There's a guy down there, Salvatore Fariniti."

"We met him."

"Hot man. He and Ethan made love. Ethan secretly videotaped it. I told Ethan that was stupid. Ethan claimed he gave the guy the only copy of the tape. I doubt it. Not the way Ethan worked."

I asked, "Fariniti knew about the porn operation?"

"Sure."

"He lied to us."

"This is a murder investigation. What did you expect?"

"Was Ethan frightened of these people?"

"When you're in an edgy, extreme business such as porn, there's always a bit of a sense of danger."

"But were people after him? Was he more worried lately?"

"He talked once in a while of getting out of the business. Not often. I didn't get the impression he was more worried than usual lately, but I hadn't talked with him in a couple of weeks."

"Is the porn mob-connected?" I asked. "Could that have had something to do with the murder?"

"Let me answer this carefully. The mob is less interested in porn than it used to be. The Internet has gotten porn beyond any single entity's ability to control it, the U.S. Congress's beliefs notwithstanding. You can show naked pictures of yourself in your own chat room anytime you feel like it. People can connect with all kinds of people with all kinds of kinks. You don't need the mob."

"But Ethan's organization was kind of big," I said. "At least he was making lots of money."

"I haven't heard of any connection between him and the mob. Nor have I heard that the mob was angry at him."

"Do you know that for sure?" I asked.

"You came to me as an expert. You can check my opinions with others. I'm not sure how easy it will be to find someone to ask. I'm not claiming what I'm telling you is anything but an expert opinion. You want certitude, try a mob-connected source. Do you know one?"

I shook my head, then said, "Some of the records are missing. We found sets of pictures that seem to be connected to blackmail."

"They didn't need money. There was no need for blackmail. Remember, porn may be sleazy and looked down on, but in most jurisdictions, it is not illegal."

Scott said, "He had a lot of old videos there. Where did he get them?"

"He brought up a bunch of old collections from companies and individuals around since the early days of porn. Back then a lot of them were pretty fly-by-night—actually, many still are. Conventional wisdom is that in the old days many that weren't mob-connected didn't stay in business long. Some just folded because they were run by a bunch of goofs."

I said, "And there was lots of kinky stuff."

"That was Ethan's specialty. If you had a kink, he had a video for it. On Ethan's Web site, he advertised, offered money for amateur stuff. Ethan paid top dollar. That's where he got a lot of the strangest videos."

"Isn't some of that stuff illegal?" Scott asked.

"Sure. They had a famous video with several sets of twins doing it together. Filming incest and selling it is very illegal. They charged premium prices for those and sold tons of them."

"All gay?" I asked.

"Absolutely not. The majority of the twin ones were sets of straight women with one guy. They also had private collections that were not advertised on the Internet. You had to know Ethan or Cormac personally to get those. They charged premium prices for them. Exactly what precise combinations of near relatives they had, I'm not sure. I don't know if there is a complete list. Even if you had model releases, I doubt if they'd list the familial relationship. If you're doing something that illegal, you're not as worried about model releases and age requirements as you might be."

"Do you know about the condo here?"

"Sure. They made videos there. There's nothing sinister in that."

"How did you meet him?" I asked.

"I was in one of his classes at the university. I fucked him on the top of his desk in the classroom one night."

Scott asked, "Why aren't you dead?"

Burnes looked shocked. "I beg your pardon?"

"Two of the people with a connection to the porn empire are dead. The third is missing. If I were you, I'd be frightened out of my mind."

"I don't know anything worth being killed for."

"Josh Durst claimed he didn't know anything," Scott said. "He's missing. Two others are dead. Why aren't you?"

"This is absurd. I have no reason to fear." Burnes glanced around uneasily.

Into the silence that began to stretch uncomfortably, I asked, "How'd you get into the porn business?"

"Ethan introduced me to people. As positions for reviewer or hanger-on opened up, I'd take them. I spend my life surfing porn sites. I go to all the video award ceremonies. I get myself onto as many porn sets as I can."

"Do you appear in videos?"

"I don't have guts enough to show my body on camera. I wish I did. I try to make personal contacts with as many people making videos as possible. For someone living in the Midwest, I know a great deal. In fact, a lot of folks in the porn industry love me. Partly they feel a need to suck up because

I'm a reviewer. Partly because I'm fair and honest in my reviews."

"We've got to tell this stuff to the police," I said.

"Fine. I'll deny I said anything."

"You don't like the police?"

"I hustled a little in college. I got hassled by some pretty nasty cops. They are not my friends. I will help you. I will not help them. Don't bother to send them."

Scott asked, "Ethan and Cormac had a live Web site or a purportedly live site. Who's keeping it up?"

"I wouldn't know."

I've watched teenagers lie for too many years not to have been suspicious of him at that moment. I said, "Why would you lie to us? Did you kill the others?"

"Hey, I agreed to help you guys. What the hell is this?"

"We're not trying to accuse you," Scott said, "but nobody we know of has any knowledge of their porn business except you. You could easily have a reason to kill them—business rivals, jealousy, something. The Web site is still running at least in part. It's got to be somebody. Why not you?"

"You can't talk to me like this."

"Sure we can," I said. As soon as Scott aired his suspicions, I glommed on to them as truth. They sounded so right.

"Where were you about eight o'clock Saturday night?" I asked.

"I wasn't invited to your wedding."

"Maybe you'll be talking to the police after all," Scott said.

"You guys are assholes."

"From stars to shits in less than an hour," Scott said, "that beats my previous record."

"We keep track of his best times," I added.

Scott said, "It's us or the police and lots of questions."

"Last Saturday I was fucking a porn star who wanted a

good review of his latest movie. I haven't been to St. Louis in ten years. I wouldn't step in that cesspool. I didn't kill anybody. I barely knew Durst."

"Who runs the porn site now?"

"I do, okay. I have the passwords. I'll shut it down if you want me to."

"We just want to know if what's on it will give a clue to the murder."

"Basically right now I've got it set on permanent loop. It's not live anymore. We advertised it that way, but, Christ, that takes a lot. There is nothing on it anyone would kill for."

"You can't be sure of that," I said. "Two people are already dead. If you won't talk to the cops, then you've got to at least have protection. We know a private detective who can help."

"You really think I'm in danger?"

"Don't you?"

"I hadn't thought so."

"The killer is desperate about something. The model releases are missing. Do you have them?"

"No, I swear."

This time I didn't sense he was lying. I said, "You're the last link. Josh Durst ran again."

"He called me," Burnes said, "Monday morning. He said people were questioning him. He didn't say it was you guys. I told him not to trust anybody and that he'd better run. He didn't tell me he had a copy of the records. I didn't know the records are what was getting people killed."

I said, "When we talked to Durst, he claimed that he had tapes of Scott pitching. We didn't see Scott's name in the athletes' list we saw."

"Durst never told me about them. If he had them, he never added them to the collection that I know about."

We used the cell phone to call Miller. He agreed about the

need for protection. While we waited for his arrival, I asked, "Was there anyone significant in his life named Michael?" I told Burnes about Ethan's last words.

"Nobody I can think of," Burnes said.

"I can't figure out what it was he wanted to come to the wedding to talk to me about."

"I can't tell you that. I don't know. He would talk about you on occasion. He always said he wanted to apologize to you. When I asked him what for, he only ever said he was a shit to you when you were kids. He said he could always trust you. I can't tell you how many times he showed me that goddamn little brown football with your initials carved on it. You do know he kept little souvenirs of many of his conquests?"

I shook my head.

Burnes continued, "He said you were the one person in his life who was honest. As for me, I never got a good impression of you from Ethan's descriptions. You seemed like someone who couldn't let go. The last time you called, he found it embarrassing. Who would cling to memories long since past and best forgotten? From what I heard, you were pretty pathetic." Burnes shrugged. "But he was desperate to apologize. I think that's why he came to town. He wanted a fresh start. I thought it was kind of silly."

When Miller arrived, we filled him in on what we'd learned, especially about Murphy and Fariniti.

As Miller was escorting Burnes away, the private eye said, "This one won't get away."

Back in our car I said, "I want to talk to Murphy and Fariniti."

"Got that right," Scott said. "I'm not sure I trust Burnes all that much."

The cell phone rang. The service said, "It's one of Mr. Carpenter's nephews. He says it's urgent."

I put it on the speakerphone expecting it to be Donny. It was Brent, Scott's sister's oldest. He sounded scared. "I just a got call from Donny. He's in trouble."

"Where is he?" Scott asked.

"I'm not sure. He said I should meet him at the corner of Clark and Diversey. I can't get there. I don't know where it is. I think he was out of his mind. He didn't give me time to say I couldn't make it. I knew I should call you."

"You could have taken a bus or a cab," Scott said.

"I don't know the city. I've never been in a cab."

"Where's your mom?" Scott asked.

"I think she's gone out with Grandma and Grandpa to talk with the private investigator."

"Stay there," Scott said. "We'll call the police. You wait there until one of the adults comes back and give them the news."

I asked, "Was he staying with you?"

A very soft, "Yes."

I decided family units closer to the kid than I could go over the stupidity of not revealing that Donny was hiding there. At least Brent had the sense to call now.

"Did he tell you to call us?" Scott asked.

"No, but after talking to all of you earlier, I realized I had to tell. I would have told him I was going to."

We called the police. The candy shop is mere blocks from Clark and Diversey. We rushed over. In the car on the way to the intersection we phoned each of Scott's relatives still in town. None of them was in. We left messages for each.

Since finding a spot on the street in that neighborhood is nearly impossible, we parked in the Century parking garage up Clark Street. We walked quickly to the intersection. We saw no one we recognized until Rohter and Hoge parked in the bus zone on Diversey west of Clark. We hustled over to them. We all scanned the never unbusy intersection.

"Why here?" Scott asked. "What the hell is he thinking? What the hell is going on?"

27

A bus drew up across the street on the south side of Diversey. When it pulled away, Donny was leaning against a no-parking sign. He was clutching his side. Scott began to run across the street. Car brakes squealed. I grabbed his arm and yanked him back. A southbound car turning right onto Diversey from Clark missed him by inches.

Traffic cleared. The cops, Scott, and I dashed across the street. I watched Donny stumble. He had both hands holding his jacket tightly to his torso. He saw us and tried to move in the opposite direction. As soon as he let go of the sign, he began to fall. A pedestrian stopped and held out a hand toward him.

By the time we reached him, the kid was on the sidewalk and gasping for breath. Rohter called for an ambulance. Hoge ran back across the street and hopped into their unmarked car. At the time I didn't pay much attention to him. Later I found out that he was chasing the bus so they could talk to the passengers about Donny.

Scott and I knelt next to the kid. He breathed heavily.

When he pulled his hand away from his side, we saw that he was rapidly losing blood. Scott tore off his own jacket, ripped off his shirt, and used it to apply pressure to the wound. The blood quickly soaked it through.

"This must have just happened," I said. "He couldn't have gone far for long on a bus without someone noticing."

Donny cried out in pain. He was panting hard. He tried to push Scott's hands away. The most bleeding seemed to be coming from a gash just below his rib cage on his far left side. I had no idea which organs were directly under that spot.

"What happened?" Scott asked.

Donny gazed at us and mumbled, "Help me." I realized this was the first time I'd heard his voice without a trace of teenage hostility. That was neither a helpful nor a comforting thought. He sounded eerily like Ethan. He put his bloody hand on top of the bloody shirt on top of his bloody wound. "Help me," he said again. I tore off my shirt and added it to the rapidly spreading red mass.

Scott cradled Donny's head and torso and murmured, "Everything's going to be fine. Just hold on. The paramedics are on their way." The kid shut his eyes. I couldn't tell if he remained conscious or not, but he was still breathing.

The paramedics did show up pretty quickly. As they worked, Scott phoned his parents' hotel room. He got hold of them. Hiram and Cynthia were with Scott's parents. We found out what hospital they were taking the kid to and told them. The paramedics loaded Donny into the ambulance. We ran to our car and raced after them.

At the hospital Donny was rushed into the emergency room. Hiram, Cynthia, and Scott's parents hurried in moments after we arrived. For once Hiram did not bluster or fulminate or foam at the mouth. He saw us, came over, and asked, "Is he all right? Where is he?"

Hiram and Cynthia were allowed to rush to the back where they'd taken Donny. We stayed in the waiting room. Hoge and Rohter arrived. The news they had was unhelpful. No one on the bus had noticed anything. It had been crowded. Six or seven people had gotten off at the stop. A number had gotten on. No one could say for sure if Donny was even on the bus or if he'd come to the corner at the same time the bus pulled up. No one claimed to remember seeing anyone approach Donny. They had found a knife in an alley half a block away.

While we waited, we told the cops about Murphy and Fariniti. "Who's your source?" Rohter demanded.

"For now, we'd like to keep confidence," I said. "We may be able to get more out of him if we need it. If his information is any good, you've got two people to question. He claims he'll deny everything he told us if you come to talk to him. He's had some unfortunate experiences with the police."

Rohter said, "We are the murder police and this is a murder investigation. You are not going to play some good-hearted amateur-sleuth crap and not tell us. Spill it or get ready to come down to the station."

I wished I had my lawyer around to consult. I said, "Call my lawyer."

Rohter swore, but refrained from arresting us. They left to pursue the leads we'd given them.

Half an hour later, Hiram came out. He nodded to us. We clustered around him.

"How is he?" Scott asked.

Hiram said, "They aren't sure he's going to make it. He hasn't regained consciousness. They don't know if he will."

Scott's father put his hand on his son's shoulder. "We'll stay with you for as long as it takes."

Scott's sister, her husband, and Scott's nieces and

nephew hurried off the elevator and joined us. As Hiram explained what was going on, Cynthia hurried down the corridor. She was crying. We all rushed to her. She clutched Hiram. She said, "They're taking him up to surgery. They couldn't stop the internal hemorrhaging."

A nurse joined us. "What's happening?" Hiram asked.

The nurse, an older woman in her fifties, said, "The doctors are going to try and . . ." She listed a series of medical things that needed to be fixed.

"Is he going to make it?" Cynthia asked.

"We'll have to see. There's been a lot of damage internally."

Hiram held Cynthia. They were both in tears. Scott's mom and dad did their best to comfort them, but they, too, looked stricken. I didn't like the kid, but there is nothing worse than losing a child.

We waited for hours. I stopped in the gift shop to pick up a book to read. When I came back, I saw Scott in a corner with Hiram. Their heads were close together. I read for half an hour. I looked up to see them hug briefly. Scott came and sat next to me. His thigh and knee leaned against mine. He took my hand. He was teary-eyed. He said, "We had a good talk. Better than we've ever had as adults."

"I'm glad," I said.

When the doctor finally emerged, she looked grim. We gathered around. She said, "We did everything we could. Several vital organs were lacerated. We're going to have to wait and see what happens in the next few hours. He's going to be in the intensive care unit."

"Will he make it?" Cynthia asked.

"I don't know. There's nothing more we can do medically. I'm sorry."

Cynthia and Hiram went to sit with their son up on the

intensive care floor. Only two people were allowed in at a time. Scott's mom and dad said they would wait outside. We stayed for another hour. Scott's sister, brother-in-law, and I decided to go down to the hospital cafeteria to eat. Mr. and Mrs. Carpenter said they weren't hungry.

Scott's brother-in-law, Mary's husband, is the manager of a convenience store in East Nowhere, Georgia. He's got an odd sense of humor. We all picked at the hospital food. They asked what we knew about the background to the attack on Donny, and what it might have had to do with the murder. We told them all we knew.

▲ 28 ▲

Scott's pager went off as we were busing our trays. Scott dialed the number. He talked for a few moments, then hung up. He turned to me. "Josh Durst is dead."

"Son of a bitch," I said. "Where is he?"

Scott said, "Miller went to Ethan Gahain's condo. He found Josh there."

"Have the police arrived?"

"Yeah."

I hesitated. "I'll stay here," Scott said. "You go and check out what's going on."

"I'd prefer to stay with you."

Scott said, "If you're in the hall with us or checking this out, it's not going to change Donny's condition."

His sister said, "Finding out what happened might be helpful to all of us. These killings must be connected to Donny in some way."

I hurried over to the condo. The night was cool. I had on only my T-shirt under my jacket. My shirt had gone with Donny into the emergency room.

I looked for a space to park in one of the best spots left in that part of the city, on School Street or Aldyne about twenty feet in from Broadway on the north side of the street. Two spaces are not metered, and no signage forbids parking at any time or requires a sticker. It's the perfect spot and seldom available. A Toyota's fading brake lights told me I'd been fifteen seconds too late for the space. I drove around for the more traditional fifteen minutes hunting for a spot. I finally found one right in front of Unabridged Bookstore, where Scott and I had first met.

I saw Miller on Buckingham just east of the condo. There was a crime scene van, lots of cop-looking officials hanging around, and a group of gawkers milling nearby. We stood apart from all these groups. Since Miller had found the body, a young uniformed cop hovered nearby.

I told him about Donny. He said several sympathetic things.

"What have you found out?" I asked.

"The cops still can't find the model releases. Ethan and company paid these people in cash. They didn't bother to submit any ten-ninety forms to the IRS for the people they hired. They did, however, report their own income to the IRS. They were actually pretty scrupulous about that. Remember, all they got Al Capone on was income tax evasion. Even if you're a crook, the government wants theirs."

"So there was no cadre of employees helping out?"

"There may have been a few helpers here and there, but nobody has any names. Cormac, Ethan, and Josh were kind of it as far as anybody can tell. Burnes seems to have been more hanger-on than any kind of employee."

"You can do thousands of dollars' worth of business with only three people?"

"How many minimum-wage people do you think you have

to hire to stuff boxes and put on mailing labels?" Miller answered his own question: "Not a lot. You figure one or two employees for a couple hours a day, the videos get sent. Before I left St. Louis, I found out about the condo from a loan officer I know at the bank that handled a lot of Ethan Gahain's accounts."

"Are they supposed to give you that kind of information?"

"No. One of the great truisms in a murder investigation is follow the money. I was trying to do that. I make it a habit to develop as many contacts as I can. I had one in the bank they used. Ethan Gahain was worth well over a million dollars. In his will it is divided equally among his children. The wives don't get a penny. The kids don't get a cent until they're twenty-one. The business was doing very well—shipping hundreds of units a week in tapes alone. They were making more money on credit card receipts from the Web site. Customer costs were fairly typical on it. Three ninety-nine per minute. People would pay a fee to join the club and another charge for every minute they watched."

"How'd you get to see the will?" I asked.

"I called wife number four and asked. She read it to me. It was a very simple thing really."

We could have done that.

I said, "His kids aren't old enough to think about killing him, are they? The oldest is only twelve or thirteen."

"The oldest is twelve. As we know, that's certainly old enough to accomplish a lot of mayhem. In this case I think it's unlikely that a kid is going to be able to do this much traveling and this much planning."

"Scott's nephew did."

"But he's fifteen, not twelve."

"It could happen."

Miller said, "Why would a twelve- or fifteen-year-old kill

all those people? I think all these murders are connected. You don't get this much random coincidence in the universe I live in."

"When we were in the condo, we didn't find any clues."

"I walked in. He was dead. It looked like his head had been bashed against the wall. He wasn't a very big guy. It wouldn't have been hard to nail him."

"He was in good shape," I said. "He wasn't huge, but he was muscular. It has to be somebody pretty strong who's killed Ethan and Josh Durst. Durst claimed there were two intruders in his house in St. Louis. Maybe there are two killers. You can't just take someone's head and bash it against something. Some of these people have to be fighting back."

"Donny got knifed, not bashed."

I said, "I still don't get how he fits in."

"If everybody is looking for something, maybe Donny knows something about it. If he was actually at the scene of Ethan's murder, maybe he took something. Maybe he knows something."

"The killer's gotta be looking for the missing data: the pictures or the model releases."

Detectives Rohter and Hoge joined us.

Rohter said, "We examined the condo just before we got the call on Donny Carpenter. Obviously, he wasn't there at the time. You guys were right about not finding anything."

"At least I didn't find this body," I said.

"You could have left it there," Hoge said.

"At this late date I would start leaving instead of finding the bodies?" Nobody else responded to the tone of light amusement I was going for in this crack.

Rohter asked the obvious: "Why was Durst here? Why did he come to Chicago? How come he knew about the condo?"

I said, "It was a staging place for homemade videos. He

was part of the crew. Durst, Gahain, and Macintire were in on something illegal, or at least it was something lethal. You've got to assume the danger extends from the connection between them, or at least it makes a great deal of sense to assume so. The connection we know about is pornographic."

"How does Mr. Carpenter's nephew fit in?" Miller asked.

Rohter said, "The kid was at the first murder scene. I don't believe in coincidences. Although the kid also might have gotten knifed by somebody who thought he was an asshole, which could be just about everybody he ever met."

I asked, "Who gains by having them dead? Blackmail gone bad has a nice ring to it."

None of us knew.

"How's your nephew?" Rohter asked.

I told him the latest.

"Did he get a chance to tell anybody what happened to him?" Hoge asked.

I shook my head.

Rohter said, "The medical examiner is reasonably certain that if Donny had called when he found Ethan Gahain, they might have been able to save him. If the kid lives, the state's attorney will probably charge him. If he didn't actually commit the murder."

The cops left.

"Did Josh Durst have family in Chicago?" I asked.

Miller said, "He's from St. Louis. I talked to his mother, a brother, and some friends. They all claimed to know nothing of any of this."

I stopped at the hospital. There was no change in Donny's condition. It was nearly dawn by the time Scott and I got home and into bed.

⟍ 29 ⟋

When we awoke, it was nearly noon. Scott called the hospital. Donny was still in intensive care.

The answering service buzzed us. My sister was on the line, but they also had a message from Douglas Clangborn, the reporter from the *Tribune*. He had invited us to a meeting of another group of athletes. After I'd noted the address, I told the service operator to switch my sister onto the line. Caroline began immediately: "What have you done?"

"I won't know until you tell me what you're upset about."

"The police were here to question Ernie. My husband did not kill his brother."

"Why did they come to question him?"

"They wanted to know when and what we knew about that condo. They could have only found out about our being there through you. They wanted to know about Ernie's movements last night and at the wedding. They said that bathroom in the hotel was wheelchair accessible, as if that made someone a suspect."

"They have to check out all possibilities. He is the brother.

It is traditional to check out the family thoroughly in these cases. I like Ernie. I think he's a good guy."

"You had at least as much reason to dislike Ethan as Ernie did."

"I had an emotional peak experience of anger at Ethan. Ernie had a whole lifetime of being pissed off."

"He didn't kill him. There was a death in St. Louis. He couldn't have done that. He couldn't have gone to St. Louis without me knowing about it."

"I believe you." This wasn't exactly a lie. What I meant was, I had absolutely no proof that Ernie killed anyone.

Caroline said, "The police kept wanting to know where we got the photos. They wouldn't believe that we simply found them in a briefcase. You gave them the photos. What did you do that for?"

"They were evidence."

"They practically accused him of working with Ethan. How dare they? He's my husband. I'm frightened. I've never been so worried. I don't like being any part of this."

"Nobody likes being part of a murder. It isn't something you run around auditioning for or seeking out."

"I want this to go away."

"I know," I said.

"Call me immediately if you learn anything."

"I will."

"How is Scott's nephew?"

"It looks pretty bad."

"Tell Scott I care."

I promised I would and hung up. I told Scott what she'd said.

Scott said, "I don't think she has anything to worry about. Ernie didn't strike me as the violent type."

"Me neither."

We called Clangborn. He said, "I've got some guys you can talk with."

We drove out to a sports bar on Madison Avenue in Forest Park just west of Harlem. We found a three-or-four-block stretch filled mostly with sports bars and beauty shops.

We parked on the street and walked into Mr. Luckey's. The bar was crammed with televisions showing sports events, some presumably live, others taped.

Clangborn waved us over to a small knot of guys in a large booth near the back. Several empty pitchers of beer sat on the table. The waitress brought over three new ones as we sat down. She brought glasses for Scott and me. Scott paid. We did a round of meet the famous baseball player. No talk about the gay stuff.

We met three more athletes with Robert Murphy in their midst. I was eager to confront him, but first I wanted to get information from the athletes. This was a much angrier bunch than was at the first place.

One was Billy McConnel from St. Louis, whom Coach Weiser had mentioned as transferring to Lafayette when Ethan had switched universities. Without preliminary, McConnel said, "I wish I'd have murdered all three of them."

"Which videos were you in?" I asked.

"I made one of their jack-off videos."

Jose Perez, another athlete said, "I did a couple with women. I never did anything with guys."

Scott asked, "You're willing to admit that in front of a reporter and your buddies?"

"Why not? The tape exists. I saw it on the Internet once. It's not like I did something with another guy. I'm not gay."

Perez's skin was the color of light chocolate. His thick hair was cut short and dyed blond, which accented his skin color. He said, "I played baseball for Carl Sandburg University. I knew I wasn't going to be a pro. What was the difference? They paid me a thousand bucks. They didn't tell me it was going to be on the Internet. I only have an old computer at home that isn't much good for anything but word processing. I don't surf porn sites. I have no reason to visit gay porn sites."

The third athlete, Emile Tanzi, had been caught beating off at a urinal. He had short, curly hair, a bushy mustache, and flawless olive skin. Emile said, "I thought the place was deserted. It was deserted. I got turned on by a girl in the stands while I was waiting to take a dive. She congratulated me after I won the competition. I went back to the locker room. You ever had a hard-on in a Speedo? It's embarrassing. Nobody was in the locker room. I never dreamed there'd be a goddamn camera."

"Everybody's angry," McConnel said. "We came up to see what could be done. Barney Natlik is gathering everybody up here. Coach Fariniti is coming to town as well."

"How'd you guys wind up making videos?"

McConnel said, "I needed money. It's not a secret a lot of us do. Josh Durst was the one who told me he had a way for me to make extra money. I figured he was gay and he wanted to get me into prostitution. I wouldn't do that kind of shit. I know gay guys who hang around sports events just to ogle the guys or who have a lot of money to pay the athletes."

"Was Ethan involved in any of that?" I asked.

"I sure never heard he was," McConnel said, "but how would we know for sure?"

None of the others had heard of it.

I turned to Perez. "How'd you get involved in making videos?"

"Durst."

"He must have been the recruiter," Scott said.

"Yeah," Perez said. "Plus I wanted to have sex. I got to

make it with a pair of nineteen-year-old twins with huge tits. It was great."

Tanzi said, "They sort of blackmailed me. I was embarrassed at what they had on tape. When they asked me to do more, I figured I had no choice."

"Did they make threats?"

"Did they need to? I was caught beating off in a public place."

"Did Coach Gahain ever attempt to have sex with any of you?" I asked.

They all said no.

The athletes left. We asked Clangborn if he would excuse us while we talked to Murphy. The reporter told us to keep in touch and reminded us of our promise to call him first. He left. I turned to the coach and said, "We talked with Marty Burnes."

Murphy glowered. "The police talked to me. I figured Burnes had to be the one to tell. I'll fix that little weasel. He's a liar."

I said, "We gave the cops your name, Burnes didn't."

"Yeah, well, I gave the cops *his* name. I knew he was in the sports program. I knew he was close to Ethan. I figured he was the rat."

My dilemma about telling the police had now disappeared. I said, "Burnes claimed you hated Ethan Gahain. That you were rivals. You lied to us. Why did you come here today? To help these athletes smear Ethan with a reporter? I want to know what the hell was going on."

"Marty Burnes is a desperate wanna-be. Why would you trust him to tell you the truth any more than you would me? Do you know him better? Do you know where he was at the time of the murders?"

I said, "Tell us about your connection to Ethan and to pornography."

"Yes, I'd caught him at it. Yes, I'd threatened to turn him in."

"And you were rivals at work?"

"Yes. He tried to undercut me in the department. He denied it, but I knew what he was trying to do. We were rivals. I saw a way of getting rid of him. I didn't care if he took porn pictures of the whole department, as long as he left. I was smarter than he was. I threatened to tell all. I had more power and influence than he did. He got the chance for the new job. I told him he had to leave."

"Why not go to the head of the department?"

"Ranklin? Ha! He's an administrator. He doesn't have a brain in his head. Until this came out in the paper, he didn't have a clue to what was going on. I found out. I had a way of getting rid of a rival. He was gone. What did I care who he had pictures of?"

Scott asked, "Why not just turn him over to the police and ruin Ethan completely?"

"I'm gay. I can't risk people asking questions and getting nosy. My name would be associated with Ethan's. Did you think that maybe Burnes had his own reasons for diverting suspicion from himself?"

"Are you saying he and Ethan were enemies?"

Murphy countered, "Burnes sure knows more about the porn operation than anyone still living, doesn't he?"

"You do," I pointed out.

Murphy said, "Fuck you both," and stormed out.

We left and drove to the police station. It was nearly six before we got a chance to talk to Rohter.

He said, "Fariniti's on his way in."

"Has he been arrested?"

"We're getting fingerprints. We want him for questioning. His lawyer is trying to cooperate."

"Can we talk to him?"

"Not a chance."

All the other amateur sleuths got to talk to the suspect if they didn't actually take part in the trapping. We must not be doing this right.

Rohter said, "We found a video he was in. He lied to the St. Louis police, and he does not have an alibi for the times of the murders."

"He must have been in Chicago yesterday."

"When I said on his way here, I didn't mean on his way from St. Louis. We found him in a motel at the airport. We got that information from the St. Louis cops, who'd checked into his whereabouts."

"It's suspicious that he was here."

"More than a bit," Rohter said.

We stopped for a bite to eat then hurried to the hospital. Still no change. We took part in the wait and worry until midnight. We were still tired from staying up most of the night before. We went home.

30

The phone woke me out of a deep sleep. It was four in the morning. Fears hammered at my heart. Calls in the middle of the night are not the harbingers of good news. I picked up the receiver. The answering service said, "It's Mrs. Carpenter for her son."

I handed Scott the phone. I whispered, "It's your mom."

He listened for a few moments, then said, "We'll be right there." He handed me the phone and I hung it up. "It's Donny. They don't know if he's going to make it through the night."

We dressed quickly and hurried to the hospital. Scott's mom and dad, his sister, and his brother-in-law were in the intensive care unit waiting room.

Mrs. Carpenter said, "Hiram and Cynthia are in with him. He hasn't regained consciousness since the operation. He's taken a turn for the worse." She dabbed at her eyes. We kept vigil through the rest of the night. As dawn rose, Hiram and Cynthia entered the room. Their eyes were red-rimmed, cheeks pale and sunken, shoulders round and slumped.

Hiram shook his head. Mrs. Carpenter buried her face in

Scott's dad's shirtfront. Scott's sister leaned heavily on her husband. She began to cry softly. Scott embraced his brother and sister-in-law. "I'm so sorry," he murmured.

I heard them both whisper thanks. It's true, there is nothing you can really say at a moment like that. Any words are not going to make the hurt and pain and loss go away. It is also true that it doesn't make a lot of difference what you say at times like that. You don't need a memorized speech or need to say the exact right thing. The murmurs of love and the closeness of caring are what make the difference. We spent several hours holding and comforting. Listening to medical personnel, and making arrangements. Hiram and Cynthia would fly their son's body back to Georgia. We did everything we could to help. Scott and I would be flying down in a few days for the funeral. Another day or two without pay paled in comparison to this tragedy.

Nobody got angry. Nobody engaged in recriminations.

When we were ready to leave the hospital, we stood in a circle in the hospital foyer. Hiram asked, "What happened? Why did he have to die?"

None of us knew. With final hugs, Scott's relatives headed to their hotel to pack and make final preparations for leaving. We drove home.

On the way we caught the news that Fariniti was in custody but had not been charged yet.

Half an hour after we'd been back in the penthouse, I wandered past the electronics room. Scott was setting back in place all the machines his nephew had moved. I didn't think this was a time for a cleaning frenzy, but it was only a few machines. Then again I'm never in favor of cleaning much at all, much less a frenzy. Cleaning is an "issue" in our relationship. He loves to do it. I hate it. Unfortunately, his love for it does not translate into a willingness on his part to do all of it. Worse luck. We'd compromised over the years. He groused less, and I cleaned more. I still had my slob room in his penthouse and in my home in the country. He only entered these sanctums under duress. I loved them.

I figured I'd better help. It couldn't be good to begin married life by reviving a spot in our relationship that needed compromise. I pitched in. He was leaning down and plugging in one of the DVD components when he held up a CD. He said, "I don't think this goes on the floor back here."

I sauntered over. For once I knew I hadn't misplaced something. I took it from his hand as he stood up. "This doesn't have a label on it," I said. I glanced around the room. "There aren't any CD cases lying around. I didn't put it there."

"So what the hell is it?"

Scott reached behind the VCR and pulled out four credit cards. They were Ethan's. I said, "The only person besides ourselves who's been in this room was Donny. We now have more than a fingerprint to prove he was in with Ethan."

Scott said, "I didn't want to believe he would rob a dying man."

The horror of that hit me powerfully. Donny had come upon someone who'd been hurt, and not only didn't he help, he'd ripped him off. Certainly I didn't want to believe someone I knew, even slightly, would do such a thing. I didn't want to believe in that kind of cruelty.

However, my wants had little to do with it. This was reality, and Scott's recently deceased nephew was not a good person.

We stuck the CD into our newest, biggest, most powerful computer. In minutes we were looking at a file of model releases for the videos that Ethan and his little gang had made.

"Ethan, Cormac, and Josh Durst each had a copy," I said. "Extra copies for protection. Obviously, not enough."

"How'd Donny get a copy?" Scott asked.

"Had to be from the murder scene."

The model release records numbered over a hundred pages. There were more pictures than we'd found in Ethan's condo. It took a minute or so for each picture to fully appear on the computer. Ours was fast, but these pictures must have required a lot of memory. Some of them were simply posed pictures, guys in various states of undress. Others were blatantly sexual with guys holding stiff pricks or scenes of guys making it together. There were a few live-action shots about ten seconds long, snippets of sexual action, all gay. We also found action loops, each about five minutes long. One of these last caught my eye.

I hit pause.

Scott said, "Is that who I think it is?"

"Who is that with him?" Coach Ranklin was in a sauna. He was there with another man whose face we couldn't see from this camera angle. "They caught him in the amateur-without-consent crowd."

Scott asked, "But why was it in with this set? I thought we were convinced the killings had something to do with blackmail."

The two men in the video shifted, and we finally saw the other person face-on. The identity of the young athlete was unmistakable. It was Shawn Ranklin, the budding Olympian, the all-American boy. I began to fast-forward it. We saw the two men drink from the same bottle of what looked to be champagne. We saw them touch and then begin to kiss.

"Oh, my," Scott said.

They rapidly proceeded from kissing to more intimacy.

I said, "We need to talk to these people now."

"We should call the police."

"He was my coach. I danced with him at my wedding. We don't know he killed anyone."

"Ethan had these pictures. He caught the two of them breaking one of the most powerful taboos in society. It's the perfect setup for murder."

We left messages for Rohter and Hoge to call us.

⌐31⌐

We drove to Carl Sandburg University. Coach Ranklin was in the locker room. His hair was damp. Sweat stains had formed under his armpits, on his back, and even the crotch of his cotton workout shorts. Must have been one hell of a lot of exercise.

"Hey, you guys," he said.

"We need to talk," I said. We moved to his cramped little office. The same one we'd been in earlier in the week. He leaned back in his chair and put his feet up on the desk. His posture made his crotch bulge more prominent and enticing, with his prick clear in outline. He twirled a towel into a tight spiral, took either end in a hand, and draped it behind his neck. He might be leaning back and look all casual, but his grip on the towel would have been tight enough to cut off its circulation if it were a human neck.

A movement behind us caught my eye. Shawn Ranklin was in the doorway. He wore tight, blue athletic shorts and no shirt. The young athlete's gorgeous muscles dripped with moisture. The hair on his legs clung to the skin in tight ringlets. Every muscle looked as if it were singing happiness.

He said, "Dad, I need to borrow some soap."

"We should talk to you as well," I said.

Shawn moved behind his dad's chair. His light gray eyes searched mine. "What's up?" With casual grace, he leaned against the back wall and hitched his butt atop a two-drawer filing cabinet. His lightly tapping left foot was the only sign that he might be experiencing strong emotions.

I remembered him from when he was a kid, the slight curl to his red hair, the shy smile.

I said, "We know this might be a little embarrassing."

Without any preliminary, Coach Ranklin launched himself at me. He didn't have far to go in the small office, so he couldn't build up a lot of momentum. Nevertheless, he pushed me backward off the chair and half knocked the wind out of me.

I scrambled away from him while trying to gulp down sufficient quantities of air. Shawn grabbed for Scott. The room was too small for broad or rapid maneuvering. The two lamps on the desk toppled to the floor when Scott and Shawn sprawled against them. Shawn aimed a kick at my head. I managed to shift enough so he didn't get a direct hit. Coach Ranklin threw the chair out of the way. He leapt toward me. His angry grimace distorted his handsome face.

I twisted sideways, cupped my hands, and slammed them against his ears. He screamed. I leapt up backward. This wasn't wrestling. This was street fighting. Any gouge or punch could mean victory or death. Ranklin leapt toward me. I instinctively raised my knee to blunt his leap. He turned sharply, but I grabbed his crotch, got a tight grip, and pulled, twisted, and compressed all at the same time. He yowled and howled as he sank to the floor, kicking feebly and continuing to scream. I didn't let go.

254

The son fought like a madman. While Scott struggled with the son, I had Coach Ranklin nearly incapacitated. I didn't let go until he ceased struggling.

Shawn Ranklin had a lamp raised high above Scott's head when three young athletes appeared in the doorway. The distraction was sufficient. Scott grabbed the wrist that held the lamp and twisted the arm high up on Shawn's back. Shawn yelped and tried to squirm. Scott applied more pressure. The lamp clattered to the floor as the kid sank to his knees. All the fight went out of him. Coach Ranklin whimpered and held his hands over his bruised balls.

Spur-of-the-moment mass murder didn't seem to be in the cards. We called the cops.

32

We sat with Shawn Ranklin in the deserted locker room. He and I had our legs straddling a bench in front of a row of empty lockers. Scott leaned against the wall about a foot ahead and to my left. The room smelled of rotting jockstraps from the laundry facility twenty feet away and chlorine from the nearby pool. Shawn was red-eyed but composed. His father had been willing to attack anyone who got near him. We eventually left him tied to a chair, locked in his own office, with a college security person on guard. Before we shut the door on him in his office, he had said, "Keep your goddamn mouth shut."

While we waited for the cops, we talked to Shawn. In the locker room he looked like a scared kid. After a few moments of silence he began to bawl.

Neither of us touched him. When he calmed down, I asked simply, "Why?"

"It was never supposed to happen. What's my mother going to think? What's everybody going to think?"

Scott said, "Four people have died."

Ranklin looked startled and gazed at Scott for a second, then hung his head. I could barely hear him as he mumbled, "That's not what I meant. Everybody's going to know. My mother is going to be crushed. She and Dad divorced years ago. I know murder is horrible, but that isn't the worst. I'll never forget what my dad and I did. We . . ."

"We saw the pictures," I said.

"That's so awful."

I asked, "How did all this get started?"

Ranklin wiped his face on a damp towel. He snuffled mightily, drew a deep breath. "It was after I won the preliminary for the Olympics. A bunch of us had a big celebration in the locker room. Somebody brought champagne. They're not supposed to. I'd been puking before the final event. I didn't have anything in my stomach. I drank only a glass or two, but it was more than I should have. I was totally wiped out from the race. I decided to take a sauna. Most everybody was gone. They have separate male and female ones. I just went in my boxer shorts. My dad joined me a few minutes later. He was wrapped in a towel. He had another bottle of champagne with him. We talked and laughed and celebrated and drank. It wasn't a very big sauna. I could feel his leg against mine. He didn't move it away." Ranklin had begun crying softly. "Neither of us meant for anything to happen. I swear. I swear. He squeezed my shoulder to congratulate me. He didn't pull away. I moved closer." Ranklin wiped his eyes and nose with the back of his hand.

He gulped and shook his head. "We never, never, talked about sex, never. Sure, when I was a kid, I thought my dad was the best-looking guy. I never thought about him sexually. I thought all kids were curious about their dads. Even as a teenager, sometimes I'd go in and take a piss while he was shaving. I wanted him to look at me. God, I'm sick."

I didn't have a clue about what to say to a guy who was confessing to incest, and we hadn't even gotten to all the dead bodies. No amateur sleuth I knew of ever had this many bodies nor the depth of sexual darkness.

"After that first time in the sauna, neither of us ever talked about it. Ever." Ranklin drew a deep breath. His whole body shuddered. He didn't bother to dry the tears. "When I took trips to Chicago, I stayed with him. It was like they say about having an elephant in the living room that nobody will discuss. Yet, I knew . . . Christ, who cares at this point . . . I knew I wanted it to happen again. One night I came home late. He was sleeping downstairs on the couch." Ranklin stopped. "We did it more than once."

"When did Ethan tell you he had the videos?" I asked.

"Pictures and videos. It started with Macintire. It was blackmail all right. Macintire wanted cash. He lost a fortune in the dotcom crash. Ethan wanted more than money. He wanted to put us on the Internet, on one of those live things they were doing. He approached me first. I told my dad. He said we had to put a stop to it.

"We offered them money. It was Ethan who said that a real incest thing could make them a lot of cash. He assured us that it would be totally anonymous. What a stupid thing to say. As if anything could be anonymous on the Internet. Even if there was a way of guaranteeing anonymity, we weren't about to permit it to be public. We had to get those photos and videos back.

"We threatened to have his whole world come crashing down on him, to expose him. He demanded sex with the two of us at the same time. We did threat and counterthreat. We burned the warehouse they moved from to send a message."

Ranklin leaned over so that his head rested against a locker. He shut his eyes. He mumbled to the floor, "We figured the pictures were in St. Louis. We got into Cormac's office before the warehouse. Cormac was easy to subdue. We kept him in our hotel room. We made him tell us where their new offices were. It took several days before he would tell. At that point we weren't into violence. We brought him with us to that storage place. We looked for a day and a half before we found anything. When my dad saw the pictures, he went nuts. We never planned on killing anyone. Cormac got free. We struggled. He managed to grab one of our guns. My dad got behind him and got hold of the gun hand. I'll never forget watching the gun inch toward Cormac's head. Another inch or two in either direction and my dad or me could have been killed. The gun went off. Cormac fell back on top of my dad. Cormac was dead. My dad got gore all over his hair and face." Ranklin began crying again.

It took several minutes before he resumed. "This was Friday night. We cleaned ourselves up. Then we kept looking. We had to. We had to find if they had anything else. We should have just burned the storage facility with Cormac in it. We had to be sure the threat was gone. We searched for hours but couldn't find what we were looking for. I looked through all the computer records. We stopped late Saturday morning. My dad was going to the wedding, so we decided to go up here and get the information out of Ethan."

"You worked with the body there?" Scott asked.

"We didn't have any choice. We discovered that, besides the stuff we found at the warehouse, Josh Durst had one set of pictures and discs and Ethan had another. There were actually three discs in each set. Once Cormac was dead, we knew we had to kill the other two. Durst was at a sport event in Oakland, California. It would have been a logistical nightmare to try to kill him out there. Anonymous plane tickets, finding out where he was staying, staking him out, hoping for an opportunity, not being noticed while we were doing it, all on turf we weren't familiar with. We had to make sure Ethan didn't come back unexpectedly and find the body. We came up to Chicago. We found Ethan. My dad was going to the wedding. He saw Ethan there and insisted on a meeting. He called me before the dinner began. I arrived after the dancing had started. My dad told me where they'd agreed to meet. I got there first."

"If Ethan was so frightened lately, why did he agree to meet you?"

"They'd been threatened by others. I know Coach Fariniti for one. We heard there was some custody shit going down. He thought he had us cornered."

"Why not threaten to expose him if he didn't give you the tapes?" I asked. "He was the one with the most to lose."

"You're wrong there. Incest? Think about it. He might lose money, but we could lose, well, everything. What would people think?" Ranklin shook his head.

"What happened in the washroom?" I asked.

"He thought he was finally going to get it on with us."

"In a public washroom?" Scott asked. "Why not a bedroom?"

"He might have thought it was just a meeting to come to an agreement, but almost as soon as I got there, he started groping me. Then my dad showed up. Ethan wanted to do it with both of us right there. He must have had like a spontaneous orgasm. I held him while my dad threatened him. Ethan was pretty scared by this point. He tried to argue and then fight. I hit him first. His head snapped back against the tile wall. Then my dad banged Ethan's head a bunch of times. There wasn't that much blood, little enough so I could just wash it off."

I remembered that most of the blood had been on the floor.

"My dad went back to the reception. I was present at the first death, but this was the first time I'd done any hitting. It scared the piss out of me. Ethan had the discs with him. I dropped a CD on my way out. I already had three of Cormac's with me. I didn't know it at the time, but the kid saw me."

Scott said, "He lied to us when he said he didn't see anyone."

Shawn said, "He picked up the CD I dropped."

"How'd he manage to have time to rob the corpse and leave a fingerprint and catch up to you?"

"I couldn't run. I had to move casually. I had to conceal little flecks of blood on the hem of my coat that I'd missed in the washroom. The hotel was jammed. I had to make sure I didn't draw attention to myself. Finding obscure ways out was not easy. He found me as I was at the corner of Wacker and Michigan. The line to get the car out of the parking garage was immense."

"How'd he know the CD was valuable?"

"What difference does the CD make? That must have been a bonus. He knew I'd killed someone."

"Ethan carried the CDs with him?"

"He'd made extra copies. We went to the condo here. We found an envelope with discs and pictures. He was right to be paranoid. He said if we killed him, someone would have copies of them to reveal to the press."

"What about Josh Durst?"

"Ethan told us he had copies as well. He thought we wouldn't kill him if we knew somebody else had copies. My dad was too angry." He added in a whisper, "So was I."

"How did my nephew figure out it was you guys who killed Ethan?"

"He told us he was listening at the door and heard the whole thing. I guess we were louder than we thought. That corridor is pretty quiet. He heard the fight. He heard my dad say we had to get out of there now. He told us he hid in one of those storage closets. He kept the door opened a crack. That's how he saw me leave. When we were gone, he ran into the washroom. He came back out and ran after me. He'd seen me on the Olympics coverage last time. I'd carried the United States flag in at the opening ceremonies."

"How did he figure out where to find you?"

"We found him. You let it slip when you were talking to my dad. You talked about not being a suspect and your nephew possibly providing an alibi. You said you were confident about not being arrested. Then the press reported that your brother and sister-in-law and nephew were at the station for questioning. Why would they bring them down? The parents were in Georgia at the time of the wedding. It had to be the nephew."

"How'd you find him?" Scott asked. "We couldn't."

"I called each of your relatives staying in town. We knew which hotel. It wasn't a secret. I pretended that I was a reporter for a tabloid and I knew he was there. It was a bluff. The second one I talked to gave him away. I told your nephew I knew he had a CD and that as a reporter for a tabloid, we'd pay a lot of money for it. He agreed to meet. He caught on pretty quick that we were the ones in the pictures. We were pretty stupid to think that he wouldn't. He was pretty stupid when he tried to blackmail us. The little fuck. We went to the meeting expecting trouble. We'd done so much killing by that point, what did another matter? We were talking in an alley off Diversey. We told him we'd meet him again. My dad got up to let him out of the car. He stabbed him, jabbed upward as hard as he could, twisted the knife into Donny's insides, and shoved him out of the car as we started up. We thought he was dead."

"You broke into our cars trying to find out if we'd found anything," I stated.

"We weren't sure if we had everything from Ethan. We were going to have to try his home. We were outside Ethan's house when you first went in on Sunday. That's how we knew you were there. We broke into his house after you guys left. We searched the house after you did, but we couldn't find anything there. We couldn't be sure what you had. We couldn't break the computer codes. We'd have to hire a computer expert to teach us how to break into them. That would take too much time."

"You didn't attack Donny until Wednesday."

"After you talked to my dad, our suspicion turned to the kid. He was a creep. He tried to be all clever. He was snarly and rude."

"Why kill him?"

"He knew we were the killers. He had the disc to hold over our heads. That was a dangerous game to play with my dad. The kid thought he was too clever by half. He had to die."

"Then why'd he still go to meet you?"

"We offered him money. He wanted that. We also told him we'd come after him. Turns out he didn't even have the disk. He told us it was in a safe place."

"He hid it in our penthouse."

We heard voices coming toward us. Detectives Rohter and Hoge arrived in the locker room. Out in the hallway, we told the cops what we knew. We gave them the compact disk with the pictures and live-action shots. They cuffed the two of them. Coach Ranklin was still cursing anybody who got within shouting distance. They took father, son, and disk away.

We were quiet in the car as we drove to my place in the south suburbs.

33

Early Saturday morning we were at a special gate at O'Hare Airport. They wheeled Donny's coffin into the belly of a plane as we watched. It was cool and cloudy. Everyone wore soon-to-be-winter jackets. My parents were there along with all the Carpenters. My mom and dad came because the deceased was a close relative of Scott's. They had never known Donny, but they knew us and it was important to them to show that they cared. Scott's mom and dad thanked them profusely. Hiram and Cynthia were pretty much in shock and said little to anyone.

While we were back in the terminal waiting for the plane's departure, Scott and I spoke with Connie, Scott's favorite niece. Everyone else went to pick up some breakfast. I asked her, "Did Donny ever say anything to you about hiding a CD with pictures on it?"

"No. Sometimes he acted like he had big deals brewing. Back in Georgia, he always talked like he knew friends who could make deals for him. He always had another scheme going. Each one was sillier or more outlandish than the next.

I don't know of any that ever amounted to anything."

"Like what?" Scott asked.

"He claimed he could get any drugs he wanted anytime. I'm not sure he even took any drugs. Most of the time he got cigarettes from Darrell. He did talk about how much he didn't like either of you."

I said, "He came to visit Scott when we were in Georgia."

"Yeah, but Scott was his uncle."

Connie retrieved cousin Brent. Brent was big and sheepish and dumb. Before I even asked a question, he said, "I didn't know. How was I supposed to know anything? I told the police everything I know. I didn't get him killed. He never said anything about murder. I didn't know what he was up to."

"Why didn't he go to you guys in the first place?" I asked. "Why did he come to us?"

"He talked about you guys a lot. He sneered a lot, but he seemed obsessed with you. Anybody who sneers that much has got to have a problem."

"How come you told a reporter that Donny was there?"

"Donny was talking about making money. The reporter offered lots of cash. I figured this was a way I could help Donny make money. He laughed about how you caught him in the electronics room. He claimed you'd never figure out what he'd been doing."

"We found the CD."

"He didn't tell me about the CD. He said he'd used your computer, and he'd thought about erasing all kinds of stuff from your hard drive. He probably would have if you hadn't interrupted him."

I said, "I bet he turned it on to see what was on the CD. I wonder how he figured out it would be useful."

Connie said, "Maybe he didn't know it would be useful until all that information started coming out about what your friend Ethan had been doing. Donny would keep something like that. I think he liked to feel sneaky and secretive. He may not have known its value, but he would have known there was something not right about it. I mean, it had pornographic pictures. He'd want to keep it quiet. He had all of the poor dead guy's money."

Scott asked, "Why did he hide the CD and not the money?"

I said, "The porn would obviously be from someplace else. The money could have been from anywhere. He'd want to keep the CD safe. He knew he couldn't keep it with him. The police would be questioning him. Who knows what runs through a teenager's mind? He wouldn't know if the cops had a witness who saw him. Even if he could have gotten into the electronics room, he couldn't take the CD with him when he left the penthouse. He and his parents were going directly to the police. He couldn't know what would happen there. The possibility might be remote that he would be searched, but he couldn't know for sure that he wouldn't be."

The cousins rejoined their parents. We talked with the Carpenters until they all boarded the plane. The police had met with Hiram and Cynthia and told them all the particulars of the boy's involvement. Mostly we murmured soft platitudes. Little could be said to ease the burden of the tragedy they were going through.

34

After they left, we hurried in from the airport. Ethan's funeral was Saturday morning at eleven. It was very private and very quiet. Certainly, the intrusion of public scrutiny into the lives of his family had been Ethan's fault. Funerals are always for the living. Obviously, the dead can't possibly care. Reporters had tried to inundate the wake the night before. Police and a squad of security people from the firm Scott and I often used had kept away the unwanted. Now, fewer than twenty people were in the church. The casket was flower-draped. Mrs. Gahain wept openly. As Watson observed, evil is the man who has not one woman to mourn him.

As Scott and I walked in, my sister beckoned me over. She pointed to the last row of the church. A man about my age sat there. His skin looked deeply tanned, more starkly so because his hair was almost white-blond. He wore a dark gray suit.

Caroline whispered and pointed, "It's a closed ceremony. He's not supposed to be here."

"Get one of the people from the church to get rid of him," I said.

"They're being horrible. The priest wouldn't come talk to my mother-in-law. We had to meet with some functionary. He wouldn't let them do the things in the liturgy they wanted. We wanted to do some eulogies, and the priest wouldn't let us."

"He can do that?" Scott asked.

"Mrs. Gahain said we had to do what the priest wanted. If she didn't want to fight, none of us was going to intervene. Mr. Gahain doesn't go to this church. He had no say-so. They're both too in shock. Tom, you've got to get him out of here. What if he's a reporter?"

I definitely didn't want that. He wasn't acting like a reporter. I wanted to say, Why me?—but there were enough overwrought, over-the-top possibilities for emotion today. I didn't need to indulge.

I walked over to the man. He sat on the edge of the pew with his head down, elbows on his knees, hands hanging loosely down. I leaned down and tapped him on the shoulder.

He looked up. Tears ran down his cheeks.

"This is a private funeral," I whispered.

"I'm sorry. I found out from a friend where it was to be held. I got here very early. I didn't know the public wasn't invited. I'll leave."

His quick compliance made me feel even more like a heel for asking him to leave. I put a hand on his shoulder. "Did you know Ethan?"

"From grade school. He and I were lovers in eighth grade."

My mind reeled. Even at his funeral Ethan was capable of reaching out and delivering one last sting. He'd always told me, always insisted, always, always, always said that I had been his first. That little virginal memory had taken on great importance for a number of years. Sure, I'd been hurt by his rejection, but I'd gotten on with my life. Our shared virginity was always one of the sacred little nubbins of memory in the back of my head that had kept what had happened between us in high school from being completely and horribly negative. My first true love had ended, and I'd gotten over it, but one of the few positive memories left was now tarnished.

Doubts surfaced. "I went to grade school with him. I don't remember you."

"I didn't go to your school. Ethan and I were in Boy Scouts together. We went to meetings and on camp-outs. The first time we had sex was the fall jamboree during our eighth-grade year. We went up to Kettle Moraine in Wisconsin. We made love for the first time on the bottom bunk of a deserted cabin on a cold October night. For six months I lived for my weekly meetings with him in the church basement. We would make out in a distant cloakroom. At first the sex was beautiful and gentle and clumsy, the way it probably is for gay or straight virgins. Certainly so for those as young as he and I were. Then my parents moved away. I haven't seen or heard from him in years. I saw on the news that he was dead. I had to come to say good-bye. I'm sorry. If this is just for family, I'll leave."

He began to stand up.

"It's okay," I muttered.

He held out his hand. "My name's Michael."

35

It had been a very long day. After the service we'd gone to the cemetery and then to a restaurant where the Gahains had rented out a room. No one had the remotest desire to do all the cooking and cleaning it would have required to have a meal at home. Not only that, reporters were still camped out on the Gahains' doorstep. I thought this was exceptionally ghoulish on the part of the press. At the restaurant people started talking about Ethan, all the funny things he'd done, the special things, the warm and fuzzy moments. Sure it was cheap sentiment, but what better time for sentimentality than at a postfuneral meal.

We spent the night at my home out in the country. I would be back to school on Monday morning. I'd spent a little time early in the evening talking to the woman who had subbed for me and finding out how my classes had been. Things seemed to have gone fine at school.

Scott and I worked out together for an hour. Then I'd read a little of the latest Barb D'Amato mystery. Scott had puttered in his workshop on his latest carpentry project. We sat over half-gallons of chocolate chocolate-chip ice cream at midnight, just before going to bed.

I said, "Let's have a quiet dinner out tomorrow. Kind of get back into a relaxed mode." I knew we'd be flying to Atlanta in midweek. I would stay just a day, he for as long as he felt he was needed.

Scott scraped the bottom of his ice cream carton and licked the spoon clean. He said, "We can't. Your wedding present arrives tomorrow."

"Doesn't that cost extra for delivery on a Sunday? Who delivers on a Sunday?"

"I do. Or at least I can have deliveries made. It was originally scheduled for tomorrow because we'd have been back. We'll have to stay home."

"All day? What is it?"

"I'm having the chef from the most famous chocolate shop in Geneva, Switzerland, come to make six of his favorite desserts for you, all sinfully chocolate, all the best in the world."

An all-dessert dinner—now there is something to truly look forward to.

"I have your present." I hurried to the bedroom and rushed back. I handed him a little box, slightly larger than the kind you put a ring in. He opened it. Inside was an ornately carved key. I knew of only one place on earth that used keys of this intricately carved, medieval design.

Scott said, "This is for Landursa."

"Room one."

He got misty-eyed. Landursa was a resort encompassing an entire tiny island in the middle of the Aegean Sea fifty miles from Athens. It was the most exclusive gay resort in the world. The service was beyond deferential, the food beyond exquisite, the rooms beyond sumptuous. We tried to go there once a year. We'd spent a passionate weekend there one New

Year's. With schedules permitting we'd tried to make it back every year since.

"I have reserved room one for us for New Year's Eve for the next twenty-five years." He had the grace not to say, Is that possible? "We don't have to go if you don't want."

"I loved the time I spent there. I think it's a perfect idea. It's idyllic. It's gay. It'll have the two of us until we're old and gray."

"Don't start to rhyme on me."

Scott leaned over and kissed me. We rinsed off the spoons we'd used and deposited our cartons in the trash. We held hands as we strolled to the bedroom. We didn't turn on any lights. We stood for several moments gazing out the windows to the moonlight streaming down onto the vast fields surrounding the house. We turned to each other. Our arms entwined. Our lips met.

◣ About the Author ◢

Mark Richard Zubro is the author of more than a dozen mysteries, including the Lambda Literary Award–winning *A Simple Suburban Murder* and, most recently, *Sex and Murder.com*. He is a high school teacher and lives in Mokena, Illinois.